This book belongs to:

PAUL SHOLTZ

Good Housekeeping's
Best Book of
Dog Stories

But Tip could not forget those burning shots . . .

Good Housekeeping's
Best Book of
Dog Stories

Edited by
PAULINE RUSH EVANS

Illustrated by
JOSEPH CELLINI

GOOD HOUSEKEEPING MAGAZINE

Distributed by
PRENTICE-HALL, INC. Englewood Cliffs, N. J.

Acknowledgements

Thanks are due to the following authors, publishers, publications and agents for permission to use the material indicated.

Appleton-Century-Crofts, Inc. for "Gulliver the Great" from GULLIVER THE GREAT by Walter A. Dyer. Brandt & Brandt for "Such as Walk in Darkness" by Samuel Hopkins Adams, copyright 1902 by Samuel Hopkins Adams. Betty Cavanna for "Scarlet's Sons" by Betty Cavanna, copyright 1943 by Betty Cavanna. Curtis Brown, Ltd. for "Lassie Come Home" by Eric Knight, copyright © 1940 by Jere Knight, reprinted by permission of the author's estate. Philip Curtiss for "The Eight Dollar Pup" by Philip Curtiss, copyright 1930 by Philip Curtiss. Lavinia R. Davis for "The Foolish Dog of Brother John" by Lavinia R. Davis. Mazo de la Roche for "Short and Merry" from PORTRAIT OF A DOG by Mazo de la Roche. J. M. Dent & Sons for "Dandy, the Story of a Dog" from A TRAVELLER IN LITTLE THINGS by W. H. Hudson. Doubleday & Company, Inc. for "Garm—A Hostage" from ACTIONS AND REACTIONS by Rudyard Kipling, reprinted by permission of the publishers, Mrs. George Bambridge and A. P. Watt & Son; for "One Minute Longer" from BUFF: A COLLIE AND OTHER STORIES by Albert Payson Terhune, copyright 1921 by George H. Doran Company. E. P. Dutton & Co., Inc. for "Dandy, the Story of a Dog" from the book A TRAVELLER IN LITTLE THINGS by W. H. Hudson, copyright, 1920, by E. P. Dutton & Co., Inc., renewal, 1947, by The Royal Society for the Protection of Birds. Hubert Evans for "Ghost-Town Dog" by Hubert Evans. Harcourt, Brace and Company, Inc. for "Far Apart" and "Reunion" from BAT: THE STORY OF A BULL TERRIER by Stephen W. Meader, copyright, 1939, by Harcourt, Brace and Company, Inc. Harper & Brothers for "Hero" from THE WAY OF A DOG by Albert Payson Terhune, copyright, 1932, by Albert Payson Terhune. Holiday House for "Sheila MacGuire" from BIG RED by Jim Kjelgaard, copyright 1945 by Jim Kjelgaard. The Macmillan Company for "Admiral Dewey Has His Fling" from ALL OVER TOWN by Carol Ryrie Brink. McGraw-Hill Book Company, Inc. for "Lazy Girl," "The Time Has Come," and "Work To Do" from ALWAYS REDDY by Marguerite Henry, copyright, 1947, by the McGraw-Hill Book Company, Inc., published by Whittlesey House. L. C. Page & Company for "Christmas Eve at

Reginald's" from BEACON HILL CHILDREN by Elizabeth Rhodes Jackson, copyright 1927, 1936, 1938, by the Rand McNally Company, copyright 1947 by L. C. Page & Company. Story Parade, Inc. for "Meals for Mickey" by Alice Dalgliesh, copyright, 1938, by Story Parade, Inc. Ruth Elizabeth Tanner for "Wild Dog" by Ruth Elizabeth Tanner. James Thurber for "Snapshot of a Dog" by James Thurber, © 1935, The New Yorker Magazine, Inc. The Viking Press, Inc. for "The Seventh Pup" from MY BROTHER MIKE by Doris Gates, copyright 1948 by Doris Gates Hall. Whitman Publishing Company for "The King and the Princess" by Jack O'Brien, copyright, 1938, by Whitman Publishing Company.

The editor and publisher have made diligent efforts to trace the ownership of all copyrighted material in this volume, and believe that all necessary permissions have been secured. If any errors have inadvertently been made, proper corrections will gladly be made in future editions.

Introduction

Some time if you really want to find out what it was like when grandfather was a boy, try asking him about his first dog. I think you will discover a good deal more than you—or grandfather—would ever have thought he remembered about those days.

Nobody, I think, ever forgets the dogs of his childhood. He may not remember the children he went to school with, but the chances are that he will be able to tell you in surprising detail the adventures and pranks of old Rex, or Rover, or Spot.

Perhaps that's why so much has been written about dogs—stories about all sorts of dogs in all kinds of places. I am sure that not all of them are *true* stories. But I do have a feeling that most in this book are based mainly on things that really happened in the life of some dog the writer once knew and never forgot.

And what dogs they are! I don't think many of them would win prizes in a show, for most of them would not have the proper pedigrees and "points." But youngsters and dogs, thank goodness, don't seem to take much stock in such things. And neither did the people who wrote

these stories. They liked dogs—dogs with real character
and personality.

Here you will find dogs of all sizes, shapes and disposi-
tions—the eight-dollar pup who is a hobbyist and a phi-
losopher, and old Reddy, a true work dog, who still
summons up the strength and courage to handle a robber; the foolish dog of Brother John who turns out to
have more sense than anybody thought he had, and the
lazy dog who at last rouses himself—to defend a kitten;
little Snap, who had fear left out of his make-up and
Lassie, the magnificent collie who displays more-than-
human devotion.

There are more than twenty dogs here, and every one
is extraordinary in his own way. I wouldn't be surprised
if among them you found one that will become your
favorite, the greatest dog in the world to you—next to
Your Own.

Danbury, Conn.   P. R. E.

Contents

Contents

Good Housekeeping's
Best Book of
Dog Stories

RUTH ELIZABETH TANNER

Wild Dog

The prairie grass was thick and soft beneath Tip's padding feet as he moved through the gathering dusk. Somewhere in the distance a mourning dove raised her voice in a sleepy *coo-coo;* now and then a grasshopper flew blindly up and away; the ceaseless throbbing of locusts filled the air.

A sudden *whirr* rose from a clump of sage as a prairie chicken shot up into the air. She floundered one-sidedly, came down again and, dragging one wing, flopped along on the ground. Tip paused to watch her for a moment, but he did not give chase, for he knew she was trying to lead him away from her nest.

Then he trotted over to the clump of sage and after a little searching found her nest cleverly hidden in the matted grass. Sorely tempted, he sniffed at the eggs. He was very hungry and, though he would never have considered eating an egg in the barn or hen house, these out on the open prairie did not seem quite the same. His hunting instinct told him to take them, they did

not belong to his master. But from generations of shepherd and collie forebears he had inherited another instinct. That was to guard faithfully, no matter what the
cost.

He licked his lips again, but with a quick shake of his
head he turned and marched away without a single
backward glance. His better instinct had won.

Two hours later, after dining on a fat prairie dog and
a quail, he started for home. When he came to the top
of a high hill he sat down, pointed his white nose to the
full moon, and sent forth the long mournful howl of a
lost or forsaken dog.

Sims, Tip's old master, had sold his ranch in New
Mexico and returned to the East. As he could not take
a half-grown dog to an apartment in a large city, he
gave Tip to a friend in Belmont just before taking the
train. But Tip did not understand. He slipped away and
traveled the twenty miles back to the only home he had
ever known. For a month he had been guarding the
empty ranch, waiting for his owner's return.

At first he had gone hungry quite a lot. But the sand-
hills south of the house were full of cottontails, and the
sage-covered prairie was alive with jack rabbits. He soon
grew accustomed to finding his own meals. Still, he was
lonely, and now he voiced all his uneasiness and his
yearning for love and companionship in his mournful
appeal to the moon.

To the north on the Flying M Ranch, old Mr. Marvin turned restlessly in his bed. "Bill! Dusty!" he called.

"Yeah," came a sleepy answer.

"Hear that dog? There are too blamed many dogs around here. From now on when you boys see a stray, shoot him. They'll be getting the calves next."

The long mournful howl of a forsaken dog.

A few evenings later, Tip paused in his wandering to watch a couple of riders coming up the coulee. He was about to make a friendly advance when—*bang!*—a shot rang out, and a bullet flicked sand into his face. *Crack!* A second shot grazed his shoulder like a hot iron.

For a moment he had been confused. Then he came to life, and fled like a tawny streak, dodging behind

brush, skimming over the open places. A man on a
long-legged black was pounding madly after him. Twice
more the rider fired at a flash of yellow and brown, but
both bullets went wild.

Finally the pursuer gave up and returned to his
companion, a lanky, sunburned boy. "He got away!
Why didn't you take a hand, Dusty?"

Dusty's gray eyes crinkled as he smiled. "I'm glad
you didn't get him. That's a good dog, a collie. He
looks like a pup that fellow Sims had."

"Anyway, I nipped him."

"Poor fellow. I'm sorry for that," Dusty said slowly.

"Boss's orders," the cowhand explained.

"The boss can shoot him if he wants to, but I won't,"
Dusty declared.

Twice more in the next week some of the Flying M
men shot at Tip, but after that he saw them first and
vanished.

Still they heard him serenading the moon. A dog
whose ancestors have for generations lived with men
and who has known a loved master cannot so easily
break the tie that binds him to mankind. He was very
lonely, but as there was no human for him to serve he
spent his energy guarding the ranch buildings. Like a
wild animal, he had formed the habit of sleeping days
and roaming about at night. Perhaps the heat and his
avoidance of chance riders started him doing this.

One evening he woke, stretched out, and, yawning

like a sleepy child, came out from under the ranch house.

"*Woof!*" he yelped, dodging to one side in surprise. Stretched across the path beside the sagging step was a four-foot rattlesnake! Tip bristled. Ordinarily he would have gladly given the snake the right of way, but this was *his own* yard; he would not stand for the intrusion.

A snarl rose in his throat and like a flash he seized the snake before it could coil. He shook and shook it, then threw it down with all the strength he had. The snake landed with a thump and was coiled like a spring, ready for battle. Tip circled about. The snake was raging with fury. His rattles buzzed. His little eyes glittered with hate. The deadly rattler's head, balanced at least a foot from the ground, swung about, ever facing the dog as Tip minced about the snake.

Finally Tip pretended to step forward, and the rattler struck with every ounce of energy in his powerful coils. His head went fully three feet through the air. His fangs brushed Tip's whiskers as the collie dodged backward. Tip walked away feeling sick. The snake had struck much farther than he had expected him to. Death had missed him only by an inch, but he was not ready to give up.

After a moment he returned to the raging snake. Again he stepped forward, but with more caution this time. As before, the rattler struck, but when he landed on the ground Tip seized him and shook him long and

hard. This performance was repeated time after time.
The snake was a powerful and experienced fighter, and
the battle was long and hard. But finally the snake failed
to recoil.

Tip waited and watched him for a moment. Then,
shaking his head distastefully, he trotted away toward
the creek to wash that hateful taste from his mouth.

The dog gravely herded away stray cattle and horses
from the ranch. But he welcomed Mollie and her calf
with a friendly, wagging tail, although they wore the
Flying M brand now. They had been sold when his old
master left, but Tip still felt they belonged here the
same as he did.

Autumn came with its yellow-brown grass and its
chilly nights. Food was not so plentiful, yet Tip had
grown in both size and cunning. He was a beauty. In
color and marking, with the white ruff about his throat,
he was like a collie. But he resembled his shepherd ancestors in his broad, powerful frame.

One evening as he scouted up wind several miles
from his home, his keen nose caught the warm scent of
freshly killed meat. A few moments later he found two
coyotes feeding upon a dead calf.

Bristling with fury, he fell upon the killers and drove
them away. Then, after hesitating for a little, he made a
good meal of the tempting meat. Nothing would have
induced him to kill a calf; all his instincts were against
it. But the calf was dead so he ate his fill. Then, circling

about the dead animal, leaving plenty of tracks, he went his way.

After that his reputation grew. A wild dog, crafty, powerful, cruel; alone he could kill a two-year-old cow! The boys at the Flying M had strict orders to "get that dog." Of all this Tip was unaware. He went his way as usual, glorying in his strength and in the art of matching his wits, both with the wild things and with men. To him it was a game.

His avoidance of men was even more than a game. He knew of their far-reaching guns and he played safe.

Then winter with its snowy blanket closed down. Dusty was to ride the upper branches of the Little Comanche Creek, keeping watch over the range cattle and sleeping in Sims' old ranch house.

"Don't let that wild dog eat you," one of the men warned him as he was getting ready to leave the main camp.

"Oh, he's no wilder'n I am. I'll have him eating out of my hand by Christmas."

"Two bits says you won't."

"Two bits. It's a bet." Gravely they called a third cowboy to witness the wager.

Tip's home was beneath the kitchen, and at first he resented Dusty's intrusion. He stayed away for two whole days, but the next night he returned. Two saddle horses were munching hay in the barn. He listened for a moment; it was such a friendly sound. Guardedly he approached the house. It seemed as before, but his sharp ears could hear the breathing of a man within. After a long, hesitating pause, he crawled under the house and curled up in his own bed.

When Dusty started for the barn the next morning, he stopped short and a slow smile spread over his face. Those fresh tracks in the snow told their story.

"I'll win that two bits yet," he said softly. After that it became a game for two. Dusty put out food every day. Tip daintily ate what he chose, though he always left Dusty's biscuits. This amused the cowboy. "If the boys knew this I'd never hear the last of it." Still he knew it was too good to keep. He would tell them sooner or later.

In turn, Tip guarded all of Dusty's things. Each morning found fresh tracks in the snow. But the month passed, and never once had the man seen his newly found friend. Then one day Dusty lost a glove. Next morning it was on the step just outside the door.

Dusty was delighted, so he dropped his old red muffler about a quarter of a mile up the trail where he knew he could find it if Tip didn't. The lost article was on the doorstep the following morning. "Old fellow, I'll bring you a rabbit today to pay for this," he promised, addressing the mouth of Tip's hole.

Staying alone in a cow camp, seeing no one for weeks at a time, is a lonely business at best. Dusty derived a great deal of amusement from Tip's actions. To some people, winning the love of a wild thing is a fascinating pastime. It was even more than that to the big, kindly cowboy. He felt that Tip had not received a square deal.

Tip had grown fond of Dusty, too. He longed to become real friends, to feel the caress of a hand on his head. Yet those burning shots could not be easily forgotten. Thus they lived until the latter part of November; each drawing a great deal of pleasure and satisfaction from his unseen comrade.

Then one cold, bitter night Dusty did not come home. As darkness fell Tip grew uneasy. He watched and listened. Dusty had never been so late before. Tip trotted to the top of the nearest hill, then back again. Time dragged, yet no Dusty. The dog grew more and more uneasy.

Some folks declare that dogs cannot reason. Perhaps they cannot, but something had brought an anxious light to Tip's eyes as he trotted restlessly about. Finally, as if he were unable to stand the suspense any longer, he picked up the trail Dusty's horse had left in the snow that morning and followed it at an easy lope. In and out among the rough, choppy hills, repeatedly doubling back to the creek, he wound. The stinging wind was rising. Sleet beat in his face and clung to his long shaggy coat.

On and on, farther into the flinty bad lands, he traveled. He was running now, sure that something was wrong. The snow was coming fast, but the trail was still readable. Then suddenly on a steep side hill he came to a big slide in the snow. His keen nose told him the story. The horse had fallen and, with his rider, had rolled to the bottom. Tip raced on a short distance to the only dark spot in the white expanse.

It was Dusty, stretched out unconscious in the snow. His hat was gone, his face was bared to the driving sleet. Tip whined softly. His fear for the moment was forgotten as he licked the boy's icy face with his red tongue.

Again he whined, but there was no answer. He poked his nose under Dusty's arm and moved it, but the arm was cold and unresponsive. Anxiously he walked about the quiet figure. He noted how one leg was stretched out in a helpless fashion. It had made a furrow in the snow. Dusty was no quitter. Battered and bruised, with a broken leg dragging painfully behind, he had pulled himself fully fifty yards before unconsciousness overcame him.

Tip sat up and howled his longest, most anguished notes. He trotted to the top of the hill and repeated them again and again, returning at intervals to try to arouse the unconscious cowboy. Once Dusty moved a little. A faint moan escaped his lips. Raising his hand, he inadvertently rubbed it against the quivering, eager dog.

In the meantime Dusty's horse, limping badly, with the bridle reins dragging and a stain of blood on the

He rolled to the bottom of the slide.

saddle, had returned to the main ranch ten miles away.
Six men, grim and steady, started out into the rising
storm on what they knew was an almost hopeless hunt.
The back trail was dim, and snow was falling fast.
Chances were ten to one they would not find Dusty
until it was too late. He might be anywhere in an area
ten miles one way by six the other. Even if they did
find him, after lying out in this bitter cold for hours,
he—they refused to think of that.

The men spread out in twos after agreeing that three
shots fired in rapid succession would mean that Dusty
was found.

After what seemed endless hours in the saddle, Mr.
Marvin turned to Bob, his companion. "Hear that
dog howl! I'd like to shoot him." Then a little later he
added, "Funny, him howling on a night like this."

"Say!" Bob brought his horse to an abrupt halt.
"Dusty bet me twenty-five cents he could tame that
dog. Do you suppose . . ."

"There's a chance," the boss muttered. When hope
is nearly dead, men will grasp at straws. Without another word they turned and urged their horses on at
a faster pace.

The long eerie howls rose faintly again, but only
once more. Then, in spite of straining their ears hopefully, desperately, nothing but the crunching of their
horses' feet and the swirling wind could be heard.
Still they fought on blindly, refusing to give up that
one faint glimmer of hope.

After wailing until his voice was hoarse, Tip gave up calling for help. He tried in vain again to rouse Dusty, then for a few moments he lay down with his warm body close beside the boy.

Presently, as if in answer to some call, he rose and trotted down wind. At the slide he came to Dusty's hat, half buried in a drift. He hesitated a moment, then picking it up he loped away in to the night.

The two men coming to a hill paused uncertainly. "Which way?" called Bob.

The boss drew rein and wiped the snow and frost from his mustache. "Say, what's that?" He pointed.

Dimly through the falling snow they saw a quick-moving shape. It hesitated, then drew near, and laid something on the ground at the feet of Bob's horse. Then it disappeared in a flash.

Bob was on the ground instantly. "Dusty's hat."

They looked anxiously about for the dog, but the gray curtain of the storm had closed. The dog had vanished. "Here, Pup! Come, Shep!" Mr. Marvin called.

From the right-hand trail came a sharp bark. They turned and followed. Bob whistled and Mr. Marvin kept on calling, "Here, Pup. Here, Shep!" Ahead came the sharp, imperative bark.

"And to think I ordered that dog shot," the boss muttered as he urged his weary horse on. "If he takes us to Dusty, I'll . . ." What could a fellow do to square himself with a dog? He couldn't think of any way just then, but he would later.

He bounded ahead when they were following.

Thus they went on through the storm. The dog's yelping grew far away on several occasions. Then he would double back with anxious inquiries, to bound ahead again when he was sure they followed.

Suddenly the horses were floundering in the deep snow at the foot of the slide. In a glance the men read the grim story of the fall! Tip raced ahead to Dusty's side to lick his hand and tell him help was coming.

Three shots were fired into the air; the men were off their horses. Shoving aside the drifted snow, they began rubbing Dusty's numb arms and feet. A roll from behind the boss's saddle turned out to be a warm wool blanket and a thermos bottle of steaming coffee. The boss took his sheepskin coat, warm from his own body, and put it on the unconscious cowboy.

Soon two other men arrived. Tip hovered about, watching. At last he saw Dusty open his eyes, choke on the hot coffee, then speak. Tip's work was done. Dusty would be all right now, he was sure, so he turned his steps homeward.

There was a certain pride in his bearing as he went his rounds about the ranch in the days that followed. Again he was gallantly taking care of the place as he waited a loved one's return, and this time he did not wait in vain.

ALICE DALGLIESH

Meals for Mickey

It's too hot to do anything," said Tim. He ran
his hands through his wet, fair hair until it stood on
end.

"But think how much hotter it is in the city," said
Robin. "In our apartment it must be simply sizzling."

Tim and his sister were sitting on the hill looking
down over their house. It was a small white house,
snuggled close on the Connecticut hillside, a comfortable little house with a gray roof and climbing roses
over the doorways. It had not belonged to the Storms
long enough for them to be quite used to it; in fact,
they had bought it only three months before. Inside
the house there was still a great deal to be done; it was
an old house and had not been lived in for years.

"Mother wants us to help her take the old wallpaper
off our room," said Robin. "She said we could wait
a day or two until it was cooler."

"I should think so!" said Tim. He looked down at
the little village that lay in the valley, far below their

own house. A bright red roof stood out from among the gray ones.

"Look, Robin! That's the new hot-dog stand. Let's go down and get a frozen custard. Haven't you a nickel?"

"Yes," said Robin, "but I was going to buy—"

"Oh, come on—it's too hot to do anything else. We'll stop and ask Mother if we can go."

A few minutes later Tim and Robin were on their way down the warm, sunny road. As they reached the main highway, a long string of cars went hurrying past, cars of people trying to escape the city heat. In front of the hot-dog stand many cars were parked. Under a large tree there were several tables. One was vacant.

"Let's eat out here instead of having a cone," said Robin. They sat down and soon were eating the cold frozen custard.

"M—m! This is the stuff," said Tim. "Make it last a long time, Robin."

Robin took a quarter of a spoonful. Then she dropped her spoon in the dish.

"Tim, look! Look!"

An enormous, tan-colored dog was coming through the doorway of the little house. Slowly it walked over to the table where the children sat. For a moment it stood looking at them, then came forward and stood beside Robin, wagging its tail.

"It's a Great Dane!" said Robin. She patted the huge head. "He's friendly."

The woman who kept the stand came out. "Don't you want a dog?" she asked.

Robin and Tim stared at her, wondering if they had heard the words aright.

"A dog? Not *this* one?"

The woman nodded. "Yes. I haven't had him long. His master moved away and couldn't take him so he gave him to us. Since we've had the stand, he's been a perfect pest. He's scared of the motorcycles—shivers when he hears one. And he frightens the customers. Gentle as a kitten he is, but how would they ever know that?"

Robin looked at Tim. "Can we take him? Shall we go home and ask Mother first?"

"If we do," said Tim, "she'll say 'no.' But if we walk into the yard with a perfectly beautiful dog, she won't have the heart to refuse. Let's try it, anyway."

"You'll have no trouble holding him," said the woman, as she snapped the leash on the big dog's collar. "He's trained to walk by you and not tug at the leash."

"What is his name?" asked Robin. Her answer made both chiddren laugh and they were still giggling as they went up the road. They took turns holding the leash, and the big dog paced alongside of them like a gentleman.

Mother was in the garden when the children and the dog turned in the gate.

"Mother," said Tim, with a confidence he did not really feel. "This is our new dog."

"Well, really!" said Mother. "Nothing much surprises me any more, but this is a little difficult. Suppose you explain!"

"Mother, this is our new dog."

It took quite a bit of explaining. Mother looked doubtful. The children looked worried. Then the dog walked up to Mother and rubbed his head against her.

"He's pretty nice," admitted Mother. "What is his name?"

"Mickey Mouse!" said Robin in a slightly choked voice, and all three of them laughed until they ached.

"Mickey Mouse!" said Mother. "It simply *can't* be. I think I'll say you can keep him if you change his name. A Great Dane named Mickey Mouse is just *too* much."

"We could call him Sir Michael," said Robin. "Mickey for short."

"Hooray! We can keep him!" shouted Tim. "Mom, you're a good sport!"

"Of course, there's Father to be thought of, too," said Mother. "It's time to go to meet the 5:55—so let's all go to the station and break the news."

Father took the news calmly but said just one thing that disturbed everyone.

"My dear young friends," he said, "have you remembered that your father is an artist and that sometimes he makes money and sometimes not? And have you thought of how much food a Great Dane eats in one day? Can't you guess?"

"How much?" asked Robin anxiously.

"Four pounds of meat," answered Father. There was dead silence. Everyone knew about the price of meat, and since they had bought the house there had not been much extra money.

"We'll have to do something to earn the money," said Tim desperately. "We'll *have* to keep him. Perhaps I could mow lawns."

"We'll think it over," said Father. "Remember you're not so good even at mowing our own lawn. Anyway, we'd better stop at the store and get the animal some food. We can't let him starve to death."

The Storms all sat around and watched Mickey have his first meal. It was all over in an astonishingly short time.

"If only his mouth were smaller, or something," said Robin. "It's like the Mammoth Cave of Kentucky."

"That wouldn't help. It's his stomach that's too big," said Tim. "I've read that if you don't eat for days your stomach shrinks. Maybe we could shrink his."

"Not a chance," said Father gloomily.

Night came and with it the question of a bed for Mickey. Mickey himself settled it, for he stretched out on the rug in front of the fire.

"He looks as if he'd always been here!" said Tim. "I guess dogs know when people really want them."

The next day the Storms began to find out that having a Great Dane in a small house is like having an elephant in a too small inclosure. One had to get used to Mickey, and even though he tried his best to be helpful about his size he was quite often in the way.

In the afternoon a friend of Mother's came to visit, a friend who owned a very small pomeranian called "Ducky." Tim and Robin called him the puffball, and did not consider him a dog at all. Somehow, when the puffball arrived, Mother forgot about Mickey. Ducky was prancing about the lawn looking like an animated powder puff when Mickey came round the corner. Ducky's mistress screamed. Mother and children sat in frozen horror, quite unable to do anything at all. Ducky stood still and Mickey bore down upon him.

A thought flashed through Robin's mind. "Mickey's mouth! The puffball will make exactly one mouthful." But Mickey's mouth did not open. The puffball stood his ground. Mickey's great tail began to wag. The dogs met. They sniffed. The puffball's tail began to wag. Away over the lawn went the two dogs, the puffball yelping joyously.

"I'll never laugh at Ducky again," whispered Robin to Tim. "He ought to have a medal or something for standing still and letting a great giant like that come up to him."

The first week went by without any mishaps except that Mickey lay down in the middle of one of Mother's pet garden beds and when he got up, there was a very large, flat place.

"Hc has only to lie down a few more times," said Mother, "and there will be no garden at all." She looked at the flattened zinnias. "A steam roller couldn't have done better."

It was a little unfortunate, perhaps, that the grocery

bill came in on the day that Mickey had sat down in the garden. "Look at it," said Mother.

4 pounds of hamburger—"for Mickey."

6 lamb chops—"those were for us."

4 pounds of hamburger—"for Mickey."

1 sirloin roast—"for us."

and so on

"Mickey eats more than we do! Something must be done about it." Mother was very emphatic.

That night Robin and Tim went to bed feeling very sad indeed. After they were in bed, they could hear Father and Mother talking things over. Bits of the conversation floated in to them (—can't possibly do it"— "another home"—"perhaps on a farm"—"the children will be upset." Robin cried herself to sleep.

The next day the weather was cooler than it had been for some time and the children began work on the wallpaper of their room. Mickey lay watching them, his head on his paws. Already, he found his new home very satisfactory.

"Robin," said Tim as he peeled a long strip of wallpaper, "Mother didn't say anything about Mickey this morning, did she? Do you think she's changed her mind?"

"I'm afraid not," sighed Robin. "O Tim, what do you suppose that funny bulge is over the fireplace?"

Tim came over to look. "It's something they used to close up the stove hole," he said.

Robin went on peeling and scraping. "Tim! It's canvas! It looks like the back of a picture."

"Sure does!" said Tim. "They've got an old piece of canvas or else a painting tacked over there. Easy, Robin! I'll get the screw driver."

Carefully they pried the canvas loose from the wall. It was sooty and dusty, but it was a picture.

"Mother!" they shouted, "come quickly! Look what we found." Mother came hurrying in. She looked at the picture carefully, took a rag and removed some of the dirt.

"It's an old portrait of a child," she said. "It might be valuable, and we'd better wait for Father. He will know just how to clean it up."

"Valuable!" Robin and Tim looked at each other, the same thought racing through their minds. Perhaps it would mean at least a dozen square meals for Mickey!

Father was even more excited about the picture than the rest of the family had been. He cleaned it carefully. It was a portrait of a little fair-haired girl in a stiff, brocaded dress.

"It must be quite old," said Robin.

"The face looks as if it didn't quite belong to the rest of it."

"It doesn't," said Father. "Traveling portrait painters used to paint the bodies and clothes of their pictures in the winter time, then in the summer the pictures were all ready to have the faces painted in.

They pried the canvas loose from the wall.

Of course the clothes didn't really suit the people who had the portraits painted. This little girl probably never wore such a handsome dress."

"How queer!" said Tim. "But, Father, do you think it's valuable?"

"I'm pretty sure it is," said Father. He looked at the large blank space over the big living-room fireplace. "It would go well there."

Tim and Robin looked at each other in despair.

"We thought—" began Robin.

"We hoped—" went on Tim.

"That we could sell the picture," said Robin. "The money would feed Mickey for at least a week."

"We must think this over," said Father. "You found it, but of course I paid for the house, and so the picture is partly mine, isn't it?"

"I suppose so," said Tim slowly. "Then we ought to share the proceeds."

"That's the right way of it," said Father. "I tell you what we'll do. I'll agree that if the picture is really valuable, one half of the money shall go to feed Mickey for as long as it will last and one half shall be used on house improvements. That means wallpaper for your rooms, you know, so you really share in that."

The children agreed that this was fair. Father rolled the picture up carefully and took it into town with him. The day seemed long, and the children got Mother and the car to the 5:55 fifteen minutes ahead of time.

They walked slowly up and down the platform, with Mickey pacing behind them. Mickey was feeling snug and comfortable inside, for he had just finished four pounds of hamburger. He knew, however, that something must be wrong because his master and mistress seemed so worried, so he tried licking their hands to see if that would help. It did not seem to help very much. Tears came into Robin's eyes and splashed on Mickey's head as she put her arm around his neck.

"You're such a lamb, Mickey, suppose the picture isn't worth much and we can't keep you?"

The train was coming down the track. It stopped and Father got off. Two children and a dog rushed up to him so fast that Father almost lost his balance.

"Steady! Steady there!"

"Father—is it?"

"Can we?"

"Was it——"

"It was," said Father as they got into the car. "Quite valuable, though not so valuable as I expected. Anyway, your share will be enough to keep Mickey for a year—maybe longer. I also went to see a man who raises dogs and he told me about a good kennel food that's cheaper than meat. He says dogs do well on it and it will save us a good deal of money. There's just one thing," he stopped and looked seriously at the children. "I am starting a bank account for you, and you may draw out enough for Mickey's food each month.

But—what about the time when Robin wants a new book, or Tim wants something for his bicycle? What about ice-cream cones?"

By this time the car had turned in the gate and stopped in front of the door. Mickey was bounding joyfully across the lawn as if he knew that this was his home forever. Robin looked down across the valley. The red roof of the hot-dog stand seemed very inviting. But Robin shook her head.

"No," she said. "Not one penny goes for anything but hamburger and dog food. And when it's all used up, we'll find a way to get some more. Mickey is going to stay!"

ERIC KNIGHT

Lassie Come Home

The dog had met the boy by the school gate for five years. Now she couldn't understand that times were changed and she wasn't supposed to be there any more. But the boy knew.

So when he opened the door of the cottage, he spoke before he entered.

"Mother," he said, "Lassie's come home again."

He waited a moment, as if in hope of something. But the man and woman inside the cottage did not speak.

"Come in, Lassie," the boy said.

He held open the door, and the tricolor collie walked in obediently. Going head down, as a collie does when it knows something is wrong, it went to the rug and lay down before the hearth, a black-white-and-gold aristocrat. The man, sitting on a low stool by the fireside, kept his eyes turned away. The woman went to the sink and busied herself there.

"She were waiting at school for me, just like always," the boy went on. He spoke fast, as if racing against

"She were waiting for me, just like always."

time. "She must ha' got away again. I thought, happen this time, we might just—"

"No!" the woman exploded.

The boy's carelessness dropped. His voice rose in pleading.

"But this time, mother! Just this time. We could hide her. They wouldn't ever know."

"Dogs, dogs, dogs!" the woman cried. The words poured from her as if the boy's pleading had been a signal gun for her own anger.

"I'm sick o' hearing about tykes around this house. Well, she's sold and gone and done with, so the quicker she's taken back the better. Now get her back quick, or first thing ye know we'll have Hynes round here again. Mr. Hynes!"

Her voice sharpened in imitation of the Cockney accent of the south. "Hi know you Yorkshiremen and yer come-'ome dogs. Training yer dogs to come 'ome so's yer can sell 'em hover and hover again.

"Well, she's sold, so ye can take her out o' my house and home to them as bought her!"

The boy's bottom lip crept out stubbornly, and there was silence in the cottage. Then the dog lifted its head and nudged the man's hand, as a dog will when asking for patting. But the man drew away and stared, silently, into the fire.

The boy tried again, with the ceaseless guile of a child, his voice coaxing.

"Look, feyther, she wants thee to bid her welcome. Aye, she's that glad to be home. Happen they don't tak' good care on her up there? Look, her coat's a bit poorly, don't ye think? A bit o' linseed strained through her drinking water—that's what I'd gi' her."

Still looking in the fire, the man nodded. But the woman, as if perceiving the boy's new attack, sniffed.

"Aye, tha wouldn't be a Carraclough if tha didn't know more about tykes nor breaking eggs we' a stick. Nor a Yorkshireman. My goodness, it seems to me sometimes that chaps in this village thinks more on their tykes nor they do o' their own flesh and blood. They'll sit by their firesides and let their own bairns starve so long as t' dog gets fed."

The man stirred, suddenly, but the boy cut in quickly.

"But she does look thin. Look, truly—they're not feeding her right. Just look!"

"Aye," the woman chattered. "I wouldn't put it past Hynes to steal t' best part o' t' dog meat for himself. And Lassie always was a strong eater."

"She's fair thin now," the boy said.

Almost unwillingly the man and woman looked at the dog for the first time.

"My gum, she is off a bit," the woman said. Then she caught herself. "Ma goodness, I suppose I'll have to fix her a bit o' summat. She can do wi' it. But soon as she's fed, back she goes. And never another dog I'll have in my house. Never another. Cooking and nursing for 'em, and as much trouble to bring up as a bairn!"

So, grumbling and chatting as a village woman will, she moved about, warming a pan of food for the dog. The man and boy watched the collie eat. When it was done, the boy took from the mantelpiece a folded cloth and a brush, and began prettying the collie's coat. The man watched for several minutes, and then could stand it no longer.

"Here," he said.

He took the cloth and brush from the boy and began working expertly on the dog, rubbing the rich, deep coat, thcn brushing the snowy whiteness of the full ruff and the apron, bringing out the heavy leggings on the forelegs. He lost himself in his work, and the boy sat on the rug, watching contentedly. The woman stood it as long as she could.

"Now will ye please tak' that tyke out o' here?"

The man flared in anger.

"Well, ye wouldn't have me tak' her back looking like a mucky Monday wash, wouldta?"

He bent again, and began fluffing out the collie's petticoats.

"Joe!" the woman pleaded. "Will ye tak' her out o' here? Hynes'll be nosing round afore ye know it. And I won't have that man in my house. Wearing his hat inside, and going on like he's the duke himself—him and his leggings!"

"All right, lass."

"And this time, Joe, tak' young Joe wi' ye."

"What for?"

"Well, let's get the business done and over with. It's him that Lassie runs away for. She comes for young Joe. So if he went wi' thee, and told her to stay, happen she'd be content and not run away no more, and then we'd have a little peace and quiet in the home—though heaven knows there's not much hope o' that these days, things being like they are." The woman's voice trailed away, as if she would soon cry in weariness.

The man rose. "Come, Joe," he said. "Get thy cap."

The Duke of Rudling walked along the gravel paths of his place with his granddaughter, Philippa. Philippa was a bright and knowing young woman, allegedly the only member of the duke's family he could address in unspotted language. For it was also alleged that the duke was the most irascible, vile-tempered old man in the three Ridings of Yorkshire.

"Country going to pot!" the duke roared, stabbing at the walk with his great blackthorn stick. "When I was a young man! Hah! Women today not as pretty. Horses today not as fast. As for dogs—ye don't see dogs today like—"

Just then the duke and Philippa came round a clump of rhododendrons and saw a man, a boy and a dog.

"Ah," said the duke, in admiration. Then his brow

knotted. "Damme, Carraclough! What're ye doing with my dog?"

He shouted it quite as if the others were in the next county, for it was also the opinion of the Duke of Rudling that people were not nearly so keen of hearing as they used to be when he was a young man.

"It's Lassie," Carraclough said. "She runned away again and I brought her back."

Carraclough lifted his cap, and poked the boy to do the same, not in any servile gesture, but to show that they were as well brought up as the rest.

"Damme, ran away again!" the duke roared. "And I told that utter nincompoop Hynes to—where is he? Hynes! Hynes! Damme, Hynes, what're ye hiding for?"

"Coming, your lordship!" sounded a voice, far away behind the shrubberies. And soon Hynes appeared, a sharpfaced man in check coat, riding breeches, and the cloth leggings that grooms wear.

"Take this dog," roared the duke, "and pen her up! And damme, if she breaks out again, I'll—I'll—"

The duke waved his great stick threateningly, and then, without so much as a thank you or kiss the back of my hand to Joe Carraclough, he went stamping and muttering away.

"I'll pen her up," Hynes muttered, when the duke was gone. "And if she ever gets awye agyne, I'll—"

He made as if to grab the dog, but Joe Carraclough's hobnailed boot trod heavily on Hynes' foot.

"I brought my lad we' me to bid her stay, so we'll pen her up this time. Eigh—sorry! I didn't see I were on thy foot. Come, Joe, lad."

They walked down the crunching gravel path, along by the neat kennel buildings. When Lassie was behind the closed door, she raced into the high wire run where she could see them as they went. She pressed close against the wire, waiting.

The boy stood close, too, his fingers through the meshes touching the dog's nose.

"Go on, lad," his father ordered. "Bid her stay!"

The boy looked around, as if for help that he did not find. He swallowed, and then spoke, low and quickly.

"Stay here, Lassie, and don't come home no more," he said. "And don't come to school for me no more. Because I don't want to see ye no more. 'Cause tha's a bad dog, and we don't love thee no more, and we don't want thee. So stay there forever and leave us be, and don't never come home no more."

Then he turned, and because it was hard to see the path plainly, he stumbled. But his father, who was holding his head very high as they walked away from Hynes, shook him savagely, and snapped roughly: "Look where tha's going!"

Then the boy trotted beside his father. He was thinking that he'd never be able to understand why grown-ups sometimes were so bad-tempered with you, just when you needed them most.

After that, there were days and days that passed, and the dog did not come to the school gate any more. So then it was not like old times. There were so many things that were not like old times.

The boy was thinking that as he came wearily up the path and opened the cottage door and heard his father's voice, tense with anger: ". . . walk my feet off. If tha thinks I like—"

Then they heard his opening of the door and the voice stopped and the cottage was silent.

That's how it was now, the boy thought. They stopped talking in front of you. And this, somehow, was too much for him to bear.

He closed the door, ran out into the night, and onto the moor, that great flat expanse of land where all the people of that village walked in lonesomeness when life and its troubles seemed past bearing.

A long while later, his father's voice cut through the darkness.

"What's tha doing out here, Joe lad?"

"Walking."

"Aye."

They went on together, aimlessly, each following his own thoughts. And they both thought about the dog that had been sold.

"Tha maun't think we're hard on thee, Joe," the man said at last. "It's just that a chap's got to be honest. There's that to it. Sometimes, when a chap doesn't have much, he clings right hard to what he's got. And honest is honest, and there's no two ways about it.

"Why, look, Joe. Seventeen year I worked in that Clarabelle Pit till she shut down, and a good collier too. Seventeen year! And butties I've had by the dozen, and never a man of 'em can every say that Joe Carraclough kept what wasn't his, nor spoke what wasn't true. Not a man in his Riding can ever call a Carraclough mishonest.

"And when ye've sold a man summat, and ye've taken his brass, and ye've spent it—well, then done's done. That's all. And ye've got to stand by that."

"But Lassie was—"

"Now, Joe! Ye can't alter it, ever. It's done—and happen it's for t' best. No two ways, Joe, she were getting hard to feed. Why, ye wouldn't want Lassie to be going around getting peaked and pined, like some chaps round here keep their tykes. And if ye're fond of her, then just think on it that now she's got lots to eat, and a private kennel, and a good run to herself, and living like a varritable princess, she is. Ain't that best for her?"

"We wouldn't pine her. We've always got lots to eat."

The man blew out his breath, angrily. "Eigh, Joe, nowt pleases thee. Well then, tha might as well have it. Tha'll never see Lassie no more. She run home once too often, so the duke's taken her wi' him up to his place in Scotland, and there she'll stay. So it's good-by and good luck to her, and she'll never come home no more, she won't. Now, I weren't off to tell thee, but there it is, so put it in thy pipe and smoke it, and let's never say a word about it no more—especially in front of thy mother."

The boy stumbled on in the darkness. Then the man halted.

"We ought to be getting back, lad. We left thy mother alone."

He turned the boy about, and then went on, but as if he were talking to himself.

"Tha sees, Joe, women's not like men. They have to stay home and manage best they can, and just spend the time in wishing. And when things don't go right, well, they have to take it out in talk and give a man hell. But it don't mean nowt, really, so tha shouldn't mind when thy mother talks hard.

"Ye just got to learn to be patient and let 'em talk, and just let it go up t' chimney wi' th' smoke."

Then they were quiet, until, over the rise, they saw the lights on the village. Then the boy spoke: "How far away is Scotland, feyther?"

"Nay, lad, it's a long, long road."

"But how far, feyther?"

"I don't know—but it's a longer road than thee or

me'll ever walk. Now, lad. Don't fret no more, and
try to be a man—and don't plague thy mother no
more, wilta?"

Joe Carraclough was right. It is a long road, as they
say in the North, from Yorkshire to Scotland. Much
too far for a man to walk—or a boy. And though the
boy often thought of it, he remembered his father's
words on the moor, and he put the thought behind
him.

But there is another way of looking at it; and that's
the distance from Scotland to Yorkshire. And that is
just as far as from Yorkshire to Scotland. A matter of
about four hundred miles, it would be, from the Duke
of Rudling's place far up in the Highlands, to the village of Holdersby. That would be for a man, who could
go fairly straight.

To an animal, how much farther would it be? For a
dog can study no maps, read no signposts, ask no directions. It could only go blindly, by instinct, knowing
that it must keep on to the south, to the south. It
would wander and err, quest and quarter, run into firths
and lochs that would send it side-tracking and back-
tracking before it could go again on its way—south.

A thousand miles, it would be, going that way—a
thousand miles over strange terrain.

There would be moors to cross, and burns to swim.

And then those great, long lochs that stretch almost from one side of that dour land to another would bar the way and send a dog questing a hundred miles before it could find a crossing that would allow it to go south.

And, too, there would be rivers to cross, wide rivers like the Forth and the Clyde, the Tweed and the Tyne, where one must go miles to find bridges. And the bridges would be in towns. And in the towns there would be officials—like the one in Lanarkshire. In all his life he had never let a captured dog get away—except one. That one was a gaunt, snarling collie that whirled on him right in the pound itself, and fought and twisted loose to race away down the city street—going south.

But there are also kind people, too; ones knowing and understanding in the ways of dogs. There was an old couple in Durham who found a dog lying exhausted in a ditch one night—lying there with its head to the south. They took that dog into their cottage and warmed it and fed it and nursed it. And because it seemed an understanding, wise dog, they kept it in their home, hoping it would learn to be content. But, as it grew stronger, every afternoon toward four o'clock it would go to the door and whine, and then begin pacing back and forth between the door and the window, back and forth as the animals do in their cages at the zoo.

They tried every wile and every kindness to make it bide with them, but finally, when the dog began to refuse food, the old people knew what they must do. Because they understood dogs, they opened the door one afternoon and they watched a collie go, not down

—a dog that lay weakly, trying to lift her head.

the road to the right, or to the left, but straight across a field toward the south; going steadily at a trot, as if it knew it still had a long, long road to travel.

Ah, a thousand miles of tor and brae, of shire and noor, of path and road and plowland, of river and stream and burn and brook and beck, of snow and rain and fog and sun, is a long way, even for a human being.

But it would seem too far—much, much too far—for any dog to travel blindly and win through.

And yet—and yet—who shall say why, when so many weeks had passed that hope against hope was dying, a boy coming out of school, out of the cloakroom that always smelled of damp wool drying, across the concrete play yard with the black, waxed slides, should turn his eyes to a spot by the school gate from force of five years of habit, and see there a dog?

Not a dog, this one, that lifted glad ears above a proud, slim head with its black-and-gold mask; but a dog that lay weakly, trying to lift a head that would no longer lift, trying to wag a tail that was torn and blotched and matted with dirt and burs, and managing to do nothing much except to whine in a weak, happy, crying way as a boy on his knees threw arms about it, and hands touched it that had not touched it for many a day.

Then who shall picture the urgency of a boy, running, awkwardly, with a great dog in his arms running through the village, past the empty mill, past the Labor Exchange, where the men looked up from their deep ponderings on life and the dole? Or who shall describe the high tones of a voice—a boy's voice, calling as he runs up a path: "Mother! Oh, Mother! Lassie's come home! Lassie's come home!"

Nor does anyone who ever owned a dog need to be told the sound a man makes as he bends over a dog

that has been his for many years; nor how a woman
moves quickly, preparing food—which might be the
family's condensed milk stirred into warm water; nor
how the jowl of a dog is lifted so that raw egg and
brandy, bought with precious pence, should be
spooned in; nor how bleeding pads are bandaged, tenderly.

That was one day. There was another day when the
woman in the cottage sighed with pleasure, for a dog
lifted itself to its feet for the first time to stand over a
bowl of oatmeal, putting its head down and lapping
again and again while its pinched flanks quivered.

And there was another day when the boy realized
that, even now, the dog was not to be his again. So the
cottage rang again with protests and cries, and a
woman shrilling: "Is there never to be no more peace
in my house and home?" Long after he was in bed that
night the boy heard the rise and fall of the woman's
voice, and the steady, reiterative tone of the man's. It
went on long after he was asleep.

In the morning the man spoke, not looking at the
boy, saying the words as if he had long rehearsed them.

"Thy mother and me have decided upon it that
Lassie shall stay here till she's better. Anyhow, nobody
could nurse her better than us. But the day that t' duke
comes back, then back she goes, too. For she belongs
to him, and that's honest, too. Now tha has her for a
while, so be content."

In childhood, "for a while" is such a great stretch of days when seen from one end. It is a terribly short time seen from the other.

The boy knew how short it was that morning as he went to school and saw a motorcar driven by a young woman. And in the car was a gray-thatched, terrible old man, who waved a cane and shouted: "Hi! Hi, there! Damme, lad! You there! Hi!"

Then it was no use running, for the car could go faster than you, and soon it was beside you and the man was saying: "Damme, Philippa, will you make this smelling thing stand still a moment? Hi, lad!"

"Yes, sir."

"You're What's-'is-Name's lad, aren't you?"

"Ma feyther's Joe Carraclough."

"I know. I know. Is he home now?"

"No, sir. He's away to Allerby. A mate spoke for him at the pit and he's gone to see if there's a chance."

"When'll he be back?"

"I don't know. I think about tea."

"Eh, yes. Well, yes. I'll drop round about fivish to see that father of yours. Something important."

It was hard to pretend to listen to lessons. There was only waiting for noon. Then the boy ran home.

"Mother! T'duke is back and he's coming to take Lassie away."

"Eigh, drat my buttons. Never no peace in this house. Is tha sure?"

"Aye. He stopped me. He said tell feyther he'll be round at five. Can't we hide her? Oh, Mother."

"Nay, thy feyther—"

"Won't you beg him? Please, please. Beg feyther to—"

"Young Joe, now it's no use. So stop thy teasing! Thy feyther'll not lie. That much I'll give him. Come good, come bad, he'll not lie."

"But just this once, Mother. Please beg him, just this once. Just one lie wouldn't hurt him. I'll make it up to him. I will. When I'm growed up, I'll get a job. I'll make money. I'll buy him things—and you, too. I'll buy you both anything you want if you'll only—"

For the first time in his trouble the boy became a child, and the mother, looking over, saw the tears that ran openly down his contorted face. She turned her face to the fire, and there was a pause. Then she spoke.

"Joe, tha mustn't," she said softly. "Tha must learn never to want nothing in life like that. It don't do, lad. Tha mustn't want things bad, like tha wants Lassie."

The boy shook his clenched fists in impatience.

"It ain't that, mother. Ye don't understand. Don't ye see—it ain't me that wants her. It's her that wants us! Tha's wha made her come all them miles. It's her that wants us, so terrible bad!"

The woman turned and stared. It was as if, in that moment, she were seeing this child, this boy, this son

of her own, for the first time in many years. She turned
her head down toward the table. It was surrender.

"Come and eat, then," she said. "I'll talk to him. I
will that, all right. I feel sure he won't lie. But I'll talk
to him, all right. I'll talk to Mr. Joe Carraclough. I
will indeed."

At five that afternoon, the Duke of Rudling, fuming
and muttering got out of a car at a cottage gate to find
a boy barring his way. This was a boy who stood, stubbornly, saying fiercely: "Away we' thee! They tyke's net
here!"

"Damme, Philippa, th' lad's touched," the duke
said. "He is. He's touched."

Scowling and thumping his stick, the old duke advanced until the boy gave way, backing down the path
out of the reach of the waving blackthorn stick.

"Thy tyke's net here," the boy protested.

"What's he saying?" the girl asked.

"Says my dog isn't here. Damme, you going deaf?
I'm supposed to be deaf, and I hear him plainly
enough. Now, ma lad, what tyke o' mine's net here?"

As he turned to the boy, the duke spoke in broadest
Yorkshire, as he did always to the people of the cottages—a habit which the Duchess of Rudling, and
many more members of the duke's family, deplored.

"Coom, coom, ma lad. Whet tyke's net here?"

"No tyke o' thine. Us hasn't got it." The words began running faster and faster as the boy backed away from the fearful old man who advanced. "No tyke could have done it. No tyke can come all them miles. It isn't Lassie. It's another one that looks like her. It isn't Lassie!"

"Why, bless ma heart and sowl," the duke puffed. "Where's thy father, ma lad?"

The door behind the boy opened, and a woman's voice spoke.

"If it's Joe Carraclough ye want, he's out in the shed —and been there shut up half the afternoon."

"What's this lad talking about—a dog of mine being here?"

"Nay," the woman snapped quickly. "He didn't say a tyke o' thine was here. He said it wasn't here."

"Well, what dog o' mine isn't here, then?"

The woman swallowed, and looked about as if for help. The duke stood, peering from under his jutting eyebrows. Her answer, truth or lie, was never spoken, for then they heard the rattle of a door opening, and a man making a pursing sound with his lips, as he will when he wants a dog to follow, and then Joe Carraclough's voice said, "This is t' only tyke us has here. Does it look like any dog that belongs to thee?"

With his mouth opening to cry one last protest, the boy turned. And his mouth stayed open. For there he

"Does it look like a dog that belongs to thee?"

saw his father, Joe Carraclough, the collie fancier,
standing with a dog at his heels—a dog that sat at his
left heel patiently, as any well-trained dog should do—
as Lassie used to do. But this dog was not Lassie. In
fact, it was ridiculous to think of it at the same moment as you thought of Lassie.

For where Lassie's skull was aristocratic and slim,
this dog's head was clumsy and rough. Where Lassie's
ears stood in twin-lapped symmetry, this dog had one
ear draggling and the other standing up Alsatian fashion in a way to give any collie breeder the cold shivers.
Where Lassie's coat was rich tawny gold, this dog's
coat had ugly patches of black; and where Lassie's
apron was a billowing stretch of snow-white, this dog
had puddles of off-color blue-merle mixture. Besides,
Lassie had four white paws, and this one had one paw
white, two dirty-brown, and one almost black.

That is the dog they all looked at as Joe Carraclough
stood there, having told no lie, having only asked a
question. They all stood, waiting the duke's verdict.

But the duke said nothing. He only walked forward,
slowly, as if he were seeing a dream. He bent beside
the collie, looking with eyes that were as knowing about
dogs as any Yorkshireman alive. And those eyes did not
waste themselves upon twisted ears, or blotched marking, or rough head. Instead they were looking at a paw
that the duke lifted, looking at the underside of the
paw, staring intently at five black pads, crossed and

recrossed with the scars where thorns had lacerated, and stones had torn.

For a long time the duke stared, and when he got up he did not speak in Yorkshire accents any more. He spoke as a gentleman should, and he said: "Joe Carraclough. I never owned this dog. 'Pon my soul, she's never belonged to me. Never!"

Then he turned and went stumping down the path, thumping his cane and saying: "Bless my soul. Four hundred miles! Damme, wouldn't ha' believed it. Damme—five hundred miles!"

He was at the gate when his granddaughter whispered to him fiercely.

"Of course," he cried. "Mind your own business. Exactly what I came for. Talking about dogs made me forget. Carraclough! Carraclough! What're ye hiding for?"

"I'm still here, sir."

"Ah, there you are. You working?"

"Eigh, now. Working," Joe said. That's the best he could manage.

"Yes, working, working!" The duke fumed.

"Well, now—" Joe began.

Then Mrs. Carraclough came to his rescue, as a good housewife in Yorkshire will.

"Why, Joe's got three or four things that he's been considering," she said, with proper display of pride. "But he hasn't quite said yes or no to any of them yet."

"Then say no, quick," the old man puffed. "Had to sack Hynes. Didn't know a dog from a drunken filly. Should ha' known all along no Londoner could handle dogs fit for Yorkshire taste. How much, Carraclough?"

"Well, now," Joe began.

"Seven pounds a week, and worth every penny," Mrs. Carraclough chipped in.

"Five," roared the duke—who, after all, was a Yorkshireman, and couldn't help being a bit sharp about things that pertained to money.

"Six," said Mrs. Carraclough.

"Five pound ten," bargained the duke, cannily.

"Done," said Mrs. Carraclough, who would have been willing to settle for three pounds in the first place. "But, o' course, us gets the cottage too."

"All right," puffed the duke. "Five pounds ten and the cottage. Begin Monday. But—on one condition. Carraclough, you can live on my land, but I won't have that thick-skulled, screw-lugged, gay-tailed eyesore of a misshapen mongrel on my property. Now never let me see her again. You'll get rid of her?"

He waited, and Joe fumbled for words. But it was the boy who answered, happily, gaily: "Oh, no, sir. She'll be waiting at school for me most o' the time. And, anyway, in a day or so we'll have her fixed up and coped up so's ye'd never, never recognize her."

"I don't doubt that," puffed the duke, as he went to the car. "I don't doubt ye could do just exactly that."

It was a long time afterward, in the car, that the girl said: "Don't sit there like a lion on the Nelson column. And I thought you were supposed to be a hard man."

"Fiddlesticks, m'dear. I'm a ruthless realist. For five years I've sworn I'd have that dog by hook or crook, and now, egad, at last I've got her."

"Pooh! You had to buy the man before you could get his dog."

"Well, perhaps that's not the worst part of the bargain."

LAVINIA DAVIS

The Foolish Dog of Brother John

Long ago, before there were any automobiles, people walked from town to town and even from one country to another. When a poor man went to find work or made a pilgrimage to a holy shrine he travelled on foot. The way from Germany to Italy led over the Swiss Alps and was one of the most dangerous walks in all the world. Many a traveller would have lost his life in the mountains if it had not been for the Brothers of St. Bernard and their wonderful dogs.

The Brothers lived and worked in a stone building called a hospice. The hospice was built high up in the mountains not far from the steepest part of the trail over the Alps. Year in and year out the Brothers cared for all needy travellers without asking for any reward for themselves. The dogs helped them in many ways but especially by finding people who had lost their way.

They were strong, brave dogs, these St. Bernards, and skilled in rescue work. They had wonderful noses which helped them to find people by smell through the deepest snow. And such a sense of direction that no matter how it stormed they always knew the way home to the hospice.

Whenever there were puppies or new young dogs at the hospice all the Brothers looked them over hoping that one would be like Barry. Barry, who was the greatest of all St. Bernards, had saved forty lives. Forty lives, mind you, and some people say he died saving the forty-first.

Now one summer day when Brother John was schooling the four youngest dogs he was very worried. Three of the dogs were neatly built with smooth hair and dark, serious eyes. They minded perfectly and worked hard, learning everything Brother John had to teach them. But the fourth dog was different.

His brown coat was shaggy and spattered with black and white patches. He was bigger than the others, clumsier, and his light eyes always seemed to be laughing. Worst of all he didn't even try to learn his lessons. He just wanted to play; or eat. Or stay close by Brother John waiting to be petted.

Brother John loved this playful, shaggy dog even though he was not in the least like Barry. He worried about him too, because he knew that when food grew

scarce in the winter the Brothers could not keep a dog
who did not even try to be useful.

Brother John sighed as he thought of it. Right away
the big dog pranced over to cheer him up. The dog's
head was cocked to one side so that his patches looked
like a paper party hat. The white fur on his big paws
looked like thick woolly socks. As he rolled over in front
of Brother John the good man had to laugh in spite of
his worries. Then he started all over again trying to
teach the dog to mind and fetch and carry.

Towards the end of summer, the Abbot in charge of
the hospice, decided the time had come to give the
four young dogs their grown-up names and their St.
Bernard collars. The collars were made of leather and
each one had a small keg of brandy fastened to it. The
brandy was to warm any half frozen traveller the dogs
might find in the mountains.

Of course the naming day, which was a sort of dog
baptism and graduation combined, was very important.
Right after early prayers the Abbot, the Brothers, all
the old dogs, and three of the young ones paraded
out to the hospice yard. Every living creature was there
—*except* the playful dog with the black and white
patches.

Brother John whistled. Instantly the dog bounded
out of the hospice and pranced toward him. The dog's
head was held high. His tail wagged proudly. And in his
big, foolish mouth was a boot. It was a new boot. It
belonged to the Abbot who was head of the hospice!

'Foolish One! Silly! Put that back!' Brother John whispered. The dog looked surprised. He dropped the boot at Brother John's feet and rolled over playing dead. 'Clown.' Brother John scolded. 'Of all the dogs in the world you are the least like the wonderful Barry.'

The foolish dog thumped his tail against the ground. He crawled on his stomach and licked Brother John's toes so it tickled. But he didn't put the boot back. Brother John had to do that himself.

The Abbot went on with the ceremony. He gave each dog his collar and blessed him. He named the three other young dogs Royal and Duke and Trusty. But when it came to the fourth dog he only shrugged his shoulders and walked away.

After that nobody thought of naming the shaggy dog with the patches. The Brothers called him 'Foolish One' or 'Clown.' When he was espicially naughty they shouted, 'Stop that, *Idiot!*'

In fact except for Brother John nobody paid any attention to him at all. Brother John went on working with him and praying for him. But even he was discouraged. 'Heaven help you, Foolish One,' Brother John said and patted the big shaggy head. 'When will you learn to be useful?'

That year winter began early. By November the Alps were white and the wind was cruel. In the path through the mountains the snow drifted higher than a

tall man's head. The good brothers of St. Bernard
worked hard and their dogs worked harder. By day and
by night, often without food or rest, the men and dogs
went through the snow to rescue travellers who had
lost their way.

The dogs worked in teams of three. When they
found a man lying hurt and helpless in the deep snow
one dog crouched on either side of him. This way they
kept off the wind and warmed him with their own
animal warmth. At the same time the third dog went
back to the hospice. He brought the Brothers to help
the traveller to safety.

In January the worst storm of all raged over the
mountains. The long night was a torment and a
misery at the hospice. Two of the Brothers tossed and
turned with a fever. All the dogs were half starved and
two of the best of them were dead, lost in a blizzard of
the week earlier.

At midnight Brother John sat by a failing fire with
only the foolish dog for company. The silly thing lay
on its back waving its big paws in the air for all the
world like a circus dog. But for once Brother John
could not laugh at such clowning. There were tears in
his eyes because the Abbot had said that in the morning the Foolish One must die. With food and firewood
so scarce that men died for the lack of them the Brothers could not keep a great hungry beast who did nothing but play.

At that moment Brother John heard a sound above the noise of the wind outside. He pushed open the door and at first the driving snow blinded him. Then he saw Trusty. The faithful dog fell at his feet half dead with the cold. Brother John pulled him inside and covered him with his own blanket.

He knew that Trusty had gone out with Duke and Royal and that now they crouched at the side of some lost traveller. Trusty had fought his way through the storm to the hospice for help. But now there was no strength left in him to guide a man back to where help was needed.

Brother John pulled on his cloak and reached for a lantern. If he went at once before more snow filled up Trusty's paw marks he might be able to find the way. He went out of the door and the shaggy dog bounced out ahead of him. 'Come back, Idiot!' Brother John tried to shout but the wind blew the words back in his throat.

The good man bent his head and pushed on step by step. There was no way to catch the Foolish One and perhaps it was just as well. Better to have him lost in the storm than to die tomorrow at the hands of a man he had thought was his friend.

Brother John had only gone a few feet before he saw that Tursty's paw marks were already covered over by the driving snow. He prayed silently and forced himself forward against the biting wind. One step. Two steps.

Brother John shook with fear and cold as he tried to decide which way to go. Everywhere he looked there was snow and ice. How could he tell where he was needed, with no paw marks to guide him? What was to keep him from tumbling into an abyss and crashing to his death? How could he tell where the snow lay deepest and where there might be a chance of going ahead?

Suddenly a strange thing happened. A big shaggy body came up beside him pushing him forward and shielding him from the wind. It was the Clown, of course, the Idiot, the Foolish One. Brother John gripped the dog's collar and they moved forward together into the storm.

In spite of the wind, and the snow, and the bitter cold they went on painfully, step by step, up into the mountains. Brother John's body grew numb and his feet were like lead. Only his courage and the great shaggy dog kept him from falling.

At last he saw a small flicker of light. It was a traveller's lantern. Beyond it sheltered by great snow-covered rocks were Royal and Duke on either side of a man's still body. As Brother John looked down at the man he thought he was already dead. He started to turn away, but the Foolish One blocked his path. The dog barked and clowned and pulled at Brother John's cloak with his teeth.

He tugged the body across the great dog's back.

For once Brother John was angry. 'Fool! Idiot!' he said. 'Must you clown even in the face of death?'

But the dog kept up his silly antics and at last Brother John understood what he wanted. He turned then and tugged the traveller's body across the great dog's shaggy back. Once more the dog barked and this time Royal and Duke obeyed him. Royal took the lead. Duke moved beside Brother John shielding him from the wind. The Foolish One with his heavy load came last of all. And so they travelled down the mountain and back through the storm.

At last they saw lights in the hospice window. The Abbot himself opened the door to them. He and another Brother lifted the traveller from the shaggy dog's back. Trusty feebly barked a welcome.

But Brother John had eyes and ears for nothing but the Foolish One who lay, scarcely breathing, at his feet. Would he live or had the terrible journey been too much for him? And if he got through the night what was in store for him tomorrow?

Across the room the traveller stirred. 'Your dogs,' he whispered. 'Your wonderful dogs have saved my life.'

Later the Abbot wrapped a blanket around Brother John's shaking shoulders and asked for the whole story of the rescue. Brother John told him everything, even how the big dog had barked and clowned at the top of the mountain.

'Your Foolish One has earned his place with us,' the

Abbot said when the story was finished. 'And tomorrow you shall name him.'

'Barry!' Brother John said and then remembering how the dog had taken the Abbot's boot he spoke more slowly. 'If he lives may I name him Barry, the Second?'

'He will live,' the Abbot said. 'And the name is well chosen. For this dog served God with his strength and his courage and even with the living foolishness which is part of his nature. No living creature can give more than the whole of himself.'

ALBERT PAYSON TERHUNE

One Minute Longer

Wolf was a collie, red-gold and white of coat, with a shape more like his long-ago wolf ancestors' than like a domesticated dog's. It was from this ancestral throwback that he was named Wolf.

He looked not at all like his great sire, Sunnybank Lad, nor like his dainty, thoroughbred mother, Lady. Nor was he like them in any other way, except that he inherited old Lad's stanchly gallant spirit and loyalty, and uncanny brain. No, in traits as well as in looks, he was more wolf than dog. He almost never barked, his snarl supplying all vocal needs.

The Mistress, or the Master, or the Boy—any of these three could romp with him, roll him over, tickle him, or subject him to all sorts of playful indignities. And Wolf entered gleefully into the fun of the romp. But let any human, besides these three, lay a hand on his slender body, and a snarling plunge for the offender's throat was Wolf's invariable reply to the caress.

It had been so since his puppyhood. He did not fly at accredited guests, nor, indeed, pay any heed to their presence, so long as they kept their hands off him. But to all of these the Boy was forced to say at the very outset of the visit:

"Pat Lad and Bruce all you want to, but please leave Wolf alone. He doesn't care for people. We've taught him to stand for a pat on the head from guests—but don't touch his body."

Then, to prove his own immunity, the Boy would proceed to tumble Wolf about, to the delight of them both.

In romping with humans whom they love, most dogs will bite, more or less gently—or pretend to bite—as a part of the game. Wolf never did this. In his wildest and roughest romps with the Boy or with the Boy's parents, Wolf did not so much as open his mighty jaws. Perhaps because he dared not trust himself to bite gently. Perhaps because he realized that a bite is not a joke, but an effort to kill.

There had been only one exception to Wolf's hatred for mauling at strangers' hands. A man came to The Place on a business call, bringing along a chubby two-year-old daughter. The Master warned the baby that she must not go near Wolf, although she might pet any of the other collies. Then he became so much interested in the business talk that he and his guest forgot all about the child.

Ten minutes later the Master chanced to shift his gaze to the far end of the room. And he broke off, with a gasp, in the very middle of a sentence.

The baby was seated astride Wolf's back, her tiny heels digging into the dog's sensitive ribs, and each of her chubby fists gripping one of his ears. Wolf was lying there, with an idiotically happy grin on his face and wagging his tail in ecstasy.

No one knew why he had submitted to the baby's tugging hands, except because she *was* a baby, and because the gallant heart of the dog had gone out to her helplessness.

Wolf was the official watchdog of The Place; and his name carried dread to the loafers and tramps of the region. Also, he was the Boy's own special dog. He had been born on the Boy's tenth birthday, five years before this story of ours begins; and ever since then the two had been inseparable chums.

One sloppy afternoon in late winter, Wolf and the Boy were sprawled, side by side, on the fur rug in front of the library fire. The Mistress and the Master had gone to town for the day. The house was lonely, and the two chums were left to entertain each other.

The Boy was reading a magazine. The dog beside him was blinking in drowsy comfort at the fire. Presently, finishing the story he had been reading, the Boy looked across at the sleepy dog.

"Wolf," he said, "here's a story about a dog. I think

he must have been something like you. Maybe he was your great-great-great-great-grandfather. He lived an awfully long time ago—in Pompeii. Ever hear of Pompeii?"

Side by side on the fur rug by the fire.

Now, the Boy was fifteen years old, and he had too much sense to imagine that Wolf could possibly understand the story he was about to tell him. But, long since, he had fallen into a way of talking to his dog, sometimes, as if to another human. It was fun for him to note the almost pathetic eagerness wherewith Wolf listened and tried to grasp the meaning of what he was saying.

Again and again, at sound of some familiar word or
voice inflection, the collie would prick up his ears or
wag his tail, as if in joyous hope that he had at last
found a clew to his owner's meaning.

"You see," went on the Boy, "this dog lived in Pompeii, as I told you. You've never been there, Wolf."

Wolf was looking up at the Boy in wistful excitement,
seeking vainly to guess what was expected of him.

"And," continued the Boy, "the kid who owned him
seems to have had a regular knack for getting into
trouble all the time. And his dog was always on hand
to get him out of it. It's a true story, the magazine says.
The kid's father was so grateful to the dog that he
bought him a solid silver collar. Solid silver! Get that,
Wolfie?"

Wolf did not "get it." But he wagged his tail hopefully, his eyes alight with bewildered interest.

"And," said the Boy, "what do you suppose was en-
graved on the collar? Well, I'll tell you: *'This dog has
thrice saved his little master from death. Once by fire,
once by flood, and once at the hands of robbers!'* How's
that for a record, Wolf? For *one* dog, too!"

At the words "Wolf" and "dog," the collie's tail
smote the floor in glad comprehension. Then he edged
closer to the Boy as the narrator's voice presently took
on a sadder note.

"But at last," resumed the Boy, "there came a time
when the dog couldn't save the kid. Mount Vesuvius

erupted. All the sky was pitch-dark, as black as midnight, and Pompeii was buried under lava and ashes. The dog could easily have got away by himself—dogs can see in the dark, can't they, Wolf?—but he couldn't get the kid away. And he wouldn't go without him. You wouldn't have gone without me, either, would you, Wolf? Pretty nearly two thousand years later, some people dug through the lava that covered Pompeii. What do you suppose they found? Of course they found a whole lot of things. One of them was that dog—silver collar and inscription and all. He was lying at the feet of a child. The child he couldn't save. He was one grand dog—hey, Wolf?"

The continued strain of trying to understand began to get on the collie's high-strung nerves. He rose to his feet, quivering, and sought to lick the Boy's face, thrusting one upraised white forepaw at him in appeal for a handshake. The Boy slammed shut the magazine.

"It's slow in the house, here, with nothing to do," he said to his chum. "I'm going up the lake with my gun to see if any wild ducks have landed in the marshes yet. It's almost time for them. Want to come along?"

The last sentence Wolf understood perfectly. On the instant he was dancing with excitement at the prospect of a walk. Being a collie, he was of no earthly help in a hunting trip; but, on such tramps, as everywhere else, he was the Boy's inseparable companion.

Out over the slushy snow the two started, the Boy

with his light single-barreled shotgun slung over one shoulder, the dog trotting close at his heels. The March thaw was changing to a sharp freeze. The deep and soggy snow was crusted over, just thick enough to make walking a genuine difficulty for both dog and Boy.

The Place was a promontory that ran out into the lake, on the opposite bank from the mile-distant village. Behind, across the highroad, lay the winter-choked forest. At the lake's northerly end, two miles beyond The Place, were the reedy marshes where, a month hence, wild ducks would congregate. Thither, with Wolf, the Boy plowed his way through the biting cold.

The going was heavy and heavier. A quarter mile below the marshes, the Boy struck out across the upper corner of the lake. Here the ice was rotten at the top, where the thaw had nibbled at it, but beneath it was still a full eight inches thick; easily strong enough to bear the Boy's weight.

Along the gray ice field the two plodded. The skim of water, which the thaw had spread an inch thick over the ice, had frozen in the day's cold spell. It crackled like broken glass as the chums walked over it. The Boy had on big hunting boots. So, apart from the extra effort, the glass like ice did not bother him. To Wolf it gave acute pain. The sharp particles were forever getting between the callous black pads of his feet, pricking and cutting him acutely.

Little smears of blood began to mark the dog's

course; but it never occurred to Wolf to turn back, or to betray by any sign that he was suffering. It was all a part of the day's work—a cheap price to pay for the joy of tramping with his adored young master.

Then, forty yards or so on the hither side of the marshes, Wolf beheld a right amazing phenomenon. The Boy had been walking directly in front of him, gun over shoulder. With no warning at all, the youthful hunter fell, feet foremost, out of sight, through the ice.

The light shell of new-frozen water that covered the lake's thicker ice also masked an air hole nearly three feet wide. Into this, as he strode carelessly along, the Boy had stepped. Straight down he had gone, with all the force of his hundred-and-twenty pounds and with all the impetus of his forward stride.

Instinctively, he threw out his hands to restore his balance. The only effect of this was to send the gun flying ten feet away.

Down went the Boy through less than three feet of water (for the bottom of the lake at this point had started to slope upward toward the marshes) and through nearly two feet more of sticky marsh mud that underlay the lake bed.

His outflung hands struck against the ice on the edges of the air hole and clung there.

Sputtering and gurgling, the Boy brought his head above the surface and tried to raise himself by his hands, high enough to wriggle out upon the surface of

the ice. Ordinarily, this would have been simple enough
for so strong a lad. But the gluelike mud had imprisoned his feet and the lower part of his legs and held
them powerless.

Try as he would, the Boy could not wrench himself
free of the slough. The water, as he stood upright, was
on a level with his mouth. The air hole was too wide
for him, at such a depth, to get a good purchase on its
edges and lift himself bodily to safety.

Gaining such a fingerhold as he could, he heaved
with all his might, throwing every muscle of his body
into the struggle. One leg was pulled almost free of the
mud, but the other was driven deeper into it. And, as
the Boy's fingers slipped from the smoothly wet ice
edge, the attempt to restore his balance drove the free
leg back, knee-deep into the mire.

Ten minutes of this hopeless fighting left the Boy
panting and tired out. The icy water was numbing his
nerves and chilling his blood into torpidity. His hands
were without sense of feeling, as far up as the wrists.
Even if he could have shaken free his legs from the mud
now, he had not strength enough left to crawl out of
the hole.

He ceased his uselessly frantic battle and stood dazed.
Then he came sharply to himself. For, as he stood, the
water crept upward from his lips to his nostrils. He
knew why the water seemed to be rising. It was not
rising. It was he who was sinking. As soon as he stopped

moving, the mud began, very slowly, but very steadily, to suck him downward.

This was not a quicksand, but it was a deep mud bed. And only by constant motion could he avoid sinking farther and farther down into it. He had less than two inches to spare, at best, before the water should fill his nostrils; less than two inches of life, even if he could keep the water down to the level of his lips.

There was a moment of utter panic. Then the Boy's brain cleared. His only hope was to keep on fighting— to rest when he must, for a moment or so, and then to renew his numbed grip on the ice edge and try to pull his feet a few inches higher out of the mud. He must do this as long as his chilled body could be scourged into obeying his will.

He struggled again, but with virtually no result in raising himself. A second struggle, however, brought him chin-high above the water. He remembered confusedly that some of these earlier struggles had scarce budged him, while others had gained him two or three inches. Vaguely, he wondered why. Then turning his head, he realized.

Wolf, as he turned, was just loosing his hold on the wide collar of the Boy's mackinaw. His cut forepaws were still braced against a flaw of ragged ice on the air hole's edge, and all his tawny body was tense.

His body was dripping wet, too. The Boy noted that; and he realized that the repeated effort to draw his master to safety must have resulted, at least once, in pulling the dog down into the water with the floundering Boy.

"Once more, Wolfie! *Once more!*" chattered the Boy through teeth that clicked together like castanets.

The dog darted forward, caught his grip afresh on the edge of the Boy's collar, and tugged with all his fierce strength; growling and whining ferociously the while.

The Boy seconded the collie's tuggings by a supreme struggle that lifted him higher than before. He was able to get one arm and shoulder clear. His numb fingers closed about an upthrust tree limb which had been washed downstream in the autumn freshets and had been frozen into the lake ice.

With this new purchase, and aided by the dog, the boy tried to drag himself out of the hole. But the chill of the water had done its work. He had not the strength to move farther. The mud still sucked at his calves and ankles. The big hunting boots were full of water that seemed to weigh a ton.

He lay there, gasping and chattering. Then, through the gathering twilight, his eyes fell on the gun, lying ten feet away.

"Wolf!" he ordered, nodding toward the weapon. "Get it! *Get* it!"

Not in vain had the boy talked to Wolf, for years, as if the dog were human. At the words and the nod, the collie trotted over to the gun, lifted it by the stock, and hauled it awkwardly along over the bumpy ice to his master, where he laid it down at the edge of the air hole.

The dog's eyes were cloudy with trouble, and he shivered and whined as with ague. The water on his thick coat was freezing to a mass of ice. But it was from anxiety that he shivered, and not from cold.

Still keeping his numb grasp on the tree branch, the boy balanced himself as best he could, and thrust two fingers of his free hand into his mouth to warm them into sensation again.

When this was done, he reached out to where the gun lay and pulled its trigger. The shot boomed deafeningly through the twilight winter silences. The recoil sent the weapon sliding sharply back along the ice, spraining the boy's trigger finger and cutting it to the bone.

"That's all I can do," said the Boy to himself. "If anyone hears it, well and good. I can't get at another cartridge. I couldn't put it into the breech if I had it. My hands are too numb."

For several minutes he clung there, listening. But this was a desolate part of the lake, far from any road; and the season was too early for other hunters to be abroad. The bitter cold, in any case, tended to make sane folk hug the fireside rather than to venture so far

into the open. Nor was the single report of a gun un-
common enough to call for investigation in such
weather.

All this the Boy told himself, as the minutes dragged
by. Then he looked again at Wolf. The dog, head on
one side, still stood protectingly above him. The dog
was cold and in pain. But, being only a dog, it did not
occur to him to trot off home to the comfort of the
library fire and leave his master to fend for himself.

Presently, with a little sigh, Wolf lay down on the ice,
his nose across the Boy's arm. Even if he lacked strength
to save his beloved master, he could stay and share the
Boy's sufferings.

But the Boy himself thought otherwise. He was not
at all minded to freeze to death, nor was he willing to
let Wolf imitate the dog of Pompeii by dying helplessly
at his master's side. Controlling for an instant the chattering of his teeth, he called:

"Wolf!"

The dog was on his feet again at the word; alert,
eager.

"Wolf!" repeated the boy. "Go! Hear me? Go!"

He pointed homeward.

Wolf stared at him, hesitant. Again the boy called
in vehement command, "Go!"

The collie lifted his head to the twilight sky with a
wolf howl hideous in its grief and appeal—a howl as
wild and discordant as that of any of his savage an-

cestors. Then, stooping first to lick the numb hand that clung to the branch, Wolf turned and fled.

Across the sharp rim of ice he tore, at top speed, head down; whirling through the deeping dusk like a flash of tawny light.

Wolf understood what was wanted of him. Wolf always understood. The pain in his feet was nothing. The stiffness of his numbed body was forgotten in the urgency for speed.

The Boy looked drearily after the swift-vanishing figure which the dusk was swallowing. He knew the dog would try to bring help; as has many another and lesser dog in times of need. Whether or not that help could arrive in time, or at all, was a point on which the Boy would not let himself dwell. Into his benumbed brain crept the memory of an old Norse proverb he had read in school:

"Heroism consists in hanging on, one minute longer."

Unconsciously he tightened his feeble hold on the tree branch and braced himself.

From the marshes to The Place was a full two miles. Despite the deep and sticky snow, Wolf covered the distance in less than nine minutes. He paused in front of the gate lodge, at the highway entrance to the drive. But the superintendent and his wife had gone to Paterson, shopping, that afternoon.

Down the drive to the house he dashed. The maids

had taken advantage of their employers' day in New
York, to walk across the lake to the village, to a motion
picture show.

Wise men claim that dogs have not the power to
think or to reason things out in a logical way. So perhaps it was mere chance that next sent Wolf's flying
feet across the lake to the village. Perhaps it was chance,
and not the knowledge that where there is a village
there are people.

Again and again, in the car, he had sat upon the front
seat alongside the Mistress when she drove to the station to meet guests. There were always people at the
station. And to the station Wolf now raced.

The usual group of platform idlers had been dis-
persed by the cold. A solitary baggageman was hauling
a trunk and some boxes out of the express coop on to
the platform; to be put aboard the five o'clock train
from New York.

As the baggageman passed under the clump of station
lights, he came to a sudden halt. For out of the darkness dashed a dog. Full tilt, the animal rushed up to
him and scized him by the skirt of the overcoat.

The man cried out in scared surprise. He dropped
the box he was carrying and struck at the dog, to ward
off the seemingly murderous attack. He recognized
Wolf, and he knew the collie's repute.

But Wolf was not attacking. Holding tight to the
coat skirt, he backed away, trying to draw the man with

*Wolf rushed up to him and seized his **coat**.*

him, and all the while whimpering aloud like a nervous
puppy.

A kick from the heavy-shod boot broke the dog's hold
on the coat skirt, even as a second yell from the man
brought four or five other people running out from the
station waiting room.

One of these, the telegraph operator, took in the
scene at a single glance. With great presence of mind,
he bawled loudly: "MAD DOG!"

This, as Wolf; reeling from the kick, sought to gain
another grip on the coat skirt. A second kick sent him
reeling over and over on the tracks, while other voices
took up the panic cry of "Mad dog!"

Now, a mad dog is supposed to be a dog afflicted
by rabies. Once in ten thousand times, at the very most,
a mad-dog hue and cry is justified. Certainly not oftener.
A harmless and friendly dog loses his master on the
street. He runs about, confused and frightened, looking
for the owner he has lost. A boy throws a stone at him.
Other boys chase him. His tongue hangs out, and his
eyes glaze with terror. Then some fool bellows: "Mad
dog!"

And the cruel chase is on—a chase that ends in the
pitiful victim's death. Yes, in every crowd there is a
voice ready to raise that asinine and murderously cruel
shout.

So it was with the men who witnessed Wolf's
frenzied effort to take aid to the imperiled Boy.

Voice after voice repeated the cry. Men groped along the platform edge for stones to throw. The village policeman ran puffingly upon the scene, drawing his revolver.

Finding it useless to make a further attempt to drag the baggageman to the rescue, Wolf leaped back, facing the ever larger group. Back went his head again in that hideous wolf howl. Then he galloped away a few yards, trotted back, howled once more, and again galloped lakeward.

All of which only confirmed the panicky crowd in the belief that they were threatened by a mad dog. A shower of stones hurled about Wolf as he came back a third time to lure these dull humans into following him.

One pointed rock smote the collie's shoulder, glancingly, cutting it to the bone. A shot from the policeman's revolver fanned the fur of his ruff, as it whizzed past.

Knowing that he faced death, he nevertheless stood his ground, not troubling to dodge the fusillade of stones, but continuing to run lakeward and then trot back, whining with excitement.

A second pistol shot flew wide. A third grazed the dog's hip. From all directions people were running toward the station. A man darted into a house next door and emerged carrying a shotgun. This he steadied on

the veranda rail, not forty feet away from the leaping
dog, and made ready to fire.

It was then the train from New York came in. And,
momentarily, the sport of "mad-dog" killing was
abandoned, while the crowd scattered to each side of
the track.

From a front car of the train the Mistress and the
Master emerged into a bedlam of noise and confusion.

"Best hide in the station, Ma'am!" shouted the
telegraph operator, at sight of the Mistress. "There's a
mad dog loose out here! He's chasing folks around,
and—"

"Mad dog!" repeated the Mistress in high contempt.
"If you knew anything about dogs, you'd know mad
ones never 'chase folks around,' any more than diph-
theria patients do. Then—"

A flash of tawny light beneath the station lamp, a
scurrying of frightened idlers, a final wasted shot from
the policeman's pistol—as Wolf dived headlong through
the frightened crowd toward the voice he heard and
recognized.

Up to the Mistress and Master galloped Wolf. He
was bleeding, his eyes were bloodshot, his fur was rum-
pled. He seized the astounded Master's gloved hand
lightly between his teeth and sought to pull him across
the tracks and toward the lake.

The Master knew dogs. Especially he knew Wolf.

And without a word he suffered himself to be led. The Mistress and one or two inquisitive men followed.

Presently, Wolf loosed his hold on the Master's hand and ran on ahead, darting back every few moments to make certain he was followed.

"*Heroism — consists — in — hanging — on — one — minute—longer,*" the Boy was whispering deliriously to himself for the hundredth time, as Wolf pattered up to him in triumph, across the ice, with the human rescuers a scant ten yards behind.

CAROL RYRIE BRINK

Admiral Dewey Has His Fling

Ardeth was a friendly child and, being the ten-year-old daughter of a small-town doctor in the early years of 1900, she knew almost everyone in Warsaw. Next to her father, she liked the new minister's boys who lived across the alley; and after them came Mrs. Dawlish, their mother; and Jenny, her father's housekeeper; and Hopper, her dog. She could go on down the list of people and animals in town almost indefinitely, naming them in the order in which she liked them. At the bottom of the list there were only two or three whom she really disliked. One of these was Mrs. Sweeney Tufton, a thin, sour lady with a sort of curdled face who preferred pug dogs to children. The other one was really not alive and scarcely belonged in the class with human beings, but Ardeth disliked him just as heartily as if he had been made of flesh and blood.

He was only the wax dummy of a little boy, dressed
in a natty suit trimmed with red braid. He was the first
thing one noticed upon entering the Warsaw Dry
Goods Store, and he was the only creature in the world
that Ardeth had ever wanted to slap. She had always
had a friendly feeling for the grown-up-lady dummies
in the store windows. They looked like helpless creatures, but with good intentions.

The little-girl dummy was rather silly, and Ardeth
thought that she should have simpered less broadly, but
it was only the smug little boy in the Buster Brown suit
which she really detested. He had large blue glass eyes
surrounded by long curly black lashes which had come
unglued at one side of the right eyelid, and he had a too
sweet smile and four pink wax dimples in his cheeks.
He wore little kid gloves on his hands, and one of these
hands was extended in welcome as if he wished you to
shake it. Once Ardeth, in a low voice, had told him
what she thought of him, and he had continued to stare
at her as glassily as ever. There was nothing one could
do about a creature like that. Scornful words wouldn't
irritate him; even the summer heat wouldn't melt him,
it seemed. Ardeth had once walked all the way downtown on the hottest day to see. Ardeth felt sure that he
would be there always, smirking and holding out his
hand, even when she was an old lady with a hundred
grandchildren.

On a warm afternoon, Ardeth and the new minister's

boys, Martin and Henry Dawlish, were crowded into the old piano box which they used for a clubhouse. Hopper, Ardeth's dog, occupied the very small space between their feet in the center of the piano box. He was a small yellow dog with short hair and a tail curled up like the handle of a jug. Now he was lazily scratching fleas, but with one ear cocked for the conversation, which he knew was about himself.

"Yes, sir!" said Ardeth. "It was just like that. I was raking leaves in the yard one fall, and the first thing I knew there was Hopper in the leaves, and just the color of them, too, except for his black eyes and nose and his red tongue. As soon as I saw him I liked him, and Hopper felt the same way about me. He's been my dog ever since."

"What kind of dog is he?" asked Martin.

"He's a *smart* dog!" said Ardeth.

"I know, but is he a pug or a black-and-tan or a St. Bernard, or what?"

"I guess he's a what," said Ardeth reluctantly. "Anyway, he's not a pug, like that little old fat dog of Mrs. Sweeney Tufton's. Poor thing, I feel sorry for him; but I wouldn't have a dog like *that!*"

"Martin! Henry!" called Mrs. Dawlish from the back porch. "Run down to the Warsaw Dry Goods Store and get me a spool of thread!"

"Oh, Mama, we're awfully busy!" cried Henry, who was really under the impression that they were. But

Ardeth loved doing errands for Mrs. Dawlish. She popped her head out of the piano box and said, "I'll go!"

Presently the three of them were clattering down the old board sidewalks from Third Street to Main, and behind them trotted Hopper, his tail curled up very tightly and his tongue hanging out, with a roving eye for adventure. Hopper knew all the possibilities of the town. He knew the mossy leak in the horse trough where a dog could drink without climbing up. He knew where the butcher threw old bones and where the feed-store man's cat hid when she didn't want to be seen. He knew what fun it was to chase the flying cash boxes in the Warsaw Dry Goods Store.

Martin and Henry were new to town, and they had never happened to go inside the Dry Goods Store before. As soon as they saw the dummy in the brown suit, they stopped short.

"Sissy!" said Henry, and Ardeth was gratified to see that both boys scowled.

"Isn't he horrid!" said Ardeth.

"What's his name?" asked Henry.

"Wilburforce," said Martin promptly.

"*Wilburforce*," repeated Ardeth admiringly. The name just suited him.

There were a good many ladies in the store this morning making purchases, and the little cash boxes flew to and fro.

The cashier sat in a small balcony up at the back of the store, and from her booth, like threads from the hub of a spider-web, went lines to the different counters. When someone made a purchase, the clerk at the counter put the money and the sales slip into a little cash box which was attached to one of these lines. Next she pulled a lever, and the cash box shot away like the wind along the line up to the cashier's booth. If there was change to be returned to the customer, the cashier put it back in the little box, pulled another lever, and away sped the box back to the counter from which it had come. This made quite an exciting atmosphere of little boxes whirring overhead, and Hopper simply adored it. Ardeth had seen him chase cash boxes before, and usually she left him outside. But this time he slipped in by accident, and the Dawlish boys were entranced at his behavior.

As soon as one of the cash boxes left the counter, Hopper started after it, barking enthusiastically. Once he was started, the excitement of the chase got into his blood, and it was almost impossible to stop him. Ardeth usually picked him up bodily, when he managed to get in, and lugged him out, his four legs waving frantically and his yelps of disappointment filling the air. But today she thought one little spool of thread would not take long, and it was fun to see how the Dawlish boys enjoyed the show.

Now it happened today that Mrs. Sweeney Tufton

was in the store to select material for a new summer dress. With Mrs. Tufton was her little pug dog, Admiral Dewey.

Dewey was small and old and very fat. Nature had constructed his nose in such a way that breathing was difficult, and, I regret to say, even when Dewey was awake, he snored. Once Dewey had been quite a gay dog, but in his later life Mrs. Sweeney Tufton had smothered him with kindness and bonbons and rules and regulations. He was only allowed to play with properly selected dogs and at times which Mrs. Tufton decided upon. He never went out except upon a ribbon-decked leash, at the other end of which was Mrs. Sweeney Tufton.

This morning Dewey was unusually bored, for he had been snoring under the empty stool to which he was tied for an hour and a half, while Mrs. Tufton looked at materials and matched samples. Therefore, when Hopper arrived and began to chase cash boxes, Dewey awoke with a pleasant feeling of excitement. Something in which he was interested had at last begun to happen. He had often looked at the flying cash boxes with an uneasy feeling that something should be done about them, and here was a dog who knew what to do. With growing excitement Dewey watched Hopper dashing to and fro and yelping. The minister's boys were clapping their hands and shouting, "That's the boy, Hopper. Sic 'em! Catch 'em!"

It was more than Dewey could endure. When the next cash box started, he gave a great snore and suddenly dashed away after it, dragging the empty stool behind him. His shrill, wheezy bark mingled with Hopper's yapping, and together they tore across the Warsaw Dry Goods Store, the stool bumping along behind.

"Oh, my little doggens!" cried Mrs. Sweeny Tufton. "Stop him! Stop him! What has happened to my little Dewey?"

"I'll catch him for you!" cried Henry, who needed only the slightest excuse to join in the pursuit. The cash box landed at the cashier's booth, the two dogs in hot pursuit. A shopper was overturned in the excitement, likewise Henry, who picked himself right up and went after Dewey.

Ardeth and Martin joined in, too, and Ardeth succeeded in grabbing Hopper and putting him out on the sidewalk. But Dewey was tasting his first liberty in a long time. Even with a stool tied to him, he could not be stopped. Around and around the store he ran. Everybody was chasing Dewey now. Mrs. Tufton and one of the lady clerks were shrieking, and the cashier was leaning out of the balcony with popping eyes. She had a bird's-eye view of what went on below, and only she could estimate the extent of the destruction. Those on the ground floor began to realize it when the notion table went over, spilling buttons, thread, hooks and eyes, garters, and safety pins all over the floor. But there

Henry, Dewey, and the stool all came down.

was worse to come, for, just as Henry managed to catch hold of a leg of the stool, Dewey circled around Wilburforce, the dummy, and started back towards the rear of the store. There was a tremendous crash, and Henry, Dewey, Wilburforce, and the stool all came down together in one struggling mass bound together by Dewey's ribbon-trimmed leash. When at last they were unwound and untangled and picked up, it was found that something dreadful had happened to the dummy. A long crack ran from his real-hair wig down his cheek.

"Oh!" shrieked Ardeth. "He's cracked his smile!"

The manager of the Warsaw Dry Goods Store came, and there were some hard words. It seemed that Wilburforce was his most beloved dummy. Nobody seemed to mind at all that Henry's nose was bleeding or that Admiral Dewey had had his fling. There was only one consolation to be had: Mrs. Sweeney Tufton was guilty, too, for it was her pug who had caused most of the trouble. There was a very uncomfortable fifteen minutes during which everybody talked at once, and finally it was decided that Mrs. Tufton would pay the damages, which were estimated at about five dollars, and that Henry should mow her lawn for her until she considered that his share in the damages was worked out. There was a good deal of talk against Hopper, too, since he had started the trouble, and it was agreed to ask Ardeth's father to contribute a dollar towards the restoration of the dummy. Then everybody turned to and helped pick up the wreckage and put things in order.

Finally the children remembered to buy the thread for Mrs. Dawlish and to get away.

"Henry," Ardeth said, "I'll help you mow Mrs. Sweeney Tufton's lawn!" She gave another skip and added, "You know, I sort of like poor Admiral Dewey, now I've got to know him. Pug dogs aren't so bad, after all. I think that Hopper's partly pug—the way his tail curls up behind!"

Always Reddy

Mr. Hoops was terribly proud of his splendid Irish Setter because Reddy was the best bird dog up and down the river. She could scent birds in weather so dry that all the other dogs just gave up. She could fly over fences and brooks as if she had wings on her feet. But now he begins to see signs of slowing down, and fears that the old dog will have to be retired. But Reddy doesn't think so. She has always loved being a worker, and she proves it most bravely in this dramatic encounter with an intruder.

LAZY GIRL

Something far more serious was happening to Reddy. It seemed every now and then as if her legs were not her own. They refused to obey her will.

Mornings when she wanted to dance on her hind feet and plant her forepaws on Mr. Hoops' shoulders, she could not make it.

It was worse on a morning after a hard workout in

the field, especially if the weather had been frosty and the birds had fallen in water. One morning she felt so stiff and sore that she could not get up until the sun found her bed and toasted her bones. Then, gradually, she limbered up and by noon she seemed as good as ever.

It was strange that Mr. Hoops suspected nothing. If Reddy failed to race and tear about the basement when he arrived, he laid it to sleepiness.

"Why, you lazy old girl!" he would say. "Pretty soft to lie abed all hours."

Then Reddy would make a great effort to rise.

"I declare!" Mr. Hoops would laugh. "You're as stilty-legged as a colt."

On dry sunny days, however, Reddy seemed livelier than ever before. She could put her paws clear up on Mr. Hoops' shoulders with no trouble at all. And she was so glad about it that she gave his ears and neck an extra good licking.

All through the hunting season Snippet gained in skill while Reddy seemed to let down, but Mr. Hoops admitted this to no one. He scarcely admitted it to himself. What if Reddy did not range out as wide as Snippet? What if she seemed to avoid fences and hedgerows? She still had a sure nose for birds and pointed them like an arrow.

One day several birds that Mr. Hoops hit fell into a creek swollen by fall rains. He watched amazed as

Reddy just stood on the bank and let Snippet retrieve them. She made no move to help him.

Mr. Hoops had to call her name out sharply before she finally splashed her way into the water and did her share of the work. Even then Mr. Hoops did not suspect.

By noon she was as good as ever.

It was the last day of the hunting season before Mr. Hoops knew.

The weather was unpromising. In spite of a crust of snow on the ground, the air was dry with a wind so fierce that it scattered all bird scent. As Snippet dashed over the rough country, Reddy seemed almost to crouch

along. Mr. Hoops wondered if rheumatism had at last
caught up with her, but he closed the little shutters of
his mind.

"She's just smart," he told himself. "Saving her
strength for a real burst of speed when she needs it."

The day wore itself out. By twilight Mr. Hoops'
gamebag was still empty. "I know we should be getting home," he told Reddy and Snippet, "but I always
like to take at least one bird to Mrs. Hoops. What do
you say to working the alder thicket once more? The
wind seems to be dying a little. Our luck is bound to
change."

Snippet wagged his tail in agreement and Reddy
seemed more eager than when they had started out. It
was almost as if she knew that this was the last hour of
the hunting season.

At a wave of the hat both dogs made a beeline for
the alder thicket. Now Snippet was clearing a split rail
fence. But Reddy! She was not going to clear it. Mr.
Hoops watched horrified as she hit the top rail, was
catapulted into the air, and then fell in a little heap in
the leaves.

It was only a matter of seconds until he reached the
spot where she lay, but to him it seemed hours. Snippet
had already found her, and when Mr. Hoops reached
them he was licking a tiny trickle of blood on her forehead.

He dropped to his knees beside Reddy and pillowed

her head in his lap. "She tried to tell me in the only way she knew. Please, God," he prayed, "don't let her die."

He glanced about helplessly. The ground was hummocky, but between the hummocks were pockets of snow. With quick hands he filled his handkerchief with the snow and placed it on Reddy's head. She made no move then nor when he felt of her legs to see if they were broken. He listened to her breathing but could hardly hear it for his own.

"Reddy," he pleaded. "If you'll get well, we'll have the best of days together. I'll rub your legs with warm liniment night and morning. You'll never have to work the fields again. And when spring comes you can lie on a warm rug in the sun and watch me plant my garden. Why, you can sleep all day if you like!"

He took off his jacket and wrapped it closely about her. How quiet the world seemed! A squirrel came to look at them with an inquiring glance, but did not even scold.

Night was closing in when Mr. Hoops felt a stirring in his arms. He pressed his ear against Reddy's muzzle to hear any faint cries of pain. There were none. Reddy was opening her eyes. She was trying to lick Mr. Hoops' face. She was trying to comfort *him!*

Joyously Mr. Hoops carried his precious burden to the car. Then he sped for the warmth of the City Hall.

"Reddy's had an accident," he told Mrs. Hoops over

the telephone. "I'll spend the night here. Yes, Hannah, there's a cot to sleep on. I'll be all right."

THE TIME HAS COME

It was long past midnight before Mr. Hoops slept. He sponged the blood from Reddy's head and cut away some of her matted hair. He bathed the wound with flowers of sulphur. Then he wrapped her in his old hunting coat and placed her near the furnace. She fell into a fitful sleep while he and Snippet looked on.

Mr. Hoops could not help noticing how Snippet had changed. In just a few hours he had grown from a playful youngster into a responsible dog. It was as if he were the parent now and Reddy the overgrown pup to be watched over.

"Snippet," said Mr. Hoops softly, "it's time you had your supper. Nothing fancy tonight. Just dry crumbles moistened with beef tea."

While Snippet cleaned his bowl, Mr. Hoops heated some milk, beat an egg into it, and added a little beef tea. Then, very gently, he lifted Reddy's jowl and poured a teaspoonful of the warm liquid between her teeth. She swallowed it and then ever so faintly began to whimper. She could stand the scratch of briers and the thwack of a fence rail, but when the master bent low over her in sympathy she cried.

Now Mr. Hoops moistened his finger in the liquid and let Reddy lick it as if she were a puppy. And soon she was lapping the milk not because she wanted it, but because it seemed to please him.

When she could drink no more, Mr. Hoops examined her carefully. Besides the gash on her head, the pads of her feet were cut by splinters and thorns.

She seemed very tired now, so Mr. Hoops covered her and let her sleep.

Meanwhile he made a table out of a barrel and spread open his dog emergency kit. With skilled fingers he cut and sewed four boots out of white leather. He made them long enough to fit well above Reddy's knees. Then he lined the insides of them with a layer of balsam salve and set them on top of the furnace to warm.

At midnight Reddy woke with a whining cry. She was ashamed of it immediately afterward, for she licked Mr. Hoops' hands as he took out the splinters and the thorns from the feathering between her toes. At last he fitted her paws into the boots he had made and covered her again with his coat. In a very few minutes she began to snore.

With a deep sigh, Mr. Hoops tiptoed upstairs to finish the night on the Mayor's cot.

Reddy's wounds healed like magic. Even her morning lameness improved now that she spent most of her time indoors where it was warm and dry. She could climb stairs as well as ever, and she could dance on her hind feet when she had a mind to. But in spite of all this, she was not happy.

All her life she had been a worker. As long as she could remember she had worked the fields for Mr. Hoops or helped him in the training of her puppies. And the harder she had worked, the happier she had been.

Now, all that was over. No one needed her, not even Snippet. She had nothing to do. And the days stumbled over each other endlessly.

Meanwhile, things began to go wrong at the City Hall. It wasn't anything big or important that happened. Just little things that added up to something big.

The high school band began to practice on the second floor of the City Hall, and every time the tuba hit a certain note Reddy and Snippet howled uncontrollably. It put the Mayor and Bessie, and even the four Commissioners, on edge.

Then Victoria had kittens in the coal room, and if either dog so much as passed her door, she leaped out like a tigress and clawed at them until the yelping was dreadful to hear.

On top of all this Reddy hunted in her dreams. Sometimes she found pheasant and partridge and quail. Then she would bark with joy. More often, however, she failed to jump over a fence, and moaned in a way that was half-human.

But the final incident that brought in a score of com-

plaints was when Snippet got his nose caught in a
mousetrap. He let out such a bloodcurdling cry that a
woman customer at Mr. Hoops' window fell to the floor
in a faint.

"Adam," said the mayor as kindly as he could, "the
time has come to find a kennel for your dogs." Then
at an imploring look from Katy he added, "Of course,
you can wait for slightly warmer days."

WORK TO DO

Mr. Hoops was a man who never went to *meet*
trouble. He waited for it to catch up with him and
tap him on the shoulder. Sometimes he even waited
until it whirled him about sharply.

"Time enough," he said to Reddy and Snippet one
Saturday night soon after the mousetrap incident,
"time enough to think about leaving here when warm
weather comes. We got through yesterday, didn't we?
All right, we'll get through tomorrow too. You'll see."

And he tried to whistle a gay tune as he stirred a pot
of mulligan. But every now and then the whistling
stopped and was a long time starting up again.

During one of these pauses, Officer O'Toole rattled
the front door. Mr. Hoops let him in and invited him
downstairs to sit awhile.

"Don't offer me any of that mulligatawny, Adam. I
could clean the whole pot, and what would the dogs

think if I did the like of that? It smells elegant!" he sniffed.

Mr. Hoops laughed. "Occasionally I sample it myself, but I always feel like a dog when I do."

Reddy and Snippet rubbed against the officer's legs.

"It was the Mayor sent me," Officer O'Toole said, as he bent over to pat the dogs. "He stops me as he drives by and says, 'O'Toole, would you be so kind as to drop in on Adam and tell him to be sure the safe is locked? I put some mighty important papers in it, O'Toole,' he says, 'and I can't remember for the life of me whether I locked it or not. 'Twould worry me all Sunday,' he says.

"Then I gives him the green light and away he goes," chuckled the policeman. "And now I've got to skedaddle too."

Mr. Hoops saw Officer O'Toole to the door. Then he tried the handle of the safe which he had locked when the five-o'clock whistle blew. This was a firm habit with Mr. Hoops. He felt more responsibility for the city's money and papers than if they had been his own. Only the City Treasurer and the Mayor knew the combination of this safe.

With a little sigh of relief at the peace and quiet, he began to jot down all of the things he wanted to do on Monday. At the very bottom of the list he wrote hurriedly, "Look up a good kennel man." He penciled this last quite faintly, almost as if he thought that the words and the need for them might vanish over the week end.

When, that same evening, Mrs. Hoops saw Mr. Hoops come home without his hat, she knew that he was worried over something. Quite rightly, she suspected it concerned Reddy and Snippet.

And then Mrs. Hoops said something which gave Mr. Hoops a jolt. "Just because *Reddy's* hunting days are over," she remarked, "just because of that is no reason Snippet should be neglected. Don't you think you should be hardening him so he'll be in condition for the hunting season?"

Mr. Hoops looked at Mrs. Hoops in wonderment. Every now and again she would come out with a suggestion that showed she understood dogs too.

So it was that on the following day, which was Sunday, Mr. Hoops took Snippet out alone. Before they set off together he stooped down and had a word with Reddy. Then with his eyes carefully avoiding hers, he smoothed her head and said good-by.

Reddy made no move to follow. Yet she seemed to believe they could not really go off without her, for she stood up now, waiting to be invited.

As Snippet bounded up the stairs after Mr. Hoops, Reddy scarcely breathed. She heard the sound of their footfalls along the corridor. She heard the door to the street close with a terrible finality. She ran over to the window to hear her name, no matter how softly it might be called. But no voice came. Mr. Hoops' footsteps were growing fainter and fainter now, and the click of Snippet's toenails on the sidewalk could no longer be heard at all. She gave one loud bark as a reminder to them, but the only answer was her own echo. So she stood there for a long time nosing the air coming in through the window. She could smell spring, and a great longing filled her.

With Snippet gone, the basement suddenly seemed hushed and chill. The ticking of the clock on the wall upstairs only emphasized the quiet.

Reddy walked slowly to her rug, but she was restless and could not sleep. Trembling a little, she got up and made her way to the coal room. Even a scuffle with Victoria and her kittens was to be preferred to all this stillness. But a sniff around the coal room revealed that Victoria and her entire family had gone out too. Miserably, Reddy returned to her own quarters.

Minute after minute ticked by. Finally, with a sigh of weariness, she flopped down on her rug. She had almost fallen asleep when suddenly she twitched and was wide awake. The door upstairs was opening. Then it clicked shut, quietly and quickly. A stranger was walking overhead with hurried steps.

Reddy was alert at once. She crept cautiously up the stairs, her hackles rising. Unmindful of any danger to herself she went into Mr. Hoops' office. A man stood

With frightening quickness he began beating at Reddy.

close to the safe, his back toward Reddy. Quietly she circled him, her nose reaching out to sift his scent from the familiar belongings of Mr. Hoops.

Instinctively she disliked him and let out a low warning growl. The man wheeled about, reaching for his gun. Then with frightening quickness he began beating at Reddy with the butt end of it. The hard steel hit her, now on the shoulders, now on the flanks. Yet the shock of the blows did not confuse her thinking. It whipped her into a fury of strength. She hurled herself at the prowler with such force that he was thrown against the wall.

And to a crash of glass and brass and bells that frightened Reddy more than the blows of the gun, the wall clock came bumping down on the thief's head. With a heavy thud, he fell to the floor.

The clock was in ruins. Coiled springs, wheels, pinions, and the big shiny pendulum were spilled over the thief's chest, and the hour hand was stuck through his hair. It gave him a rakish look.

Reddy stood there puzzled. She was covered with fine splinters of glass, but none had penetrated her coat. She shook herself, stepped carefully over the glass and wire, and made her way to the man. He lay very still.

She stood guard over him. Her shoulders ached from the blows, but she did not mind the pain at all. At last she had work to do. She must hold this stranger until her master returned. Steady. Steady. He would come.

How still everything seemed! Even the ticking noise
had stopped. Outside, a Sunday quiet hung over the
street. Only a few sparrows were making twittering remarks to each other. The prowler groaned, but made
no move.

Finally the streets began to liven with men and
women and children coming home from church. But
Reddy never wavered. Even when the lock turned, she
stood rigid, though she knew in a flash that it was Mr.
Hoops and Snippet.

Anxious to see how Reddy fared, Mr. Hoops walked
hurriedly down the corridor. He gave only a passing
glance into his office, but that was enough to show him
the opened safe, and the thief with Reddy on guard.

At that very instant, the thief opened his eyes, but
when he saw *two* red dogs where before he had seen
only one, he closed them quickly again.

"Steady, Partner! Steady!" breathed Mr. Hoops. He
reached for the telephone and called Officer O'Toole
and the Mayor. Officer O'Toole came running, his dinner napkin still stuffed between his brass buttons. Close
on his heels followed the Mayor and two of the four
Commissioners.

There was such a hubbub in the crowded cage that
Mr. Hoops and his dogs slipped downstairs unnoticed.

Reddy gave one glad cry when she and Snippet and
Mr. Hoops were back together again. She began to leap
and run in circles around Mr. Hoops, and there was an

air of importance in the very way she wagged her tail. It reminded him of the way she used to act after a good day of hunting when things had gone just right.

Upstairs, Mayor Twitterton was saying to Policeman O'Toole, "I'm sorry I asked Adam to move his dogs out. Reddy has done the citizens of Belleville a great service today. I had no idea that the City Hall needed a watchdog. So long as I am Mayor, she and her pup shall live right here in City Hall."

And since he had already been Mayor for a dozen years, and since his campaign for Congress was not going along too well, it looked as if he would go right on being Mayor for another dozen years.

With the thief handcuffed and the two Commissioners on watch, the Mayor and Policeman O'Toole went downstairs to break the good news to Mr. Hoops.

But they got only as far as the landing. There they stopped suddenly, realizing that he must have overheard the Mayor's announcement.

"Did you hear that? Everything's going to be all right." Mr. Hoops was telling Reddy. "Snippet can take over the field work, and you have a new job guarding City Hall." Then a look of triumph crossed his face. "Why, you've got about the most important job in all Belleville!"

Too happy to say more, he swooped the great gangling dog into his arms and danced a funny little jig, in and out among Katy's mops and pails.

JACK O'BRIEN

The King and the Princess

The King lay stretched in the warm sun on the east side of the cabin. At times he moaned and his legs jerked as he dreamed of rabbits racing through the tall grass. The Princess eyed him from the corner, then hobbled over, squatted down and playfully whacked the King on the nose with her wooden leg. He awoke violently, sat up; then, seeing who had annoyed him, yawned and stretched out again. The Princess curled between his paws.

Sounds crazy, doesn't it? Kings—and cabins. Dreaming of rabbits. Lying in the sun. Princesses—with wooden legs. Well, it was crazy, and I'd like to tell you the strange story of this particular King and this particular Princess.

Up in the big timber country of the Northwest, Dad Wilson and his son Bob built and maintained a hunting lodge. Both of them were first-class woodsmen. Their cabin was located in what is perhaps the finest hunting and fishing country in the whole United States, and men from all over the country used to go up there for their vacations.

One rainy afternoon Bob came into the big cabin room where his father was seated before the fire reading. Young Bob had just paddled out from town and was wearing a raincoat. He tossed his hat on a chair and walked over to the table, a grin on his face.

"Look, Dad," he said. His father's book dropped to his knees as Bob pulled out of his pockets two of the fattest squirmiest pets ever seen in the North. A kitten, as black as night with a single white star on her forehead, and a puppy, so fat he fell in a heap when he tried to walk.

"Where in the world did you get 'em, Son?" exclaimed Dad Wilson.

"I got them from Mrs. Round at the boarding house in town. They're moving south so they turned them over to me. Watch."

Bob put out his finger. The kitten, not at all frightened after its curious ride in a raincoat pocket leaped daintily upward, back arched and tail straight in the air, then minced sideways until near enough to pounce upon the pointing finger. The pup, not to be outdone, rumbled into action like a baby truck, ploughing across the oilcloth on stomach as well as feet, bringing up

with a *plop* against Bob's hand, one huge paw planted
across the kitten's neck.

With a squeal the kitten pulled her head out from beneath the paw and then, with all the spirit of a bantam
fighter, slapped the clumsy puppy across the face with

That was the beginning of their curious friendship.

one front paw. That was a signal for a free-for-all and
around the floor the two of them tumbled, locked in
fierce combat, biting each other without effect, for tiny
teeth could not pierce the thick fur that grew on each
small body. Bob and his father roared at their antics.

That was the first appearance of the pair and the beginning of their curious friendship. The puppy was

named King and the kitten dubbed Princess on the spot. Everyone thought the names most appropriate.

The two youngsters thrived and grew rapidly. The King, of course, was destined to become a big dog and soon towered over little Princess. But that difference was in size only. She had the pep of a small tiger and battled King around the floor, across the porch and out on the ground whenever she felt in the mood—which was nearly every time she saw him. And he loved it. He never grew rough with her, seeming to understand the great difference and advantage he held in strength.

The King would often lie on his side and with half-open eyes pretend to sleep. The Princess, noiseless as a drifting feather, crept closer and closer, maneuvering like a dark shadow until she reached an advantageous point from which to pounce upon her pal. Then down she'd come and around they'd thresh, King's big paws exerting just enough pressure to hold her and his long jaws clamped about her in mock ferocity, while the Princess yowled as though she were being killed.

When he would release her, she would spank him across the nose and scamper away, leaping to the mantel. There she'd sit calmly eying King who raged beneath her, daring her to come down. She'd come down —in her own sweet time, sometimes landing on his back. Then, while he whirled and raced about the place in sheer delight, the Princess clung to his thick fur like a monkey.

That fall during the hunting season, there was a party
of three up from Chicago, among them Doctor Mason,
a famous surgeon. I was staying there, too, on a survey-
ing job in the neighborhood.

One night after supper as we sat before the fire
smoking and talking, we heard a low wail like the sobbing of a child. King, who had been dozing in front of
the fire, came to his feet like a flash and was at the
door, Bob right behind him. We knew that wail. It was
the Princess.

In a few moments Bob reappeared, bearing the black
cat in his arms. King pranced at his side, head high,
whining at the burden the man bore. We stood aside as
he laid the Princess gently on the table. Her right front
paw was badly mangled and she whimpered in pain as
Bob held her head and Doctor Mason worked over her.

"Someone must have left a trap beneath the porch
steps," Bob explained. His lips were drawn tight as he
spoke. "She hopped off the steps and landed right in
it."

Doctor Mason looked up and said briskly, "Get
plenty of hot water. I've got my kit. I'll amputate. It's
the only way to save her."

For the next hour that cabin room resembled a hospital. The Princess was put to sleep while King paced
up and down the floor. Men spoke in whispers. Bob and
I helped the Doctor and it was an education to watch
him. Those fine, sure fingers whose skill brought fees

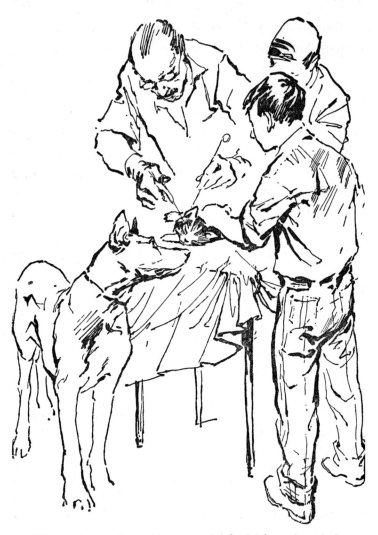

For an hour the cabin room looked like a hospital.

of thousands of dollars, flew about the mangled paw
with as much dexterity and gentleness as though he
were working on a baby.

Well, pretty soon it was all over and the Princess was
laid in a little box, strapped so that the wound could
heal. Her leg had been amputated just above the first
joint.

"Unless infection sets in, she'll be all right," Doctor
Mason explained.

"But how will she ever walk, Doctor?" Bob wanted to
know. The surgeon smiled.

"I'll attend to that, Son—in the morning." And he
did. While all hands kept coming to Princess' bed, talking to her as though she were human, and King took up
his post right beside the box never leaving even for food,
the Doctor was busy whittling on a piece of hickory.
When at last he'd finished, there was perfected and
waiting for the Princess the neatest peg leg you would
ever want to see.

But it was weeks before Princess was well enough
to use it. When he was sure that the wound was healed,
Doctor Mason fitted the peg leg into place with a little
harness across her shoulder. It was awkward at first and
Princess had trouble getting around. Her first few attempts were laughable, yet nobody laughed as they
watched her. The first time she fell in the middle of the
floor, she looked up and cried. King walked over, picked

her up with his teeth, and carefully carried her back to her box.

But as time went on, she grew accustomed to it and it wasn't long before she was thumping about the place making life miserable for the King again. She had a weapon now, for when she'd slap his face with that peg it would really sting and he'd draw back, crouch and bark at her until the pain had gone.

And so life went on in the little cabin just as it had always done, until one day the sun was dimmed and we smelled smoke. Standing on the porch we looked toward the east.

"Fires," muttered Dad. "Forest fires—but bad. Think they'll reach us, Bob?" His son shook his head.

"There's no wind. They'll burn out before they get this far." But Bob was wrong. The wind came up and the fire roared toward the cabin. It was about two o'clock at night when the alarm was shouted by one of my men. As we dressed hurriedly, the reflection from the flames danced on the inside walls and it was getting hot.

"Save what you can carry and get out," Dad ordered. So we packed what we could and ran down the road, never stopping till morning at the side of the lake. Then, as we sat having coffee and biscuits, the King emerged from the brush, tired-looking and covered with ashes. We glanced at each other, knowing what had happened.

His pal was gone. In our desperate haste, we had forgotten her. The big dog dropped down beside us and
soon fell asleep.

Late that afternoon the fire burned out and we
started back, disheartened by the disaster. King alone
seemed strangely happy. He raced ahead barking at us
as though urging us on. Then he'd run back and leap up
at Bob, trying to get him to hurry.

We came at last to the cabin clearing and saw one of
these miracles that sometimes occur in the woods. The
shack was still standing, untouched by flame. The fire
had swung down to a point right behind it; then perhaps the wind had died and the draft had ceased. Whatever had happened, the Wilson home was intact. We
moved in again and set our things in order.

But King was not to be silenced. Back and forth he
ranged, between the door and Bob, whining and barking and pleading. At last the man gave in. Tossing aside
a jacket he had started to mend, he called to me.

"Come on, Jack. This fellow has got something on
his mind. Let's see what it is."

We went outside. The King, overjoyed, raced
straight for the river bank. Stopping on the shore he
turned and waited until we came up. Then satisfied that
we were with him he barked once and plunged into
the stream. Bob and I watched in silent wonder.

In the middle of that stream—it wasn't very wide—
was a small bar, a sort of island. On the island stood the

stump of a tree. It had been a splendid oak once but lightning had cut it down, leaving a blistered fragment perhaps four feet high.

Straight to the island swam the King and crawled up on the sandy beach. He shook himself once, then trotted to the stump. Here he stopped, reared up on his hind legs and with his forefeet against the post, cocked his head to one side looking down into the hollow.

We watched, and what we saw made us want to shout. Slowly and with great dignity the white-starred face of the Princess rose from the little nest at the top of the stump, then her shoulders and peg-leg harness came into view.

For a long minute she looked straight at the King as though scolding him for being late. He waited without moving a muscle. At last the little black lady struggled to the edge of the nest, felt her way cautiously onto King's broad head and clung to his neck. Steadily he lowered himself to his four feet, turned and walked back to the river. He never even paused at the water's edge but moved steadily into the stream and swam toward us.

Perched gaily on his back, her tail lashing happily, her peg leg stuck securely behind the King's ear, Princess rode in state back to the landing place in front of the cabin.

Neither Bob nor I spoke as the dog walked sedately up to us. Wilson took the kitten from her perch and set her on the ground. Relieved of his burden, King's nose lowered toward her, to assure himself of her safety. She banged him with her wooden leg, and hobbled away toward the cabin, the big dog rocking along beside her. Bob looked at me for a long time, a slow smile on his lips.

At last he said, "No one can ever tell me that the King didn't hide her out there. That's just the sort of stunt that bucko would pull for a pal."

WALTER A. DYER

Gulliver the Great

It was a mild evening in early spring, and the magnolias were in bloom. We motored around the park, turned up a side street, and finally came to a throbbing standstill before the Churchwarden Club.

There was nothing about its exterior to indicate that it was a clubhouse at all, but within there was an indefinable atmosphere of early Victorian comfort. There was something about it that suggested Mr. Pickwick. Old prints of horses and ships and battles hung upon the walls, and the oak was dark and old. There seemed to be no decorative scheme or keynote, and yet the atmosphere was utterly distinctive. It was my first visit to the Churchwarden Club, of which my quaint, old-fashioned Uncle Ford had long been a member, and I was charmed.

We dined in the rathskeller, the walls of which were completely covered with long churchwarden pipes, arranged in the most intricate and marvelous patterns; and after our mutton-chop and ale and plum pudding, we filled with the choicest of tobaccos the pipes which the old major-domo brought us.

Then came Jacob R. Enderby to smoke with us.

Tall and spare he was, with long, straight, black hair, large, aquiline nose, and piercing eyes. I disgraced myself by staring at him. I didn't know such a man existed in New York, and yet I couldn't decide whether his habitat should be Arizona or Cape Cod.

Enderby and Uncle Ford were deep in a discussion of the statesmanship of James G. Blaine, when a waiter summoned my uncle to the telephone.

I neglected to state that my uncle, in his prosaic hours, is a physician; and this was a call. I knew it the moment I saw the waiter approaching. I was disappointed and disgusted.

Uncle Ford saw this and laughed.

"Cheer up!" said he. "You needn't come with me to visit the sick. I'll be back in an hour, and meanwhile Mr. Enderby will take care of you; won't you, Jake?"

For answer Enderby arose, and refilling his pipe took me by the arm, while my uncle got into his overcoat. As he passed us on the way out he whispered in my ear:

"Talk about dogs."

I heard and nodded.

Enderby led me to the lounge or loafing-room, an oak-paneled apartment in the rear of the floor above, with huge leather chairs and a seat in the bay window.

Save for a gray-haired old chap dozing over a copy of Simplicissimus, the room was deserted.

But no sooner had Enderby seated himself on the window-seat than there was a rush and a commotion, and a short, glad bark, and Nubbins, the steward's bull-terrier, bounded in and landed at Enderby's side with canine expressions of great joy.

I reached forward to pat him, but he paid absolutely no attention to me.

At last wrigglings subsided, and he settled down with his head on Enderby's knee, the picture of content. Then I recalled my Uncle's parting injunction.

"Friend of yours?" I suggested.

Enderby smiled. "Yes," he said, "we're friends, I guess. And the funny part of it is that he doesn't pay any attention to any one else except his master. They all act that way with me, dogs do." And he pulled Nubbins's stubby ears.

"Natural attraction, I suppose," said I.

"Yes, it is," he answered, with the modest frankness of a big man. "It's a thing hard to explain, though there's a sort of reason for it in my case."

I pushed toward him a little tobacco-laden teak-wood stand hopefully. He refilled and lighted.

"It's an extraordinary thing, even so," he said, puffing. "Every dog nowadays seems to look upon me as his long-lost master, but it wasn't always so. I hated dogs and they hated me."

Not wishing to say "Really" or "Indeed" to this big, outdoor man, I simply grunted my surprise.

"Yes, we were born enemies. More than that, I was afraid of dogs. A little fuzzy toy dog, ambling up to me in a room full of company, with his tail wagging, gave me the shudders. I couldn't touch the beast. And as for big dogs outdoors, I feared them like the plague. I would go blocks out of my way to avoid one.

"I don't remember being particularly cowardly about other things, but I just couldn't help this. It was in my blood, for some reason or other. It was the bane of my existence. I couldn't see what the brutes were put in the world for, or how any one could have anything to do with them.

"All the dogs reciprocated. They disliked and distrusted me. The most docile old Brunos would growl and show their teeth when I came near."

"Did the change come suddenly?" I asked.

"Quite. It was in 1901. I accepted a commission from an importing and trading company to go to the Philippines to do a little quiet exploring, and spent four months in the sickly place. Then I got the fever, and when I recovered I couldn't get out of there too soon.

"I reached Manila just in time to see the mail steamer disappearing around the point, and I was mad. There would be another in six days, but I couldn't wait. I was just crazy to get back home.

"I made inquiries and learned of an old tramp

steamer, named the Old Squaw, making ready to leave for Honolulu on the following day with a cargo of hemp and stuff, and a bunch of Moros for some show in the States, and I booked passage on that.

She was the worst old tub you ever saw. I didn't learn much about her, but I verily believe her to have been a condemned excursion boat. She wouldn't have been allowed to run to Coney Island.

"She was battered and unpainted, and she wallowed horribly. I don't believe she could have reached Honolulu much before the regular boat, but I couldn't wait, and I took her.

"I made myself as comfortable as possible, bribed the cook to insure myself against starvation, and swung a hammock on the forward deck as far as possible from the worst of the vile smells.

"But we hadn't lost sight of Manila Bay when I discovered that there was a dog aboard—and such a dog! I had never seen one that sent me into such a panic as this one, and he had free range of the ship. A Great Dane he was, named Gulliver, and he was the pride of the captain's rum-soaked heart.

"With all my fear, I realized he was a magnificent animal, but I looked on him as a gigantic devil. Without exception, he was the biggest dog I ever saw, and as muscular as a lion. He lacked some points that show-judges set store by, but he had the size and the build.

"I had seen Vohl's Vulcan and the Württemberg

breed, but they were fox-terriers compared with Gulliver. His tail was as big around as my arm, and the cook lived in terror of his getting into the galley and wagging it; and he had a mouth that looked to me like the crater of Mauna Loa, and a voice that shook the planking when he spoke.

A Great Dane he was, named Gulliver.

"I first caught sight of him appearing from behind a huge coil of cordage in the stern. He stretched and yawned, and I nearly died of fright.

"I caught up a belaying-pin, though little good that would have done me. I think he saw me do it, and doubtless he set me down for an enemy then and there.

"We were well out of the harbor, and there was no

turning back, but I would have given my right hand to be off that boat. I fully expected him to eat me up, and I slept with that belaying-pin sticking into my ribs in the hammock, and with my revolver loaded and handy.

"Fortunately, Gulliver's dislike for me took the form of sublime contempt. He knew I was afraid of him, and he despised me for it. He was a great pet with the captain and crew, and even the Moros treated him with admiring respect when they were allowed on deck. I couldn't understand it. I would as soon have made a pet of a hungry boa-constrictor.

"On the third day out the poor old boiler burst and the Old Squaw caught fire. She was dry and rotten inside and she burned like tinder. No attempt was made to extinguish the flames, which got into the hemp in the hold in short order.

"The smoke was stifling, and in a jiffy all hands were struggling with the boats. The Moros came tumbling up from below and added to the confusion with their terrified yells.

"The davits were old and rusty, and the men were soon fighting among themselves. One boat dropped stern foremost, filled, and sank immediately, and the Old Squaw herself was visibly settling.

"I saw there was no chance of getting away in the boats, and I recalled a life-raft on the deck forward near my hammock. It was a sort of catamaran—a double platform on a pair of hollow, water-tight, cylindrical buoys. It wasn't twenty feet long and about half as broad, but it would have to do. I fancy it was a forgotten relic of the old excursion-boat days.

"There was no time to lose, for the Old Squaw was bound to sink presently. Besides, I was aft with the rest, and the flames were licking up the deck and running-gear in the waist of the boat.

"The galley, which was amidships near the engine-room, had received the full force of the explosion, and the cook lay moaning in the lee scuppers with a small water-cask thumping against his chest. I couldn't stop to help the man, but I did kick the cask away.

"It seemed to be nearly full, and it occurred to me that I should need it. I glanced quickly around, and luckily found a tin of biscuits that had also been blown out of the galley. I picked this up, and rolling the cask of water ahead of me as rapidly as I could, I made my way through the hot, stifling smoke to the bow of the boat.

"I kicked at the life-raft; it seemed to be sound, and I lashed the biscuits and water to it. I also threw on a coil of rope and a piece of sail-cloth. I saw nothing else about that could possibly be of any value to me. I abandoned my trunk for fear it would only prove troublesome.

"Then I hacked the raft loose with my knife and shoved it over the bulwark. Apparently no one had seen me, for there was no one else forward of the sheet of flame that now cut the board in two.

"The raft was a mighty heavy affair, but I managed to raise one end to the rail. I don't believe I would ever have been able to heave it over under any circumstances, but I didn't have to.

"I felt a great unheaval, and the prow of the Old Squaw went up into the air. I grabbed the ropes that I had lashed the food on with and clung to the raft. The deck became almost perpendicular, and it was a miracle that the raft didn't slide down with me into the flames. Somehow it stuck where it was.

"Then the boat sank with a great roar, and for about a thousand years, it seemed to me, I was under water. I didn't do anything, I couldn't think.

"I was only conscious of tremendous weight of water and a feeling that I would burst open. Instinct alone made me cling to the raft.

"When it finally brought me to the surface I was as nearly dead as I care to be. I lay there on the thing in a half-conscious condition for an endless time. If my life had depended on my doing something, I would have been lost.

"Then gradually I came to, and began to spit our salt water and gasp for breath. I gathered my wits together and sat up. My hands were absolutely numb, and I had to loosen the grip of my fingers with the help of my toes. Odd sensation.

"Then I looked about me. My biscuits and water and rope were safe, but the sail-cloth had vanished. I remember that this annoyed me hugely at the time, though I don't know what earthly good it would have been.

"The sea was fairly calm, and I could see all about. Not a human being was visible, only a few floating bits of wreckage. Every man on board must have gone down with the ship and drowned, except myself.

"Then I caught sight of something that made my heart stand still. The huge head of Gulliver was coming rapidly toward me through the water!

"The dog was swimming strongly, and must have leaped from the Old Squaw before she sank. My raft was the only thing afloat large enough to hold him, and he knew it.

"I drew my revolver, but it was soaking wet and useless. Then I sat down on the cracker tin and gritted my teeth and waited. I had been alarmed, I must admit, when the boiler blew up and the panic began, but that was nothing to the terror that seized me now.

"Here I was all alone on the top of the Pacific Ocean with a horrible demon making for me as fast as he could swim. My mind was benumbed, and I could think of nothing to do. I trembled and my teeth rattled. I prayed for a shark, but no shark came.

"Soon Gulliver reached the raft and placed one of his forepaws on it and then the other. The top of it stood six or eight inches above the water, and it took a great effort for the dog to raise himself. I wanted to kick him back, but I didn't dare to move.

"Gulliver struggled mightily. Again and again he reared his great shoulders above the sea, only to be cast back scratching and kicking, at a lurch of the raft.

"Finally a wave favored him, and he caught the edge of the under platform with one of his hind feet. With a stupendous effort he heaved his huge bulk over the edge and lay sprawling at my feet, panting and trembling."

Enderby paused and gazed out of the window with a big sigh, as though the recital of his story had brought back some of the horror of his remarkable experience.

Nubbins looked up inquiringly, and then snuggled closer to his friend, while Enderby smoothed the white head.

"Well," he continued, "there we were. You can't possibly imagine how I felt unless you, too, have been afflicted with dog-fear. It was awful. And I hated the brute so. I could have torn him limb from limb if I had had the strength. But he was vastly more powerful than I. I could only fear him.

"By and by he got up and shook himself. I cowered on my cracker-tin, but he only looked at me contemptuously, went to the other end of the raft, and lay down to wait patiently for deliverance.

"We remained this way until nightfall. The sea was

comparatively calm, and we seemed to be drifting but slowly. We were in the path of ships likely to be passing one way or the other, and I would have been hopeful of the outcome if it had not been for my feared and hated companion.

"I began to feel faint, and opened the cracker-tin. The biscuits were wet with salt water, but I ate a couple, and left the tin open to dry them. Gulliver looked around, and I shut the tin hastily. But the dog never moved. He was not disposed to ask any favors. By kicking the sides of the cask and prying with my knife, I managed to get the bung out and took a drink. Then I settled myself on the raft with my back against the cask, and longed for a smoke.

"The gentle motion of the raft produced a lulling effect on my exhausted nerves, and I began to nod, only to awake with a start, with fear gripping at my heart. I dared not sleep. I don't know what I thought Gulliver would do to me, for I did not understand dogs, but I felt that I must watch him constantly. In the star-light I could see that his eyes were open. Gulliver was watchful too.

"All night long I kept up a running fight with drowsiness. I dozed at intervals, but never for long at a time. It was a horrible night, and I cannot tell you how I longed for day and welcomed it when it came.

"I must have slept toward dawn, for I suddenly became conscious of broad daylight. I roused myself,

I felt that I must watch him constantly.

stood up, and swung my arms and legs to stir up circulation, for the night had been chilly. Gulliver arose, too, and stood silently watching me until I ceased for fear. When he had settled down again I got my breakfast out of the cracker-tin. Gulliver was restless, and was evidently interested.

" 'He must be hungry,' I thought, and then a new fear caught me. I had only to wait until he became very hungry and then he would surely attack me. I concluded that it would be wiser to feed him, and I tossed him a biscuit.

"I expected to see him grab it ravenously, and wondered as soon as I had thrown it if the taste of food would only serve to make him more ferocious. But at first he would not touch it. He only lay there with his great head on his paws and glowered at me. Distrust was plainly visible in his face. I had never realized before that a dog's face could express the subtler emotions.

"His gaze fascinated me, and I could not take my eyes from his. The bulk of him was tremendous as he lay there, and I noticed the big, swelling muscles of his jaw. At last he arose, sniffed suspiciously at the biscuit, and looked up at me again.

" 'It's all right; eat it!' I cried.

"The sound of my own voice frightened me. I had not intended to speak to him. But in spite of my strained tone he seemed somewhat reassured.

"He took a little nibble, and then swallowed the biscuit after one or two crunches, and looked up expectantly. I threw him another and he ate that.

" 'That's all,' said I. 'We mut be sparing of them.'

"I was amazed to discover how perfectly he understood. He lay down again and licked his chops.

"Late in the afternoon I saw a line of smoke on the horizon, and saw a steamer stove into view. I stood up and waved my coat frantically, but to no purpose. Gulliver stood up and looked from me to the steamer, apparently much interested.

" 'Too far off,' I said to Gulliver. 'I hope the next one will come nearer.'

"At midday I dined, and fed Gulliver. This time he took the two biscuits quite without reserve and whacked his great tail against the raft. It seemed to me that his attitude was less hostile, and I wondered at it.

"When I took my drink from the cask, Gulliver showed signs of interest.

" 'I suppose dogs get thirsty, too,' I said aloud.

"Gulliver rapped with his tail. I looked about for some sort of receptacle, and finally pulled off my shoe, filled it with water, and shoved it toward him with my foot. He drank gratefully.

"During the afternoon I sighted another ship, but it was too distant to notice me. However, the sea remained calm and I did not despair.

"After we had had supper, I settled back against my cask, resolved to keep awake, for still I did not trust Gulliver. The sun set suddenly and the stars came out, and I found myself strangely lonesome. It seemed as though I had been alone out there on the Pacific for weeks. The miles and miles of heaving waters, almost on a level with my eye, were beginning to get on my nerves. I longed for someone to talk to, and wished I had dragged the half-breed cook along with me for company. I sighed loudly, and Gulliver raised his head.

" 'Lonesome out here, isn't it?' I said, simply to hear the sound of my own voice.

"Then for the first time Gulliver spoke. He made a deep sound in his throat, but it wasn't a growl, and with all my ignorance of dog language I knew it.

"Then I began to talk. I talked about everything— the people back home and all that—and Gulliver listened. I know more about dogs now, and I know that the best way to make friends with a dog is to talk to him. He can't talk back, but he can understand a heap more than you think he can.

"Finally Gulliver, who had kept his distance all this time, arose and came toward me. My words died in my throat. What was he going to do? To my immense relief he did nothing but sink down at my feet with a grunt and curl his huge body into a semicircle. He had dignity, Gulliver had. He wanted to be friendly, but he would not presume. However, I had lost interest in conversation, and sat watching him and wondering.

"In spite of my firm resolution, I fell asleep at length from sheer exhaustion, and never woke until daybreak. The sky was clouded and our raft was pitching. Gulliver was standing in the middle of the raft, looking at me in evident alarm. I glanced over my shoulder, and the blackness of the horizon told me that a storm was coming, and coming soon.

"I made fast our slender provender, tied the end of a line about my own waist for safety, and waited.

"In a short time the storm struck us in all its tropical fury. The raft pitched and tossed, now high up one end, and now at the other, and sometimes almost engulfed in the waves.

"Gulliver was having a desperate time to keep aboard. His blunt claws slipped on the wet deck of the raft, and he fell and slid about dangerously. The thought flashed across my mind that I might soon be rid of the brute.

"As I clung there to the lashings, I saw him slip down to the further end of the raft, his hind quarters actually over the edge. A wave swept over him, but still he clung, panting madly. Then the raft righted itself for a moment, and as he hung there he gave me a look I shall never forget—a look of fear, of pleading, of reproach, and yet of silent courage. And with all my stupidity I read that look. Somehow it told me that I was the master, after all, and he the dog. I could not resist it. Cau-

"Then I began to talk. I talked about everything . . ."

tiously I raised myself and loosened the square rope I had saved. As the raft tipped the other way Gulliver regained his footing and came sliding toward me.

"Quickly I passed the rope around his body, and as the raft dived again I hung on to the rope with one hand, retaining my own hold with the other. Gulliver's great weight nearly pulled my arm from its socket, but he helped mightily, and during the next moment of equilibrium I took another turn about his body and made the end of the rope fast.

"The storm passed as swiftly as it had come, and though it left us drenched and exhausted, we were both safe.

"That evening Gulliver crept close to me as I talked, and I let him. Loneliness will make a man do strange things.

"On the fifth day, when our provisions were nearly gone, and I had begun to feel the sinking dullness of despair, I sighted a steamer apparently coming directly toward us. Instantly I felt new life in my limbs and around my heart, and while the boat was yet miles away I began to shout and wave my coat.

" 'I believe she's coming, old man!' I cried to Gulliver. 'I believe she's coming!'

"I soon wearied of this foolishness and sat down to wait. Gulliver came close and sat beside me, and for the first time I put my hand on him. He looked up at me and rapped furiously with his tail. I patted his head—a little gingerly, I must confess.

"It was a big, smooth head, and it felt solid and strong. I passed my hand down his neck, his back, his flanks. He seemed to quiver with joy. He leaned his huge body against me. Then he bowed his head and licked my shoe.

"A feeling of intense shame and unworthiness came over me, with the realization of how completely I had misunderstood him. Why should this great, powerful creature lick my shoe? It was incredible.

"Then, somehow, everything changed. Fear and distrust left me, and a feeling of comradeship and understanding took their place. We two had been through so much together. A dog was no longer a frightful beast to me; he was a dog! I cannot think of a nobler word. And Gulliver had licked my shoe! Doubtless it was only the fineness of his perception that had prevented him from licking my hand. I might have resented that. I put my arms suddenly around Gulliver's neck and hugged him. I loved that dog!

"Slowly, slowly, the steamer crawled along, but still kept to her course. When she was about a mile away, however, I saw that she would not pass as close to us as I had hoped; so I began once more my waving and yelling. She came nearer, nearer, but still showed no sign of observing us.

"She was abreast of us, and passing. I was in a frenzy!

"She was so near that I could make out the figure of the captain on the bridge, and other figures on the deck below. It seemed as though they must see us, though I realized how low in the water we stood, and how pitifully weak and hoarse my voice was. I had been a fool to waste it. Then an idea struck me.

" 'Speak!' I cried to Gulliver, who stood watching beside me. 'Speak, old man!'

"Gulliver needed no second bidding. A roar like that of all the bulls of Bashan rolled out over the blue Pacific. Again and again Gulliver gave voice, deep, full, powerful. His great sides heaved with the mighty effort, his red, cavernous mouth open, and his head raised high.

" 'Good, old man!' I cried. 'Good!' And again that magnificent voice boomed forth.

"Then something happened on board the steamer. The figures came to the side. I waved my coat and danced. Then they saw us.

"I was pretty well done up when they took us aboard, and I slept for twenty-four hours straight. When I awoke there sat Gulliver by my bunk, and when I turned to look at him he lifted a great paw and put it on my arm."

Enderby ceased, and there was silence in the room save for the light snoring of Nubbins.

"You took him home with you, I suppose?" I asked.

Enderby nodded.

"And you have him still?" I certainly wanted to have a look at that dog.

But he did not answer. I saw an expression of great sadness come into his eyes as he gazed out of the window, and I knew that Jacob Enderby had finished his story.

W. H. HUDSON

Dandy:

The Story of a Dog

He was of mixed breed, and was supposed to have a strain of Dandy Dinmont blood which gave him his name. A big ungainly animal with a rough shaggy coat of blue-gray hair and white on his neck and clumsy paws. He looked like a Sussex sheep dog with legs reduced to half their proper length. He was, when I first knew him, getting old and increasingly deaf and dim of sight, otherwise in the best of health and spirits, or at all events very good-tempered.

Until I knew Dandy I had always supposed that the story of Ludlam's dog was pure invention, and I dare say that is the general opinion about it; but Dandy made me reconsider the subject, and eventually I came to believe that Ludlam's dog did exist once upon a time, centuries ago perhaps, and that if he had been the laziest dog in the world Dandy was not far behind him in that respect. It is true he did not lean his head against a wall to bark; he exhibited his laziness in other ways. He barked often, though never at strangers; he

They would coil up by Dandy's side.

welcomed every visitor, even the tax-collector, with tail-waggings and a smile. He spent a good deal of his time in the large kitchen, where he had a sofa to sleep on, and when the two cats of the house wanted an hour's rest they would coil themselves up on Dandy's broad shaggy side, preferring that bed to cushion or rug. They were like a warm blanket over him, and it was a sort of mutual benefit society. After an hour's sleep Dandy would go out for a short constitutional as far as the neighboring thoroughfare, where he would blunder against people, wag his tail to everybody, and then come back. He had six or eight or more outings each day, and, owing to doors and gates being closed and to his lazy disposition, he had much trouble in getting out and in. First he would sit down in the hall and bark, bark, bark, until some one would come to open the door for him, where upon he would slowly waddle down the garden path, and if he found the gate closed he would again sit down and start barking. And the bark, bark would go on until some one came to let him out. But if after he had barked about twenty or thirty times no one came, he would deliberately open the gate himself, which he could do perfectly well, and let himself out. In twenty minutes or so he would be back at the gate and barking for admission once more, and finally, if no one paid any attention, letting himself in.

Dandy always had something to eat at meal-times, but he too liked a snack between meals once or twice a

day. The dog-biscuits were kept in an open box on the
lower dresser shelf, so that he could get one "whenever
he felt so disposed," but he didn't like the trouble this
arrangement gave him, so he would sit down and start
barking, and as he had a bark which was both deep and
loud, after it had been repeated a dozen times at intervals of five seconds, any person who happened to be in
or near the kitchen was glad to give him his biscuit
for the sake of peace and quietness. If no one gave it
him, he would then take it out himself and eat it.

Now it came to pass that during the last year of the
war dog-biscuits, like many other articles of food for
man and beast, grew scarce, and were finally not to be
had at all. At all events, that was what happened in
Dandy's town of Penzance. He missed his biscuits
greatly and often reminded us of it by barking; then,
lest we should think he was barking about something
else, he would go and sniff and paw at the empty box.
He perhaps thought it was pure forgetfulness on the
part of those of the house who went every morning to
do the marketing and had fallen into the habit of returning without dog-biscuits in the basket. One day
during that last winter of scarcity and anxiety I went to
the kitchen and found the floor strewn all over with the
fragments of Dandy's biscuit-box. Dandy himself had
done it; he had dragged the box from its place out into
the middle of the floor, and then deliberately set himself to bite and tear it into small pieces and scatter them

about. He was caught at it just as he was finishing the job, and the kindly person who surprised him in the act suggested that the reason of his breaking up the box in that way was that he got something of the biscuit flavor by biting the pieces. My own theory was that as the box was there to hold biscuits and now held none, he had come to regard it as useless—as having lost its function, so to speak—also that its presence there was an insult to his intelligence, a constant temptation to make a fool of himself by visiting it half a dozen times a day only to find it empty as usual. Better, then, to get rid of it altogether, and no doubt when he did it he put a little temper into the business!

Dandy, from the time I first knew him, was strictly teetotal, but in former and distant days he had been rather fond of his glass. If a person held up a glass of beer before him, I was told, he wagged his tail in joyful anticipation, and a little beer was always given him at mealtime. Then he had an experience, which, after a little hesitation, I have thought it best to relate, as it is perhaps the most curious incident in Dandy's somewhat uneventful life.

One day Dandy, who after the manner of his kind, had attached himself to the person who was always willing to take him out for a stroll, followed his friend to a neighboring public-house, where the said friend had to discuss some business matter with the landlord. They went into the taproom, and Dandy, finding that the business was going to be a rather long affair, settled himself down to have a nap. Now it chanced that a barrel of beer which had just been broached had a leaky tap, and the landlord had set a basin on the floor to catch the waste. Dandy, waking from his nap and hearing the trickling sound, got up, and going to the basin quenched his thirst, after which he resumed his nap. By-and-by he woke again and had a second drink, and altogether he woke and had a drink five or six times; then, the business being concluded, they went out together, but no sooner were they out in the fresh air than Dandy began to exhibit signs of inebriation. He swerved from side to side, colliding with the passers-by, and finally fell off the pavement into the swift stream of water which at that point runs in the gutter at one side of the street. Getting out of the water, he started again, trying to keep close to the wall to save himself from another ducking. People looked curiously at him, and by-and-by they began to ask what the matter was. "Is your dog going to have a fit—or what is it?" they asked. Dandy's friend said he didn't know; something was the matter, no doubt, and he would take him home as quickly as possible and see to it.

When they finally got to the house Dandy staggered to the sofa, and succeeded in climbing on to it and, throwing himself on his cushion, went fast to sleep, and slept on without a break until the following morning. Then he rose quite refreshed and appeared to have forgotten all about it; but that day when at dinner-time some one said "Dandy" and held up a glass of beer, instead of wagging his tail as usual he dropped it between his legs and turned away in evident disgust. And from that time onward he would never touch it with his tongue and it was plain that when they tried to tempt him, setting beer before him and smilingly inviting him to drink, he knew they were mocking him, and before turning away he would emit a low growl and show his teeth. It was the one thing that put him out and would make him angry with his friends and life companions.

I should not have related this incident if Dandy had been alive. But he is no longer with us. He was old—half-way between fifteen and sixteen: it seemed as though he had waited to see the end of the war, since no sooner was the armistice proclaimed than he began to decline rapidly. Gone deaf and blind, he still insisted on taking several constitutionals every day, and would bark as usual at the gate, and if no one came to let him out or admit him, he would open it for himself as before. This went on till January, 1919, when some of the boys he knew were coming back to Penzance and to the house. Then he established himself on his sofa, and we knew that his end was near, for there he would sleep all day and all night, declining food. It is customary in this country to chloroform a dog and give him a dose of strychnine to "put him out of his misery."

But it was not necessary in this case, as he was not in misery; not a groan did he ever emit, waking or sleeping; and if you put a hand on him he would look up and wag his tail just to let you know that it was well with him. And in his sleep he passed away—a perfect case of euthanasia—and was buried in the large garden near the second apple-tree.

BETTY CAVANNA

Scarlet's Sons

Scarlet was the most beautiful collie that Prue had ever seen. When Gerald Lonsdale brought her to the farm in the long shining car, she stepped down form the seat beside her master with the delicacy and breeding of a queen.

"She'll be better off out here in the country with you than anywhere else," Mr. Lonsdale told Prue's father, while Scarlet, aware that all was not as usual, nudged her master's hand gently with her slim muzzle.

"Aye," said Sam Ferguson, with jut a trace of a Yorkshire accent, "and when the pups come, it'll be better for them, too." He looked with tenderness and admiration at the collie. A finer one he had never seen, even at home in northern England. "I'll treat her like she's my own, sir!"

And Gerald Lonsdale, owner of the famous Lonsdale kennels, knew that he could trust Sam as he would himself.

That evening, after the supper dishes were washed,

Sam took down a grooming brush and a cloth from the closet shelf and, kneeling on the rug, began working expertly on Scarlet's coat. He rubbed the rich, deep sable fur with the cloth, cradling the aristocratic muzzle carefully in one hand. Then he brushed the snow-white ruff and fluffed out the "leggings" and the "apron" and the "petticoat." All the while he talked, explaining to Prudence the points that made Scarlet an outstanding show dog.

Then suddenly, tragically, when Scarlet's four puppies were only three days old, the mother died. Sam had called Mr. Lonsdale long distance when the collie was taken sick.

"A blood-stream infection, sir!" he had explained. "A bad one. I doubt if we can save her!"

"If you can't save her, with the help of the best vet in the country, I know that no one can. Do what you can, Sam, and I'll know it's been your best!"

The night that Scarlet died Sam could eat no supper. "The finest bench dog the Lonsdale kennels ever produced," he muttered, "and in the prime o' life!" Then he turned his attention to the puppies, so lost, so tiny, with their tight-shut eyes and their hungry mouths. "Run down to the village, Prue, and buy some bottles and some nipples. We'll do what we can for them!"

Sam taught his daughter to bottle-feed the babies. He mixed their formula himself. An ordinary kennel man might not have saved one of the pups, but Sam pulled three of them through, with Prue's help, and in six weeks they were as sturdy and sweet as though Scarlet herself had nursed them.

Prue thought that she had never seen anything more adorable than the three plump balls of fur. She named them when they were ten days old—the day their eyes opened—not kennel names, of course, just pet names— Sistie and Cocoa and Sonny. She crouched down in the cool barn by their low box and talked to them, telling them to hurry up and grow, so that they could run about the farm and play with her. She forgot that she was a junior in high school, almost grown up. She talked like a child again.

By the end of June, the puppies were three months old. "And every one o' thim a beauty in its own right," Sam said.

"Unless I miss my guess, they'll each of them be as fine a dog as Scarlet, or maybe finer!" exclaimed Mr. Lonsdale when he saw the litter. He arranged to leave the pups at the farm until they were six months old, when he would select one to keep and offer the other two for sale. "There's a spirit to a dog who grows up in a family that you don't get in a kennel-bred dog," he explained.

It was hard for Prue to realize that the puppies would not always live at the farm. They seemed like her own. "Maybe," she said hopefully to her mother, "he'll take his pick and then leave that dog with us a little longer, anyway."

"Maybe," said Mrs. Ferguson, but her voice held little of the conviction that Prue would have liked to feel.

For some reason, Sonny was Prue's favorite.

With every added week of life, the young collies grew both in stature and in personality. Their short muzzles lengthened; their puppy coats became less downy and more silky; their eyes grew bright and understanding when Prue issued familiar commands. Cocoa was the rascal of the three, chasing chickens with gay abandon, leaping hedges much too high for his short legs. Sistie was dainty and feminine, behaving with the coy assurance of a debutante, but as she grew older, she developed a slight droop to her left ear, which Sam feared would spoil her chances as a bench dog. Sonny, for some reason that she couldn't quite put into words, was Prue's favorite. He had a joyousness, a quick intelligence, that she loved.

"You can talk to Sonny," she told her dad. "He knows what you're saying." And Sam Ferguson nodded. "It's Sonny I'd be keepin' if I was Mr. Lonsdale," he said.

The second week in September the school bus began to joggle down the hill that lay to the right of the farm. Prue again ran down the path in the morning, her books and her lunch under her arm.

"A good thing school's started," muttered Sam to his wife. "She was gettin' that attached to the collies, it'd fair kill her to have 'em taken."

Being a junior was much better than being a sophomore. Freshman year everything had been new and different and exciting, but sophomore year had been sort of in-betweeny, like being neither bird, fish, nor good red herring. Now, as an upperclassman, Prue began to feel a new sense of responsibility and importance. But it didn't make her any less anxious to get back to the farm afternoons to see her pups.

One day when the first of the falling maple leaves were blowing high on the wind, Prue saw, as she climbed the hill, the familiar Lonsdale car parked by the barn. Her heart tightened and beat with sharp premonition, and her eyes, try as she would, filled with tears.

"Now don't be ridiculous," she told herself. "They aren't your dogs. They never were. They're part of Daddy's job, that's all." But she turned at right angles to the path and cut down to the lower field, where the brook ran past an old bent apple tree. Flinging her books down on the grass, she lay flat on her stomach, as she had so often in the days of braids and pinafores. She stayed there until she heard the Lonsdale car go down the road.

When she finally went into the house, Sam Ferguson was standing by the window turning the pages of a newspaper, and her mother was rolling out hot biscuits on a floured board. Prue went on through the kitchen to the living room and dropped her books on the worn sofa. She was sorry, now, that she had not had the courage to come right on up to the house and out to the barn while Mr. Lonsdale was there. At least she could have been brave enough to say good-by to her brood. Then finally she could stand it no longer. She ran back to the kitchen and cried, "Dad, what about the pups?"

"Cocoa's been sold to a fine kennel in Connecticut," said Sam, "and Sistie goes to a Chicago breeder."

"And Sonny?" Prue whispered.

"Fir the time bein'," Sam went on, a twinkle appearing in his eye, "Sonny stays with us."

It was almost too good to be true. Prue went out to the barn and put her arms around the big puppy's neck and told him how terribly, terribly glad she was. And Sonny licked her hand and barked and pawed Prue's clean sweater with his muddy forepaws.

But now, in spite of her delight, a hint of sorrow lingered in the crisp fall air for Prudence. She knew, every afternoon when Sonny waited for the returning bus at the end of the lane, that it could not last forever —this companionship between herself and a dog which was so much more satisfying than any other friendship she had ever known. Someday, next month or next year, Mr. Lonsdale would drive up to take Sonny away. There would be essential justice, Prue knew, in the parting, for Sonny was born to a great heritage. She understood now how rare a champion show dog was, and that Sonny would be a champion she was sure.

Already Sam was beginning to teach the puppy to stand properly, to walk with graceful dignity, to obey standard spoken commands. Eagerly Prue watched her father work with the dog. Then she copied his technique.

It seemed to Prue that Sonny obeyed her more quickly than he did her dad. "That's natural," said Sam. "He feels that you're his mistress. He knows your voice an' your touch better'n mine." He was proud of the way his slim, tall daughter handled the dog. "They make a right pretty pair," he confided to his wife. "Prue with her hair almost the color of Sonny's coat."

The winter passed. Wind and cold rain and snow swept over the fields of the farm, and Sonny's coat grew long and thick, so that by the spring, when he was a year old, he was even more beautiful than the remembered Scarlet.

Still Mr. Lonsdale did not come for his dog. "I'm not planning to enter him in the spring shows," he wrote Sam. "I'd rather hold him until he gets his full growth and show him first in the fall."

So Prudence had Sonny for a second summer, and when she worked at her chores, the collie was always at her heels. But all the time, she tried to think of Sonny only as a loan, not as a possession or a member of the family.

So when Mr. Lonsdale came for his dog it was no shock; it was simply a deep-rooted sorrow that Prue was well aware she must bear alone. She was up in the back field hoeing and cultivating the truck patch, when the car drew up, and Sonny was lying asleep under an oak tree. Immediately she whistled the dog to her, and with a quick gesture she knelt and buried her face in the collie's ruff. Then she walked quickly down toward the barn, with Sonny gamboling ahead of her on his quick, slender legs.

"He'll not need much grooming, or much training

either, for the Philadelphia show in September," Sam Ferguson was saying to Mr. Lonsdale. "Prue's seen to that."

"I'm sure she has," said Mr. Lonsdale with a quick look of appreciation in the girl's direction. "What is it you call him?"

"Sonny," said Prue, and the collie's ears pricked to attention.

"Sonny," repeated Mr. Lonsdale. "Let's see. For a kennel name we could make it Scarletson. How would that look on a show list, Sam? 'Lonsdale's Scarletson'?"

"I think it would look fine, sir," said Sam, but all the time he was watching Prue.

Then, with the suddenness of catastrophe, Sonny was gone, and Prue, for all her careful acceptance of the loss, could not choke down her dinner. The August fields were empty, and autumn seemed already upon them. Prue began to look forward to the opening of school, so that this seeping loneliness would be less.

There was nothing Sam could say to Prue to comfort her. She never mentioned Sonny, and somehow he could not bring himself to say the dog's name either. Mrs. Ferguson looked at the two of them with a sympathy that only bordered on understanding.

"We could buy a dog, maybe," she offered one evening after she had counted the small hoard of change which she called "kitchen money." Prue was upstairs studying, and Mrs. Ferguson was alone with her husband. "Mabye not as fine a dog as Sonny, but a dog's a dog, after all."

Sam shook his head. "It wouldn't be the same," he said.

The very next day, in the R.D. box at the end of the lane, there was a letter from Mr. Lonsdale. Prue, coming home from school, carried it up to her father, who was repairing a chicken coop in the back of the barn. When he opened it, two green tickets fell out. Prue picked them up and saw that they were tickets for the dog show.

Sonny was entered, Mr. Lonsdale said, and he had high hopes for him, though he was still finding the adjustment to kennel life difficult to make. "He may be grieving a bit for the farm," was the way Sonny's owner put it. The tickets were sent in the hope that Sam would be able to get down to Philadelphia with his wife on the day of the show.

That night at supper Sam read the letter aloud. "I'll take ye, Mother," he said, "if ye'd like it."

"Nonsense!" returned Mrs. Ferguson. "You'll take Prudence here. What do I know about dog shows?"

Prue's hands were cold with excitement when she and her father entered the huge stuffy hall reverberating with the noise of yapping dogs. A gray haze hung low over the lofty room, with its milling crowds of kennel men, handlers, owners, judges, and spectators.

Show rings were surrounded by aisles of dog boxes, to which were chained the hundreds of entrants.

Sam, with a dog man's sixth sense, went straight to the section reserved for collies, and Prue searched the boxes eagerly for a glimpse of Sonny, but the section labeled "Lonsdale Kennels" was empty. "He must be in the ring already," said Sam, pushing his way through the crowd.

A group of collies were indeed being judged, and Prue gave a little gasp when she saw her dog, waiting patiently with his handler at the edge of the ring. She clutched her father's sleeve. "There he is! There's Sonny!"

Sam was buying a program. He flipped through the pages hastily. "Look, lass, who's running against him. His own brother!"

Prue's eyes left Sonny to alight on the handsome collie being walked before the judge. "Not Cocoa!" she cried.

"Cocoa Colonel of Sweetbriar," Sam read, "is the way he's listed, but it's Cocoa all right. Look at the markings on his muzzle."

Prue would never have recognized the full-grown dog, so distinguished and so mannered, as the bounding six-months-old pup who had been into everything at the farm. But she saw now that he was a fair match for his brother—more than a fair match, perhaps.

When the handler led Sonny out, he carried himself with the familiar sure dignity. Prue watched eagerly. Though his coat shone in the blazing electric lights and his head was held high on his arching neck, didn't his eyes lack a little of their old sparkle? Didn't his ears prick up less quickly at his handler's signal than they had when she spoke up at the farm?

Impulsively, Prue started to edge forward toward the barrier that encircled the ring, but Sam grasped her arm and held ber back. "Don't let the dog see you!" he cautioned. "Ye'd throw him off his form."

"Of course!" Prue shrank against her father's arm and watched the handler parade Sonny before the judge. He moved beautifully, with that silky precision that she knew so well, but she missed something —the joyousness, the animation of the Sonny that had met her after school and frolicked around her in an ecstasy of delight.

"They're judging for best of breed," Sam was explaining. "Cocoa looks mighty good. It'll be a close race."

It was. Again and again the judge reviewed the points of the two collies, after dismissing their competitors from the ring. Cocoa showed more spirit than Sonny. Even Prue had to admit it. But Sonny's superior coat and carriage finally won out. When the judge handed the blue ribbon to the Lonsdale handler, everyone clapped, and Prue jumped up and down in excitement and pleasure.

He reached Prue in three bounds.

Mr. Lonsdale himself came over to Sam after the judging. He looked more concerned than pleased. "This qualifies him for entry into the working-dog group," he told Ferguson. "By rights he should be in line for a blue there, too, but he isn't showing to advantage. He seems to lack spirit." Then he turned thoughtfully to Prue. "Want to go back and see him?"

Prue's eyes answered his question before she could breathe a "Yes!" She could have run to the boxes.

When they finally reached the Lonsdale sign, the handler was just chaining the collie fast. "Sonny!" Prudence cried the dog's name with a little catch in her voice.

Suddenly the collie, standing languid and panting in the open-sided box, stiffened. His sharp ears pricked to attention. Then he saw her!

With a leap he broke from his handler. Hauling his dragging chain, he reached Prue in three bounds, and as he came, he barked that sharp cry of happiness that dogs sometimes achieve. His mouth stretched wide. His plumed tail told her how glad he was, how relieved, how right his world had suddenly become.

Sam, Mr. Lonsdale, and the handler all stood motionless and watched. This was something more than a dog's greeting of a well-loved playmate. This was a return of a collie to his one true master. And the three men, who all knew dogs and loved them, understood.

The girl and the dog seemed alone in the vast show

room. They were conscious only of their reunion. They spoke to each other in the language that had developed between them, and their happiness shone in their eyes.

Sam Ferguson looked from his daughter to Mr. Lonsdale. "I'd no idea," he said.

The kennel owner spoke slowly. "I left him with you too long," he said, but there was no bitterness in his voice. "This is why he lacked spirit in the ring. I'm afraid I'll never make a champion of Sonny." A note of sadness crept into his voice. He was looking at the finest collie he had ever bred, and calling it a day.

Prue caught the last remark. She turned to face Mr. Lonsdale. Her hands still stroked the collie's head, but she leaped to his defense.

"Mr. Lonsdale! Sonny is a champion. He's everything a collie should be! Let me handle him this afternoon. I'm sure we can win!"

Sonny's owner looked at Sam questioningly. Sam replied with a shrug. "The girl could do it," he said. "She's learned all I know, but she's never been in a show ring in her life."

"We have three hours," muttered Mr. Lonsdale, taking out his watch. "I'd be willing to chance it."

When Sonny entered the ring with Prue that afternoon, he looked like a different dog. His tail was carried with a spirit, and his eyes held a fire that had been lacking in the morning. He went through his paces like a master showman, an old hand at the game, and it sur-

prised few of the onlookers that he carried off the blue
ribbon from under the nose of the spaniel who had
been considered the "comer."

"That settles it," sighed Mr. Lonsdale as he turned
to Sam. "You may as well take Sonny home with you.
On the condition, of course, that you allow Prudence
to continue to show him when I should want him entered."

Sam was looking at Prue and the dog coming toward
them around the outside of the ring. "There's only one
answer to that," he said. "Take a look at the girl and
the tyke now! Ye can see they belong together."

HUBERT EVANS

Ghost-Town Dog

Ken Hayward, relief operator at Government Telegraph Cabin Number 13, was desperate for company. Otherwise he would never have provided food and shelter for the battered old Airedale.

Ken had never dreaded winter solitude before. The hushed stillness of the snow-laden forest, the aloof mountains of the northland, and the winding rivers sealed in ice were all part of his life. But the brooding silence of this ghost-town at the Forks was different. The deserted cabins and empty, straggling street of the abandoned gold-rush camp were getting on his nerves. And then seemingly from nowhere, the starving terrier had appeared at the cabin door.

Now as Ken listened idly to a batch of messages going through from the north to the railhead, forty miles away, he glanced at the grizzled old vagabond beside the heater and grinned.

"I've changed my mind, fella," he said, as the Airedale turned a tousled head toward him. "I said that

soon as you were fit to travel, you'd get the bum's rush
out of here. But we seem to hit it off, and maybe I'll
let you stick around."

Beside the stove the ownerless terrier rose and shook
himself. It was good to be out of the driving snow,

The old dog started to follow.

good to be warm and fed after those desperate weeks
no dog of softer breed could have lived through. Slowly
he stalked across the room and laid his whiskered muzzle on the young operator's knee.

"Sure, I mean it," Ken assured him. "This ghost-
town was like to get me down, but with you to talk
to—"

He broke off suddenly as, turning the worn collar about the dog's neck, he found a battered brass name plate with the one word *Derry* showing faintly through the tarnish.

"So you've got a name? Somebody, somewhere, thought a lot of you. I wonder—"

There the Morse of Ken's station call interrupted him. It was the operator at Cabin Number 14 calling.

"Line to railhead gone dead," he tapped. "See if you can raise them."

But out of the south beyond the canyon no answer came along that vital strand of wire connecting the north country with the outside.

"Maybe another windfall in that patch of burned timber a mile south of here." Ken tapped back to the worried operator at Number 14. "I'll go see. Hold everything. I'll be back inside an hour."

He dressed hurriedly for the short mush to the swath of brulee. As he stepped to the door, the old dog whom someone years ago had known and loved as "Derry" got up to follow.

"You stay put, fella," Ken advised him. "Don't worry. You aren't losing your meal ticket. I'm coming back. Here." He got some scraps from the cupboard and tossed them to the terrier.

Five minutes later, with a low-drawn, contented exhalation, the Airedale stretched out beside the heater again. Had Ken heard, he would have thought it nothing more than the appeased sigh of a dog who had wangled a meal. But Ken would have been wrong, for Derry's hunger was not the kind mere food could appease.

Of recent years the world had not been kind to Derry. And in the drifting life of northern camps, his characteristic reserve, his inability to fawn and win temporary friends, had made existence vastly harder for him than for the usual shallow-natured camp dog. Where he came from no one knew, and when he was forced to wander on again probably no one would care.

No outstanding attraction of his, nothing in his appearance or rough, uncompromising manner, could ever serve to win him an honored place in a human home. Outwardly he was just a tramp, and even Ken Hayward had failed to perceive the rugged qualities that made the terrier a potential comrade.

In days past, Derry had known well the thrill of human friendship. But construction jobs end and boom camps all too soon become ghost-towns, and time after time the dog had found himself homeless and masterless again.

And now Derry, the independent, was growing old. yet he could not beg for shelter nor respond to the advances of men he did not like—his cold reserve soon repelled them. In Ken Hayward, however, he had sensed a master he could serve, just as he had once served another lean young fellow whom fate had taken where he could not follow. And it was this deeper hunger that had brought him to the Forks three days before.

Stretched out there, after Ken's hurried departure, for ten minutes the old Airedale did not move a muscle. But when the sounder broke into urgent signals again, the dog became uneasy. Always before, Ken had been there to go to the clattering thing. Now he had left it unguarded. Derry got up and stood beside the table, legs braced, the muscles of his broad chest taut.

The sounder clattered on, and Derry's uneasiness increased. Something was wrong with this thing that belonged to his self-selected master—and the master wasn't there. Derry rushed to the door, clawed it vainly, then broke into a deep-throated bark. Poised and alert, he lowered his scarred head to the crack and listened for the crunch of snowshoes that would tell him Ken was coming back.

Not a sound outside, and there was no seeing through that heavy door. The big dog turned, sprang to the table, and looked through the window into the swirling curtain of snow. He whined pleadingly, but there was no Ken.

Bent on finding him, Derry sprang from the table, and a hind foot, skidding, upset the instrument and scattered papers. He paused an instant, looking back over his shoulder. Then, with his need of Ken increased, he charged the door, prodding it with stiff forelegs and hurling himself against it until suddenly the loosened latch dropped, and the door swung open.

Circling, he found Ken's snowshoe trail and, charging breast deep through the soft snow, started in pursuit.

Ken was nearing the camp clearing after his hurried trip to the patch of burned timber when he saw the terrier struggling toward him. He frowned. Now how did that dog get out? Had he broken a window? The mutt was going to be just one more thing to bother about.

Ken was worried enough already, for he had found the line clear through the brulee, and that meant only one thing—there had been a snowslide in the canyon eight miles to the south, and perhaps for days the north would be cut off from the outside.

He looked sternly at the dog, and demanded, "What you doing here?"

Derry sensed the reproof but, tail still high and ears resolutely back, he turned and led the way to the cabin. Here was the master, and now all would be well.

But it wasn't. When Ken saw the open door, he growled, "If you can open doors, why can't you shut them? Want to freeze us out?"

Ignoring that, Derry trotted hurriedly in. Ken followed, and when the worried young operator saw the sounder tumbled to the floor and the scattered papers, now sodden with the snow which had swirled into the cabin and melted on the table and floor, his irritation blazed into anger.

"You worthless mutt," he fumed. "Went wild to get out, did you, and tore up the place!"

Derry's tail went down. Yet he did not cower and back away, nor was there any hint of guilt in his clear eyes. Instead, unyielding determination showed in the set of jaws and head.

"I should have known better than to take you in," Ken snapped. "You're a tramp and a bum. Well, I'm through being soft. You've had your chance. Get out." He opened the door again.

For an instant the old dog did not understand. Ken pointed to the open door and repeated the command. "Get out! Scram."

Forlornly, Derry padded out.

Ken was still fuming over what seemed to him a rank betrayal of trust when he got the sounder connected again and rapped out Number 14's station call.

Instantly the other operator broke in with the signal that a message was coming. Ken snatched up a message pad, and as he began to write, his consternation mounted. But not until he had checked the message and held it to the late afternoon light of the window to read it through again, did he fully realize its fateful meaning.

The telegram was from the distant Beaver Lake Mission and read:

ELEVEN INDIANS ALREADY DEAD OF FLU STOP EPI-
DEMIC SPREADING TO WHITES STOP RUSH HELP BY
PLANE STOP GOOD LANDING ON ICE ONE MILE EAST OF
MISSION.

A trilling whine, pleading and desolate, came from
the dusk of the ghost-town street outside the cabin.
But Ken paid no attention. Methodically he began making up his pack for loading on the light, broad-run-
nered hand sled—two days' grub, sleeping bag, tools,
batteries, and fifty pounds of extra wire.

Then he called the operator at Number 14 and
tapped out: "Slide in pass must have carried out line.
Am taking extra wire and batteries. If it is a long job
will mush through to signal cabin below canyon and
tap line there. Tell mission to watch for plane tomorrow
if storm clears."

Outside while the boy lashed his load to the sled,
Derry stood at the corner of the cabin watching intently. Many a time he had traveled in harness. He
edged forward, hoping to have Ken put him between
the traces.

But the boy eyed him coldly. "You stay here. Understand?" he warned.

Without sullenness, but with no trace of apology
for what he had done, the old Airedale looked up at
him.

"I won't see you starve, but don't ever think I'm
packing grub for the likes of you. Here," Ken strode

into the cabin, brought out a couple of bannocks, and tossed them toward the terrier.

A moment later, twisting his feet into the lashings of his long Stikine snowshoes, the young operator passed the sled rope over his shoulders and started down the telegraph trail. Five minutes later he looked back. There was the dog, floundering close behind the sled.

"Can't you get it through your thick head I'm finished with you?" Ken yelled. "You're no good to me— or anybody else." He pointed in the direction of the cabin. "Mush—*klataws!*"

A dog of softer spirit would have whined and come crawling alongside the sled, appealing to be allowed to come. But Derry could never cringe. He knew that Ken didn't want to have anything more to do with him. He knew that he had made an enemy and not a friend; yet he stood there four-square on the trail with something grimly splendid in the set of his old shoulders.

With eyes that were almost fierce in their intensity, Derry watched the sled swing into the gloom of the snow-burdened spruce trees. Then, deliberately defying the boy's last command, he stalked along the trail. Ken Hayward could do what he liked, say what he liked, but Derry would not submit to being cast aside.

More than most dogs, the Airedale has a mind of his own. Perversely loyal, this breed defies adversity. Easy-going subservience is foreign to them, and by their blend of loyalty and headstrong independence, the members of this rough-and-ready clan are capable of bringing either heartbreak or adoration to a human comrade.

Hour after hour Ken kept breaking trail toward the canyon, wholly unaware that, half a mile behind, the old dog, still scorning his command, was following him. Snow and wind had ceased and already a few stars showed like pinpricks through the black canopy of night.

Along the high cut-bank, then down a wooded draw to the flat beside the ice-locked river, the lone musher trudged. The breaking was heavy but, with an ominous suggestion of mildness in the still air, he dared not halt for a rest and mug-up beside a hastily kindled fire. After any heavy snowfall the canyon, with its thousand-foot walls flanking the river, was anything but a healthy spot. But to be caught there when a warm chinook wind was cutting into the countless tons of snow poised on those rock faces might mean the end.

More and more the surface snow was clinging to Ken's snowshoes, clogging the fine babiche at toe and heel, balling up on the main filling of grizzly hide.

He reached a group of tumble-down shacks beside the telegraph trail and recognized them as the fishing camp used by Indians during the fall salmon run. The canyon mouth must be just ahead. Out of the darkness of the nearest shack, three Indian dogs sidled furtively, snarling.

Ken hurried on. It was going to be a close thing, he knew. There was a soft threat in the air, and from the high peaks there descended the faint drone of rising wind, as the chinook raced inward from the North Pacific.

His snowshoes swung, crunched, and lifted as he drove himself on. He had a job to do. *Eleven Indians already dead . . . epidemic spreading to whites . . .* At any time now the heavy slides might start. Those towering walls were loaded with death. But this was his job, and he must go on.

Still snarling, the mongrels back at the shack were slinking into shelter when from down the trail they heard a sound that made their hackles rise in anger— the short-clipped, anxious bark of a lone white man's dog.

Shouldering through the trampled snow, Derry neared the abandoned fishing camp. He traveled hurriedly, sensing menace in that softness of the air and bent on keeping close to that lean young fellow who scorned the loyalty he was rebelliously determined to bestow.

Suddenly, with an outburst of snarls, the three dogs, who had crouched like brigands beside the dark trail, jumped him. It must have seemed to them that it would be easy enough to kill this lone stranger, then tear and feast upon his body.

Caught off guard, the old dog went down in a

The Airedale seemed to be all over the mongrels.

smother of snow; and as he fell, the thunder of the
first avalanche inside the canyon came to him.

The three mongrels were all over him, slashing and
ripping with their sharp fangs. Yet already they were
learning that their victory was to be no easy one. For
to all the dashing tactics of his breed, the Airedale had
added the fighting tricks of those other northland dogs
which, down the years, had been both foes and com-
rades to him. MacKenzie River Huskies, the Male-
mutes of the Yukon, the Huskies along the Alaskan
coast, all had taught him much. And from his forebears
he had inherited a spirit that never knows the meaning
of surrender.

The battered head flashed sideways, and the foremost
dog was seized below the shoulder and sent spinning.
The paw of the second was curshed to a pulp—and
then the black-and-tan fury was upon his enemies. Age
had blunted his fangs, but the strength and lightning
speed of jaws and neck remained.

Slashing, swerving, pouncing in and away, the Airedale seemed to be all about the mongrels. Cunningly
the leader retreated, then sprang at him from behind.
But a second later, screaming, the mongrel attacker
dragged himself on three legs to the door of the nearest
shack. His two companions followed. Derry shook himself and stood for a moment as if listening to the shud-
dering echoes of the avalanche from the canyon close
ahead. Then he pushed on.

When he reached the tons of hard-packed snow that had thundered down the trail, the old dog halted. A slash in his forehead was bleeding badly. He shook the blood from his eyes and mounted the snow wall. Over and around the lumps of rock-stained snow he wove his way. Sniffing, listening anxiously, he crossed the slide, and when he saw snowshoe and sled tracks proceeding from its farther edge, he yipped excitedly.

A gust, startlingly warm, smote him as he started on —the chinook had swooped, and the canyon was filled with the turmoil of its passing. Snow burdens from the tossing trees filled the air with a choking whiteness, but with head low the panting Airedale plunged on.

Above the turmoil, from the far side of the canyon, there came a gathering roar, and a minute later gusts of swirling wind caused by this second slide all but swept him from his feet.

Then, midway through the canyon, he found Ken Hayward. Silently he pushed forward and thrust his head against the boy, and silently Ken accepted his presence.

The two thrust on. Under the warm blasts of the treacherous chinook, the snow-filled trail was all but impassable. No single human being could battle forward long. At each plunging step Ken's shoe was loaded with heavy snow that had to be shaken free before the other foot could be driven forward. The wet snow balled up on the toe bar of his shoes until he had to drop to his knees and claw the lumps from under his moccasins.

Shouldering past the struggling boy, the old dog took his turn at breaking, just as he had done many times on trails he had traveled with that other, long-lost young master who had given him his name. Charging, struggling, fighting the clogging whiteness as if it were a living enemy, the four-footed veteran of the trails became the spearhead of the desperate fight for safety.

And then, through the storm's mad symphony, Ken caught a rumbling undertone that told him the fight was lost. Out of the darkness high above came an ominous, deep-throated sound with a thunderous crescendo the next slide was swooping on them.

"Mush, Derry!" Ken panted, and tried to spurt ahead, his eyes on the blackness through which the churning wall of death was hurtling to blot out the trail. "Mush, boy!"

But there was no need to warn the terrier. Torn and bleeding though he was, he drove his weary body forward, ploughing a narrow trench through the snow for Ken to follow.

The air was throbbing with the discord of rushing sounds. The ground beneath them seemed to tremble, and then from above and behind them a churning wave of rock and snow roared into sight. Above the mighty inferno of sound, Derry's voice rang out with all the fiery challenge of a bugle call. The seething edge of the

slide swept past Ken, tripping him, rearing to engulf
him, then spewing him aside in a huddled heap.

Snow devils spun and danced in the shaken air as
Derry bounded back to muzzle the limp form appeal-
ingly. He licked Ken's face, prodding him with first one
forepaw and then the other, demanding that he rise
and renew the struggle and get out of the canyon before it was too late. But when the dazed boy swayed to
his feet, he clutched his knee and crumpled helplessly
on the snow.

"You go, old fellow," he gasped.

But already Derry, trained and canny old sled dog,
was tugging at the rope of the overturned sled, breaking it out of the snow that all but buried it, tugging
until it lay within reach of Ken's hand. It was then
that Ken, in one soul-searing flash of revelation, saw the
true nature of this grand old outcast who had all along
been offering him allegiance.

"Derry!" was all he could say, but in that one word
there was something that gave new power to the dog
who heard it.

With fumbling hands Ken cut a thong from the sled
lashing and knotted it into a rough harness across the
black and tan shoulders. Lurching to the sled, he felt
the dog leap into the traces. The sled moved. With
both arms and his good leg Ken gave all the help he
could, pushing the sled, clearing the banked-up snow
from before the broad runners.

Battling forward, the boy forgot about the threat of

other slides, forgot the many places where only that sixth sense of the trained sled dog prevented them from floundering off the winding trail. A strange exultation possessed him. It was as if the mighty courage of this new partner fortified him—as if together they could not be beaten.

They were on the downgrade now. Evergreens began to show beside the trail again. And then, unbelievably, the squat signal cabin loomed before them.

Ten minutes later Ken, in spite of his crippled condition, had the batteries connected and with eager fingers had sent the SOS from Beaver Lake Mission speeding on its way. Then the sounder on the table began to talk again, and the superintendent at the railhead was calling.

"Great work, Hayward!" the official tapped. "We're starting out now with a trouble-shooting crew. Wait there. I want to hear more about this night's work."

When Ken had the fire going, he slumped to the floor and drew the old Airedale to him. "Believe me, he'll hear all right—he'll hear about you. Old-timer, I never knew—I never—"

Fumbling for words, he tried to tell the dog what was in his heart. "From now on we stick together. From now on we're partners, see?"

Derry sat there, stiff and awkward, his fearless old eyes half closed. But clumsily he pressed his scarred head into the hands that held it—he had found the home he longed for in Ken's heart.

DORIS GATES

The Seventh Pup

In some ways Billy Bent was a very lucky boy, and he knew it. But in other ways he wasn't so lucky. That's the way it is with nearly everybody, only it was more so with Billy.

First of all, Billy loved dogs. What boy doesn't? But Billy loved dogs in a special way. All he really cared about was dogs. He had already decided that when he grew up, he was going to earn his living training them. That wouldn't happen for quite a while, though, because Billy was only nine years old.

But already he had a way with dogs, and an eye for them, too. At least that's what Mr. Riggs said, and he should have known. For Mr. Riggs raised fox terriers and sold them to people who came from miles around to buy them. And Billy lived next door to Mr. Riggs.

The people he lived with were paid by the county to take care of Billy because he was an orphan. That was not lucky. But living next door to Mr. Riggs was. Billy spent most of his time there.

Now one day, Queenie, the best dog at the Riggs kennel, presented her owner with a litter of puppies. Billy happened to be right at Mr. Riggs' side when he discovered Queenie's new family.

"Well, old lady," Mr. Riggs said kindly, and Queenie wagged her stump of a tail and looked at him with adoring eyes. "How many babies have you this time?"

He moved Queenie out of her box and there, in a black and white heap, were seven puppies cuddled closely together. They were beautiful puppies, with strong, healthy bodies and perfect markings. All but one. He was little and all his markings were in the wrong places. The black spot that should have fitted neatly over his back had slid down on one side. One half of his face was black and the other white. And on the white side he had a black ear, and on the black side a white ear. In short, he couldn't have been more sadly mixed up.

"Well," said Mr. Riggs again, "it won't be hard to decide what to do with that seventh pup." He had put the six good puppies in the box and the seventh was sitting all by himself on the floor of Queenie's pen.

"What do you mean?" asked Billy, but in his heart he knew exactly what Mr. Riggs was going to say.

"Queenie won't have milk for more than six puppies, and that seventh one isn't any good anyway. I'll just have to kill him."

Billy looked at the seventh pup, and all at once he

knew that he loved him better than all the rest of Queenie's litter put together. Perhaps it was because the puppy wasn't wanted that made Billy love him so. He could understand how the pup might feel about that, because nobody cared much about him, either.

There is a great difference between having a home of your own and being cared for by people who are paid to do so. Billy always had enough to eat and a good bed to sleep in. Just the same, he knew what it was not to be wanted. So now he wanted the seventh pup. He wanted him more than anything in all the world.

"Yep, I'll have to kill him," Mr. Riggs repeated. "But he's so homely, it won't be much of a loss."

Then Billy spoke. "Don't kill him," he begged. "Give him to me."

Mr. Riggs looked at Billy in surprise. "He's too little to take away from his mother," he said. "You couldn't feed him, son."

"Yes, I could," Billy insisted. "I'll feed him with a baby's bottle. And if he doesn't keep well and strong, then—then, why then I guess you'll have to kill him."

Mr. Riggs could think of nothing to say against Billy's plan, so he gave him the pup. Billy lifted it from the floor while Mr. Riggs held on to Queenie. She didn't care if the puppy was homely, either. Then Mr. Riggs gave Billy one of the nursing bottles which he kept at the kennel for emergencies, and Billy went proudly home, the seventh pup cuddled close in his

"He's too little to take away from his mother."

arms. This was his first dog, and it was the dog among all dogs which he had most wanted for his very own.

The man the county paid for keeping Billy was sitting on the front porch when Billy reached the house. He lowered the paper he was reading to glance at Billy as he came into sight. He started to raise the paper again when his eyes fell upon the seventh pup.

"Where on earth did you find that?" he demanded, in a voice which said as plain as day that he didn't think much of it.

This was the moment Billy had been waiting for. "How do you like my dog?" he asked.

"What do you mean, *your* dog?" The man's voice had a sharp edge to it now.

"Mr. Riggs just gave him to me for keeps," explained Billy.

"Well, you can just take him right back," said the man. "What made you think you could have a dog?" He gave the paper an angry shake. "Besides, he's about the homeliest mutt I ever had to look at."

"I'll keep him out of sight," begged Billy. "I'll feed him and take care of him, and he won't be a bother to anybody."

"Yeah?" said the man. "And who'll pay for his grub? You eat more than your keep right now. There isn't any extra for a dog."

Billy swallowed hard. "He's not a very big dog," he

insisted. "He wouldn't eat much and I'll share what's coming to me with him."

"Talk's cheap," said the man, going back to his paper. "You do as I say and take him back to Mr. Riggs."

So Billy turned right around and walked sadly back to the Riggs place with the pup. But Mr. Riggs wouldn't take him back.

"He's your dog," he told Billy, who was trying to wipe the tear stains off his cheeks. "When I give a dog, I give him for good."

"But he," Billy nodded toward the house next door, "he won't let me keep him. He won't let me have the food for him and I couldn't let the puppy starve." Billy spoke the words in a shaky voice.

"I haven't said he would starve," said Mr. Riggs. "I only said he was still your dog. How would you like to have him board and room over here?"

"I haven't any money to pay for his keep," explained Billy hopelessly.

"I haven't asked for money," said Mr. Riggs and smiled. "How would you like to earn the pup's keep?"

Billy looked with surprised eyes at Mr. Riggs. How?" he asked.

"I've noticed for some time now, that you have a way with dogs," Mr. Riggs explained. "I need a little extra help now and then, especially since this new litter

arrived. Suppose you come over whenever you get the
chance and mix feed and clean kennels, and I'll board
the pup for your pay."

Billy's face broke into a smile so bright that Mr.
Riggs couldn't face it and had to look down at the
ground for a minute. Would he work for the pup's
board! Would he! Why he'd rather be fussing around
dogs than doing anything else in the world anyway.
And just by fussing around dogs, he could keep the
pup.

"Gee, Mr. Riggs," he said with a long happy sigh.
"Gee, thanks."

In a couple of days, Mr. Riggs cut off the puppies'
tails because people expected fox terriers to have short
tails. But Billy wouldn't let him touch the seventh pup.

"He's so homely anyway it won't matter a bit if his
tail is too long," he explained. "I don't want him hurt."

"He'll be a funny-looking fox terrier with a too-long
tail, all right," said Mr. Riggs. Then he added with a
chuckle, "But then, he's funny-looking anyway."

Billy hadn't listened to a word since Mr. Riggs had
said "too-long tail." For the past two days, ever since
he had had him, in fact, Billy had been trying to think
of a name for his pup. Nothing seemed good enough.
Spot, Trixy, Pal. They were all ordinary and none of
them seemed to fit. But now, suddenly, Mr. Riggs had
given him a name.

"That's it," Billy shouted. "That's his name."

"What's his name?" demanded Mr. Riggs.

"Why, 'Too-long.' It's perfect. He's a dog with a too-long tail, and so 'Too-long' is his own special name."

Mr. Riggs grinned and walked away. And from that day, the seventh pup was known as "Too-long."

The weeks passed and then the months. Too-long grew, and his tail grew with him. From the first he thrived on Billy's care. And it seemed as if his too-long tail had been one reason for his good start in life. For while the other puppies were licking their sore stumps and waiting for their shortened tails to heal, Too-long frisked gaily at his master's heels as Billy went faithfully about his kennel chores.

It turned out to be lucky after all that the people he lived with didn't care much about Billy. If they had, they might not have wanted him to spend so much time away from home.

As it was, Billy spent more time at the Riggs place than he did at his own. As soon as school was over, he dashed next door, where Too-long fell upon him with sharp barks of welcome. And whenever Billy had a chance he worked with the pup, teaching him the things a well-trained dog should know.

By the time Too-long was six months old, he had learned to follow at Billy's heels, to lie down when told to do so, and to bring a ball right to his master's feet. Even Mr. Riggs had to admit that Too-long, for all his bad looks, was as sharp as a needle.

By the time he was a year old and Billy ten, Too-long stayed wherever you told him to, jumped over a broomstick to bring the ball, spoke, shook hands, and rolled over. Billy thought he was the most wonderful dog in the world.

"You've done a good job with him," Mr. Riggs told Billy. "It's too bad you've taken all that trouble with a dog that can't ever go into the show ring. He could be a champion with what he knows if he just had the looks."

Then, one day just a week before the dog show, bad luck decided to pay a visit to Mr. Riggs. The only dog that he had planned to enter in the show that year took a bad cold. How it happened nobody knew. Mr. Riggs' face looked as long as Too-long's tail.

That's the way it is with the people who own kennels. If they don't have a dog to put in the show, they feel as if the whole year had been lived in vain. Never before, since he had been raising fox terriers, had Mr. Riggs failed to bring home a blue ribbon, which means first prize. And this year, he would have no ribbon at all. Not even a second or a third, which, though they are only yellow and white, are better than no ribbon at all.

Billy, noticing how sad Mr. Riggs looked, began to

put his brain to work. He knew a thing or two about dog shows. That very day, with Too-long at his heels, he went down town to the dog-show office. He didn't say a word about it to Mr. Riggs. But the evening before the show day, he bathed and brushed Too-long within an inch of his life. Then he went over with him again all the things he had taught him. Then he went home, still without saying a word of his plan to anyone.

The next morning, Billy borrowed a collar and rope from the kennel office, and he and Too-long started for the dog show.

Two hours later, Mr. Riggs, wandering about among the barking dogs and crowding people, came at last to the ring where the Obedience Trials were being held. A large crowd was gathered there, for this event was for boys and girls who handled their own dogs, and he had a little trouble at first in seeing what was going on.

When at last he could get a view of things, his jaw dropped in astonishment. For there, going through his trials as easily and perfectly as he did in his own back yard, was Too-long. And with him was Billy.

In the ring were other dogs, held a little to one side by their masters while Too-long was having his turn. All kinds of dogs, big and little, fine and homely. But the homeliest of them all was Too-long. Mr. Riggs remembered then that there was one part of every dog show where looks didn't count. That was the Obedience Trials. Just so a dog carried out his master's orders perfectly, nobody cared what he looked like. And if he were perfect enough, he could even win the blue.

Mr. Riggs felt his eyes grow misty as he watched the little dog, his spots all wrong and his tail held out straight and long behind him. There was such an eagerness in the way he tried to do just what Billy wanted that it seemed as if he knew he had a chance of bringing home a prize ribbon today.

Billy was as eager as the dog. He never once looked at the crowd. He never even heard the applause when Too-long jumped the hurdle and brought Billy the make-believe bone. He was too busy trying to send a thought message to Too-long that the hurdle was only a broomstick.

Too-long obeyed every command. Each time this happened, his too-long tail beat his sides in joyful thanks for the attention. The homely little dog had captured the hearts of the audience, as had the boy with the patched jeans.

At last it was over and, after a check-up, a man approached Billy and handed him a blue ribbon. Too-long had won the blue!

Mr. Riggs caught up with Billy outside. "I saw you in there," he said. "I was proud of you."

Billy held out the blue ribbon. "You can put it in the glass box with the others," he said. "The kennel will have a ribbon to show for this year, too. Too-long's blue," he added.

Mr. Riggs took the ribbon. "Thank you, Billy," he said. "I appreciate what you've just done. Another thing. Too-long is big enough to earn his own keep. He's worth his weight in rats and is every inch a terrier. How would you like to work for wages instead of his board?"

"For you?" asked Billy, a light coming into his face.

"For me," said Mr. Riggs.

"You bet," said Billy. "I'd like that fine."

"Then you're hired as my right-hand man," said Mr. Riggs, and laid his hand on Billy's shoulder. Under it, he could feel Billy pull his shoulders up very straight.

Ahead of them, Too-long frisked and galloped, his too-long tail wagging happily. It is doubtful if he knew any more than did Billy that seven is really a very lucky number!

ALBERT PAYSON TERHUNE

Hero

They named him "Hero." This was when he was only two months old and his loud barks defied the world. He was such a fearless little fluff of gold-brown fur that the name seemed to fit every active inch of him. A year later, however, the name "Hero" fitted him as a double-width woolen blanket might fit a ladybug.

The Marriotts had been very proud of the rabbit-sized collie baby. But the Marriotts were very ashamed of the rabbit-hearted collie giant that Hero had grown into.

True, he was beautiful. But his deep-set dark eyes had not the "look of eagles" a collie's eyes should have. In them was gentleness, but not a hint of spirit.

"I don't mind his being gentle," grumbled Rance Marriott. "Gentleness is the grandest thing in the world. But if it hasn't spirit and strength behind it, it isn't gentleness at all."

"But Hero's so obedient and friendly," protested

Hilda Marriott. "He's never the least bother, and—"

"And never the least joy, either," added her husband.

"I hate a quarrelsome dog!" put in Hilda.

"So do I," agreed Rance. "But one wants his dog to be something more than a sheep. Whenever I'm walking with him and we pass the Brendas', that husky police dog of Sam Brendas' comes charging out. He tackled Hero in earnest, the first time. Nowadays he does it for a joke. He sails into Hero and knocks him over and rolls him in the gutter and nips him, until I interfere. Does Hero take his own part? He does not! He just sprawls there meekly and lets himself be roughhoused. Then when the police dog has been driven off, Hero gets up and trots along with me, not at all ashamed that he's been licked. It's the same when a cur half his size tackles him. Hero just curls up and lets himself be thrashed."

Out on the veranda bounded the big bronze collie, his expression almost excited—for Hero. Up to Rance and then to Hilda he capered, barking and galloping back to the front door, and returning to repeat the performance.

"What's happened?" wondered Rance. "He looks almost alive. Is it a new game he's invented or—"

"He wants us to go somewhere with him," said Hilda. "See how he runs from one to the other of us and back to the hallway. Come along."

As they started toward the hall, Hero gamboled delightedly ahead to the top of the cellar stairs. There he waited only long enough to make certain his owners were close behind him. Then down the stairs he pattered.

"Come along!" begged Hilda, as Rance hesitated. "Let's see what he's trying to show us."

"A man-eating mouse, probably," suggested Rance. "But, no, that can't be. For he'd never have the sublime courage to approach a mouse, of his own accord."

The dog came running up the steps, whined eagerly, and trotted down again. This time the Marriotts followed. At the foot of the stairs Rance turned on the electric switch, flooding the shadowy place with light.

Hero was standing proudly above a pile of soft rags in a far corner. On the rag couch lay the Marriotts' gray Persian cat, Fathma, blinking lazily up at them. Cuddled against her furry underbody squirmed four tiny and vari-colored newly born kittens.

Fathma was strangely easygoing, for a Persian. She and Hero had been brought up together. They had always been on comfortable terms, their mutual mildness serving to avert quarrels.

Now, Hero was excited at discovering Fathma's children. As soon as Rance and Hilda bent over the rag bed to look at the kittens, the collie rushed up the back cellar stairs to the kitchen. Presently he reappeared, coaxing the cook down to view the newcomers.

Fathma lay there and purred, blinking sleepily. Now and then she licked one or another of her babies with a rough pink tongue.

That night Hero did not sleep on his rug outside Hilda Marriott's door, where he had slept ever since he was a puppy. Instead, he stretched his mighty bulk on

She and Hero had always been on comfortable terms.

the concrete floor of the cellar, as close as might be to Fathma and her babies.

"He's found his true role in life, at last," sneered Rance. "As a collie he is a grand kitten-nurse."

Hilda did not join in her husband's mirth. To her there was something pathetic in the huge dog's absorbed interest in the family of newly born baby cats and in his air of protection over them. True, it was undoglike, and especially was it uncollie-like. But it did not seem funny to her.

That was the beginning. Every day, and practically all day, and every night and all night, Hero lay or sat or stood guard over the litter of Persians. Gravely he would survey the fast-growing kittens, sometimes touching them gingerly with his forepaw or sniffing at them.

He was in misery when a load of coal rattled noisily down the chute, and he interposed his own bulk between it and the corner where the kittens were.

One day he and Fathma had their first quarrel. Playfully Hero rolled one of the kittens over with his nose. He was unintentionally rough. The kitten squalled in protest. Fathma flew to the rescue, side-swiping Hero across the nostrils with sharp claws.

The dog fled, howling, until he reached the top of the cellar stairs. There he stood, in comic dismay, slapping alternately at his scratched and bleeding nose, and peering tearfully down at the scene of his ill-treatment.

Step by step, at long intervals, he descended to the cellar and crept trembling along the floor until once more he was near the nest. Fear of further punishment made him shake as with a chill. But the craving to return to his duty as guard overcame his dread.

To his relief, Fathma made no attempt to renew the strife. Nor did Hero make further playful advances toward the kittens. He contented himself sniffing at them now and then, and lying quietly with head between his forepaws, watching.

Rance often took guests down to the cellar to see the kittens' canine nurse. With all a collie's odd sensitiveness, Hero seemed to realize he had become an object of ridicule. He winced and cringed when laughter greeted the spectacle of a great bronze dog brooding over a nestful of kittens. But he did not desert his post.

The babies grew larger and stronger. No longer did they content themselves with huddling in the nest. Now, with sprawling feet and unwieldy little fat bodies, they set forth on exploring expeditions along the cellar floor. A pretty sight it was to watch the fluffy mites crawling about the delighted big dog, while their sleepy mother looked placidly on.

One of them in particular, a snow-white kitten with china-blue eyes, picked Hero as her own chum. She would climb over his paws or cuddle against his chest or play with his plumed tail.

Pleased and proud was Hero of this distinction. He would lick the kitten all over. He would lie uncomplaining as her sharp claws dug playfully into his sensitive tail. The other kittens did not show any great interest in him. Thus, from the start, he and the white kitten were exclusive play-fellows and pals.

Fathma was a good mother, as Persian mothers go. But she was a family pet, and her place had been up-

stairs with the humans of the household. When her
kittens were able to get along without her for an hour
or two at a time, she would leave them with Hero and
would run daintily upstairs to seek out Hilda or Rance
or the servants.

When the kittens were graduated from the cellar to
the woodshed and were allowed to play daily on the
lawn in the spring sunshine, Hero and the white kitten
had gorgeous romps together. Their friendship was
pretty to watch. Even Rance Marriott grinned with
grudging approval of their play.

"Of course, it was just like the poor fool to pick out
the kitten we're selling first," Rance said. "I suppose
Hero will mope around and look more like a sick calf
than ever, when she's gone. I'm sorry for him. For he's
found the one creature on earth that doesn't either
bully him or despise him."

"I don't bully him," denied Hilda, "and I don't de-
spise him. And I wish you hadn't promised Sam
Brendas that particular kitten. You know how fond
Hero is of her, and—"

"And I had promised Sam his choice of the four,"
interrupted Rance. "I'm sorry to have to disappoint the
noble Hero. Sam is sending for the kitten tomorrow
afternoon. Will you have her brushed up a bit before-
hand, please? And stick Hero in a closet or somewhere."

Mid-afternoon, next day, Hilda Marriott came out

on the lawn, where Hero snoozed with the white kitten huddled up asleep between his paws. Picking up the furry wisp in her arms, Hilda whistled to the dog. Happily he trotted indoors after her and his kitten pal. There, to his pained surprise, he was lured into an upper room and the door was shut behind him.

He scratched plaintively at the door, but nobody came to let him out. In a little while he heard voices downstairs—Hilda's voice and another woman's.

Readily the dog recognized this second voice. It belonged to a guest who came often to the Marriotts'. She lived in the house where that snarling police dog lived—the dog that mishandled Hero so unmercifully.

Failing to scratch his way through the door, the collie amused himself by trotting to the window and gazing down into the street. Then Hero's interest sharpened. Mrs. Sam Brendas had left the Marriott house and was walking down the street. In her arms she was carrying something.

As she turned the corner, Hero saw what the "something" was. It was his chum, his pal, his idol—the tiny white Persian kitten!

Something went queer in Hero's gentle brain.

The spirit of his brave collie ancestors suddenly seemed to assert itself. These collies had guarded with their lives their masters' belongings. They had known stanch loyalty to their friends.

Back to the door Hero ran, tearing at its panels with claws and teeth. It stood firm.

To the window he dashed. The room was on the second floor, just above the side veranda. But, for all Hero cared, it might have been on the thirtieth story of a skyscraper. It offered the only means of escape—and he took his chance.

With a great diving leap he flung himself at the glass pane. Through the brittle barrier he crashed with all the driving force of his seventy pounds. He struck against the steep veranda roof, rolling and sliding down it to the edge, then bouncing out into space again. His falling body struck the center of a thick, high lilac clump, just beyond the porch. The branches broke his fall, so that he landed on the grass unhurt.

By the time he hit the lawn he was on his feet and in flying motion. Across the yard he sped and down the street, galloping with his glass-cut body close to earth and with hackles bristling. He knew well where Mrs. Sam Brendas lived, and where she was carrying his kitten friend. Not an inch did he swerve from his route.

Men were beginning to stroll up the street on their way home from business. They gave wide berth to the bleeding, savagely onrushing collie.

A dog or two came running out from dooryards. Hero whizzed past them, unheeding. Some of them started to chase him. But no dog, save a racing greyhound, can hope to catch up with a collie that is running at full speed.

Hero came in sight of his goal in time to see Mrs. Brendas open her own front door and disappear in the hallway. She was carrying the sacred white kitten. The kitten was scared because a giant police dog had sprung up from the mat and had come toward her. "Down!" Mrs. Brendas ordered the dog sharply and took the kitten indoors.

As the door shut behind her, Hero came dashing up the walk. The police dog's temper had been ruffled by the scent of the strange kitten and by his owner's curt rebuff. The collie had invaded the sanctity of the front yard and was rushing toward the sacredly guarded veranda. The insolence of his act called for a drastic and dramatic punishment. As Hero leaped up the veranda steps, the police dog dashed savagely after him.

Perfect love casteth out fear.

In all his despised young life Hero had never found anything worth losing his temper over. He had seen no need to fight. He had had no desire in his gentle heart to harm anyone or anything.

When he had been attacked and bullied by other dogs, their enmity had puzzled and pained him. He had seen no reason for fighting back. It had been easier to submit gently to their onslaughts and then to get himself out of their way as soon as he could.

But today he had something to fight for. His fluffy little white playmate had just been carried into that house, and an ugly giant dog was trying to bar him from following and rescuing her. The dog, and every other obstacle, must be gotten rid of before Hero could continue his search for the kitten.

Instead of the meekly crouching collie, the police dog found his charge met by a devil swathed in shimmering bronze fur. Grappling, roaring, slashing, rending, the two combatants rolled down the steps together. As their falling bodies hit the flagstones of the path below, they flashed apart and to their feet, flinging themselves at each other's throats.

This was the sight which confronted Rance Marriott and Sam Brendas, as together they rounded the corner of the street. This was the sight which made Mrs. Brendas drop the white kitten and run to the front door in consternation.

The police dog was a renowned battler and a veteran of many bloody frays. But a fighting collie is not like any other fighter in all dogdom.

Hero was everywhere in general and nowhere in particular. Now he was stabbing with lightning speed under the rearing enemy's forelegs, and slashing the other's fawn-colored underbody. Now he was slipping eel-like from what threatened to be a death grip and was raking the police dog's tawny shoulder. So do wolves fight.

A fighting Collie is unlike any other fighter in dogdom.

Once and again the larger dog tried to down Hero by sheer weight and ferocity. Once and again the collie eluded the charge, and countered with deep bite or slash. Twice Hero was knocked off his flying feet. But a collie down is almost never a collie beaten.

He fell with his feet bunched under him; and by the time he hit ground he was either springing to one side, slashing as he leaped, or rolling compactly out of range of the frightful jaws.

It was a beautiful exhibition of science against bull strength. Roaring and foaming, the police dog drove once more for the throat. The collie ducked under the great lunging head and dug his teeth with wrenching force into one of the fawn-hued forelegs of his foe. Thus does the wolf seek to cripple an antagonist by breaking his legs.

With a screech, the police dog released his grip on Hero's neck, and tried to seek safety in retreat.

Hero stood for a moment, panting and eying the victim. Then he seemed to remember his mission at that house. Up the steps he rushed, pushing past the panic-stricken Mrs. Brendas and into the hallway.

In another second he emerged. Between his bloody jaws he carried tenderly a fluff of white fur. He had found and rescued his little chum after overcoming the dragon which guarded the door. Now he was bearing her home where she belonged.

Past the men he cantered, deaf to Marriott's call.

Two minutes later he laid the kitten gently at Hilda Marriott's feet. Then, apparently, he remembered that his master had called him and that he had not obeyed. Licking the kitten's tousled fur once in rough good-fellowship, Hero left her there and cantered out of the house.

Meantime both men had found their tongues.

"I get the whole idea!" Rance declared. "Hero loves that kitten as he doesn't love anything else. He came here after it. Your dog stopped him, but he couldn't stop him for long. Then Hero went in and got what he came for. You can guy me, if you like, you people. Hero fought for her and he won her, fair. You can have your cash back or you can have any two of the three other kittens instead. But you can't have the white one. Neither can anyone else. She belongs to Hero. Is that understood?"

Sam Brendas looked up from his task of tending his police dog's hurts.

"All right," he agreed. "We can settle the terms later on. Now give me a hand in carrying Hindenburg indoors, while Mary phones for the vet."

As Marriott came out of the Brendas' house three minutes later on his way home, a figure arose stiffly from the police dog's favorite porch mat and came in gay good-fellowship to greet him.

Rance stared down at his collie. Not at the cuts and other hurts that decorated his splendid body, but at

the deep-set dark eyes upraised to his. Those eyes
flashed with a queer light that changed the whole expression of Hero's classic face.

"The true collie look!" babbled Rance foolishly, as
he caught the hurt head lovingly between his two
hands. " 'The look of eagles!' Hero—"

His voice thickened in his throat. But Hero understood. Wagging his plumed tail, he led the way out of
the gate and toward home. As they turned the corner into their own street, a neighbor's dog swaggered
blusteringly out. This was a mongrel dog that delighted
to chase Hero under the Marriott veranda every time
he could catch him in the roadway.

In something less than half a minute, now, the mongrel aggressor was *ki-yi*-ing, in astonished flight, to the
safety of his own kennel.

"Hero!" rebuked Marriott fondly, as he called his
frisking collie back to him. "You'd be a grand walking
companion if it wasn't that you have one bad fault—
you're too quarrelsome. Try to get over the habit of
going around with a chip on your shoulder, you—you
glorious pal of mine!"

ELIZABETH RHODES JACKSON

Christmas Eve at Reginald's

Perhaps it's because Reginald was a real Christmas puppy, born on Christmas Eve, that he has so much love in his heart for everyone and has so many friends.

When he goes walking with us, perfect strangers that we meet are not strangers to him at all. Boys in the street that we have never seen before say, "Hello, Reggie, old boy," and very proper old ladies in old-fashioned hats pat him very gently and say, "Good morning, doggie. How nice to see you again!"

Once he ran right up to a lovely young lady who was sitting talking at the Esplanade and put his paws on her white dress. She wasn't even annoyed. She shook hands with him, and the young man with her said, "Is that your dog? We've known him a long time and we wondered where he belonged." And the young lady said, "He's one of our best friends."

After that, almost every time we went to the Esplanade, we used to see them. No matter how earnestly they were talking together, they would stop to pat Reginald. But one day the young man was sitting there alone, looking very gloomy. Beany, who sometimes says

But Reginald loves everyone.

the wrong thing, asked him, "Where's the young lady?" and he said shortly, "She hasn't come." After that we never saw the young lady, but we often saw the young man alone and he always rubbed Reginald's ears very kindly.

One day—it was Election Day—Reginald was walking with Jack and me and we passed a voting place.

Reginald recognized the policeman outside and poked his nose into the policeman's hand to be petted, and the policeman said to him:

"You ought to be after running for office yourself today. As popular as you are, you'd carry the ticket."

We were very much surprised because we had thought that that policeman didn't like Reginald. He had been very cross one day because Reginald followed and came running after us into the Public Garden when we were going to the swan boats. The policeman had stopped us and said, "Don't you know you can't bring that dog in here? There's a sign at the gate, 'No dogs allowed except on leash.'"

"Yes, we saw it," said Beany politely, "but Reginald didn't. At least, he couldn't read it."

"Don't tell me that dog can't read," said the policeman. "As smart a beast as he is!" So we really had thought the policeman didn't like Reginald.

But Reginald loves everyone and he goes all over Boston by himself to make new friends. He crosses the street with the traffic lights to get to Boston Common. He likes to watch the children swimming in the Frog Pond and bark at the squirrels that chatter at him from tall elms. We never go to the West End because once when Jack went there to look at a beautiful ship model in the window of an antique shop, a big boy knocked him down and took ten cents away from him. But our ash-barrel man told Beany he often meets Reginald in the West End, and the children playing in the street pat him and love him.

Once, just before Christmas, he was gone all night, and in the morning we went up and down Beacon Hill, asking at every door, "Have you seen a dog named Reginald? White with black spots?"

Most of the people said, "Why, I know Reginald. I do hope you'll find him."

One very stately lady with white hair and a Paisley shawl was just getting into her car when we asked her. "Dear, dear!" she said. "How sorry I am! He is such a good dog."

Then we came to a house where there is a beautiful white door with a fanlight and a shiny brass knocker. It is our favorite house on the Hill. On Christmas Eve it is always brightly lighted, and the curtains are drawn back at the window to show a great painting of the Christ Child.

We lifted the knocker, and after a moment the door was opened by a very straight butler. I asked, "Have you seen a dog named Reginald? White with black spots?"

He cleared his throat and looked embarrassed. "Why, the fact is, Miss," he said, "there was a dog answering to that description on the front steps yesterday, and I was given orders to take it away, and . . ." he stopped and coughed as an old gentleman came into the paneled hall behind him.

"What's this? What's this?" said the old gentleman. "Don't hold the door open, Bates. What's this all about?"

"The young lady is asking about her dog, sir," said the butler very respectfully.

"Dog?" said the old gentleman. "You took it to the Animal Rescue League, I hope, Bates, as I ordered you to?"

"Yes, sir, quite so, sir," said the butler.

"Quite right," said the old gentleman. "I've contributed to the Animal Rescue League for years. About time I made some use of it. Proper place for a lost dog."

"But Reginald isn't a lost dog," said Beany. "He knows his way home."

The old gentleman looked at Beany very hard. "Well, well!" he said. "If he knows his way home, why does he spend his time sitting on my doorstep?"

"Probably he sat down to rest," said Beany. "Probably he likes your house. Probably he admires your fanlight."

Beany choked a little, and Jack and I knew he was thinking of Reginald shut up in a cage and hoping we would come for him. Jack said comfortingly, "Anyway, now we know he's safe and we know where to go for him."

"And we do thank you," I said to the old gentleman. "We know you meant to be helpful."

The old gentleman looked at Beany and from him to Jack and then at me. It reminded me of the surprised way Beany looked, the first time he saw a giraffe at the circus.

"Most extraordinary!" said the old gentleman. "Bates, you may order the car."

"Yes, sir," said Bates.

In just a minute or two the car was in front of the house and we all went out and got it. Jack sat in front with the chauffeur and Beany and I sat in back with the old gentleman. We drove through Park Square to the Animal Rescue League on Carver Street, and sure enough, there was Reginald. When they brought him in to see us, he rippled from his nose to the tip of his tail and jumped all over us and even tried to jump up to kiss the old gentleman. Then we all rode home together. When we got out of the car and said good-by, the old gentleman took his hat off as if I were a grown-up lady.

The next day the lady in the Paisley shawl came to our house to see if we had found Reginald. She was so glad when he got up from the fireplace rug and stretched himself to welcome her. She stayed and talked a while with Mother, and they had tea, and when she went she said, "They say the fashion of making calls is out of date, but Reginald has revived it. I hope you and your children and Reginald will soon return my call."

After she had gone, Beany said, "I wish all Reginald's friends would call on us, don't you, Mother?"

"Mercy!" said Mother. "You don't realize how many friends he has. We'd have a constant procession of callers."

"Well," I said, "why can't we give a party and have them all at once?"

"Oh, let's have a party," said Beany. Beany loves parties and thinks we all ought to have birthdays twice a year.

"Couldn't we, Mother?" I said. "Reginald has gone to dinner with so many people—it really is his turn to invite them."

"I know what," said Jack. "Christmas Eve is Reginald's birthday. Let's have 'open house' for him with candles in the windows and all his friends invited."

Mother looked doubtful. "How could you invite them?" she said. "You don't know who his friends are."

"But he knows," said Beany. "Let's tie the invitation to his collar, and everywhere he makes his calls, they'll read it and come."

We got out our box of Christmas cards and wrote the invitation that very day. We chose a card with three camels across the top, and Jack printed on it: "Reginald invites all his friends to Open House on Christmas Eve from seven to eight-thirty," and the address. Then we tied it to Reginald's collar with a green-and-red Christmas ribbon. Reginald seemed to like it and he went off proudly with his head in the air.

I don't know how many people read the invitation, but after a few days it was very much soiled and a little bit torn, and we wrote a fresh one. This time the card had a Christmas tree on it. When that card got worn out, we gave him one with Santa Claus in a sleigh with reindeer.

Sometimes he would come home with a note tied on, "Thanks. I'll be there," or "We accept with pleasure." And one said, "Sorry, I can't come. I've got the measles."

Reginald and Beany met the gloomy young man one afternoon on Beacon Street. Reginald, of course, stopped to greet him, and the young man saw the card. It was the Christmas tree one.

"What's all this?" he said. "Whose Christmas package are you?"

Then he read the invitation and his gloom vanished.

"I say," he said. "Is this true about Reginald's Christmas Eve?"

"Oh, yes," said Beany. "He's inviting all his friends."

"I say. That gives me an idea," said the young man. "I'd like to borrow Reginald for a while. Don't be worried about him. I'll see that he's safe." Reginald trotted happily along with him and didn't turn up till evening.

The week before Christmas is a very busy one. There are always last things to do to get our presents finished and write the labels and mail Christmas cards and un-

pack the tree ornaments. This time we were especially
busy the day before Christmas, getting ready for Reginald's open house. I helped Mother make sandwiches
and cut them star-shaped, and Jack put the candles into
their holders and set them in rows on the window sills
and sashes, and Beany polished the silver. We were all
working hard when the knocker sounded at our apartment door, and Beany went to open it.

We heard a voice say, "I cain't come to the party
Honey, 'cose my folks is having open house their-
selves. But I sure did appreciate getting invited. Reginald walked into my kitchen with the butcher's boy,
and he turned his haid for me to read the invite as
much as to say, 'You is personally invited.' So I done
made a birthday cake for the party, with the compliments of the season."

It was a beautiful cake, all frosted, with Reginald's
name in red icing on top. We put the cake in the middle of the mahogany table on Mother's best lace table-
cloth. There was a bowl of holly at each end and the
silver candlesticks with tall red candles. Mother was to
serve the coffee and I was to pour the cocoa. Jack would
pass the cups, because Beany sometimes spills, and
Beany could hand the sandwiches, and Daddy said he
would take care of the doughnuts.

When we heard the church bells chiming, "Noel,
Noel," and saw houses up and down the street shining
out in a blaze of light, we knew that Christmas Eve

The policeman was carrying a little boy.

was beginning. Soon the streets would be crowded with people who had come into town to hear the carolers singing on candle-lighted Beacon Hill and visit their friends who were keeping open house. While we were lighting the candles in our windows, a band of carolers went by singing, "Oh, Little Town of Bethlehem," and Beany whispered to me, "Can you believe that it really is Christmas Eve at last?" and I knew just how he felt. Then someone lifted our knocker and we all ran to open the door to Reginald's first guest.

It was the cross policeman. He was carrying a little boy in his arms and behind him was an anxious-looking woman.

"This is my boy, Jimmy," said the policeman. "And nothing would do but he must come to the dog's party. So I said to the Missus I'd bring him myself, and I'll be after coming for him a little later. Where can I put him down, ma'am?"

Then we saw that the boy couldn't walk. He had iron braces on his legs. Mother moved the cushions and made a place for him on the sofa, and Reginald jumped up and lay down beside him.

Jimmy's mother said, "That's what he always does—cuddles down on the bed next to Jimmy. It soothes him something wonderful when he's fretful after one of his bad nights, awake with the pain and too sick to listen to the radio."

The next visitor was the pretty young lady. "I had to

come," she said, "because Reginald came all the way to
my house to invite me. I heard him barking at the door.
He must have shut himself into the vestibule in some
way, and he was so glad when I opened the door to
him." Reginald heard his name and wagged his tail as
he lay on the sofa.

Then the lady came who wears the Paisley shawl,
and she brought Reginald a Christmas box of barley-
sugar dogs. She was just drinking her coffee when the
old gentleman came in who had sent Reginald to the
Animal Rescue League. The Paisley lady said to him,
"So, James Saltonstall, you're another of Reginald's
friends!" And the old gentleman said, "By all means.
Consider it an honor." And then he said to Mother,
"Most extraordinary dog. Comes and sits on my doorstep regularly. Admires my fanlight, your surprising
son said. Unusual architectural appreciation."

All the evening people kept coming until the room
was all one hum of pleasant sound, and Cheerio, my
canary, began to sing so loud we couldn't hear the
carolers outside. The butcher's boy came. He couldn't
stay because he was so busy delivering turkeys, but he
brought a big bone for Reginald tied with a red paper
bow. The boy from the West End who had taken Jack's
ten cents came. He was very much surprised and embarrassed to see Jack. But Reginald greeted him for
an old friend, and the boy accepted a big piece of the
birthday cake and asked for another.

The Admiral came, too. He lives on Brimmer Street, and, of course, everyone in the neighborhood knows who he is. We were very proud that our Reginald had gained the friendship of such a brave and distinguished man.

When Jimmy saw him, he almost stood up. "Gee, Admiral," he said. "Can I shake hands with you?"

Reginald heard "shake hands" and he lifted his paw, too, and the Admiral shook hands with both of them and then pulled a chair up close to the sofa.

"Say, Admiral," said Jimmy, "that was great stuff, that broadcast. I didn't miss one of them. I could hear the ship a-creaking and the waves swashing and the wind, and I felt just like I was at the Antarctic myself. When I grow up—and get well, you know—do you think I could go along? I could be a cabin boy or something, couldn't I?"

I didn't hear what the Admiral answered, because our knocker sounded just then, and I opened the door to the young man who had borrowed Reginald. "Merry Christmas!" he said, and then he saw the young lady near the door.

"You came," he cried.

"Of course, I came," she said. "Reginald asked me specially."

"I know," said the young man. "I shut him into your vestibule. I had to see you. I had to explain. I say, you

must let me explain. Where can we go to talk?" he said
to me rather wildly.

I showed him the bay window with the wide seat.
"Really," said the young lady coldly, "I don't see that
there's anything to explain." But she sat down with
him in the window seat, apart from the others. Reginald followed them and nuzzled into their hands, trying to get them to pet him, but they didn't seem to
know he was there.

When it was nearly half-past eight, Mother went to
the piano and played some carols and we all stood
around her and sang. The boy from the West End had
quite a good voice, and the policeman, who had come
again to carry Jimmy home, came in strong on the bass.
Then people began to leave. Just as the old gentleman
was going, he put a package into my hands. "Merry
Christmas to Reginald!" he said. "Most remarkable
dog!"

It was a fine leather collar, and on the plate was en-
graved Reginald's name and address, and underneath,
"He is not a lost dog. He knows his way home."

The policeman carried Jimmy out very carefully with
his mother trailing behind and calling back, "God
bless you and a merry Christmas," and we heard Jimmy
telling his father, "Gee, Dad, you can bet I won't forget
this Christmas Eve."

"Now everybody's gone," said Jack as we closed the
door, "let's hang up our stockings."

And then we saw that not everyone was gone. The young lady and the young man were still in the window seat.

"Oh, we thought you had gone," said Beany.

"Oh, are we the last?" said the young lady, very much surprised, and they got up quickly.

Beany realized he hadn't sounded very polite.

"Oh, don't hurry," he said. "Do stay. Because as soon as you go, we shall have to go to bed."

But they did go at last. At the door the young man shook hands with Reginald and said, "Thanks a lot, old chap, for the Christmas present you gave me."

And the young lady's face got pink and she took Reginald's head in both her hands and kissed him on the black spot between his ears.

Then Reginald in his shining new collar lay down on the hearth rug with his nose between his paws, and went to sleep. We blew out the candles in the window and on the tree, and we hung our stockings at the fireplace. We could hear the carolers in the distance singing, "God rest you merry, gentlemen," and when it ended we heard the chime of church bells on the frosty air. But nothing disturbed Reginald. Only his tail moved very gently in his sleep, so probably he was having happy dreams about his friends.

Reginald always wears his new collar now, to tell everyone he knows his way home, so we are sure no one will ever take him for a lost dog again.

from STEPHEN MEADER'S

Bat

You could hardly blame June Faulkner for mourning as long as she does for her lost dog. Not only was the big white bull terrier a championship show dog—he was the bravest, the smartest, and most devoted companion a girl ever had. When Bat is stolen by two gangsters, he breaks away and is found by a little lame Italian boy, Tony Donato. He and his sister Marie treat the dog kindly, but Bat, renamed Beppo, never stops yearning for his first love. When Marie comes across an advertisement for Bat, she writes to June. But the same two gangsters also read about the $1000 reward and steal the dog from Tony. Again Bat makes his escape, and after many hardships, returns to Ventnor, the Faulkner summer home, only to find it deserted. Bat spends as much time as possible waiting on the porch for his beloved mistress. But during the time when June and her father return briefly, the famished dog is out on the beach searching for food.

FAR APART

Ramsdell Faulkner stood inside the broad windows of the sun-porch at Devon, and looked out into the storm-drenched twilight. It was the third day of the northeaster—a belated equinoctial gale that had been whipping the coast with more than customary fury—and it was getting on his nerves. He could hear June at the piano in the drawing-room. She was playing without notes, shifting from one melancholy fragment to another, always in low-pitched, mournful minor chords. At last she broke off in the middle of a sobbing melody and he heard her impatient fingers go up the keyboard in an abrupt run. Then silence fell.

He frowned, stroking his chin in thought. It was so unlike June—this moody restlessness that had dropped like a pall over her gay spirits. Except for that single day of half-hysterical joy when the letter, forwarded from Ventnor, had come from the Italian girl, his daughter had been like this for nearly a month now. And after the bitter disappointment of finding that the terrier had disappeared again, he was really frightened about her health.

Something, he thought, would have to be done to take June's mind off that dog.

He heard a scurry of feet behind him and Candy bounced in the air to caress his fingers with a wet tongue. The little black spaniel was doing his best to fill the place Bat had held in their affections. After a moment the girl's slow step sounded in the library.

"Out here all alone in the dark, Daddy?" she yawned. "Ugh, what a night! Did the paper say anything about its clearing?"

He turned and took her listless hand. "Yes, dear," he told her. "The barometer's rising. Ought to be all over before morning." An idea struck him. "How'd you like to drive me down to the shore, if it's fair? They say this storm has played the devil with property down there. We'd better go and see if the cottage is still standing."

"All right," she replied without enthusiasm. "I'm not crazy about going back to the shore, but a drive anywhere would help, after being cooped up in the house so long."

They got off by ten, riding through the new-washed, sun-brightened morning with the top down and Candy on the seat between them. There had been dire reports of the storm's ravages in the early editions of the papers.

"Half a million in property damage, they say," Mr. Faulkner was remarking. "Those things are usually stretched a bit but I'm anxious just the same. Wouldn't want anything to happen to the Ventnor place—we've had too much fun there, eh, June?"

The girl drove automatically, her eyes somber, fixed on the road. For a moment she did not answer. Then,

"Let's not talk about that, Dad," she said. "You know it won't ever be the same again."

Ramsdell Faulkner took the rebuff in silence, but he was too fond of his daughter to see her making herself unhappy without putting up some sort of a fight. He marshaled his thoughts before he spoke again, and when he did there was gentleness in his voice.

"I know how you feel, June," he said, "but I honestly think it's better for you if we do talk about it. There isn't a thing on earth that we can blame ourselves for. Bat lived a happy life. He wouldn't have enjoyed it half so much if we'd kept him tied up or watched him every minute."

He waited to see how she would take it, but her face was still expressionless.

"When we missed him," he went on, "I did everything that could be done. There was no time lost, either. By that same evening the police had traced him as far as that garage in South Philadelphia, but all the evidence they could get seemed to point to his having been killed. If he went down fighting, June, it wasn't a bad end for a bull terrier. Maybe—it's the way he'd have liked it."

He paused, clearing his throat of a certain huskiness. "Well," he continued, "there's never been any real proof of that, of course. I kept the advertisement running in the papers on the chance that he might still be alive. The Donato girl's letter sounded genuine enough and it's possible—just possible—that the dog her brother found was Bat. If that story of his could be believed, about the masked stranger who stole his dog, it would lend some color to the idea. But you know— a child's imagination—"

June shifted impatiently behind the wheel. Her face was stormy. "They were telling the truth," she said. "Both of them. Remember, I talked to them. I'd trust that girl any time, and Tony—why, his heart was broken!"

Her father tried to be tactful. "It's like you, my dear, to believe in people," he smiled. "I'm glad you feel that way. But you'll remember the police didn't find a trace of any dog when they got that tip and broke into the house a few hours afterward. Of course, I've still had hopes that the thief—if there is such a person— would try to collect the reward. But now I'm afraid we'll have to face the facts. Bat's gone. I'd like to— well," he fumbled for words, knowing he was being clumsy, "if it would help, June, I'd like to get you another dog—any kind you want."

The girl's gloved hands gripped the wheel tighter. "Father!" she said sharply. "Don't—please."

After that they rode in a troubled silence, broken only when they spoke of inconsequential things.

The first glimpse of the resort city on its island was reassuring. The sun, high over the sea, glinted in golden flashes on each rain-washed tower. It was all so brave and gay that June gave her father a puzzled look.

"I expected to see crumbling walls and people wading in the streets," she said. "Did they really have a storm down here?"

As soon as they reached Pacific Avenue her question was answered. From the boardwalk, a block away, came a steady sound of hammering, and through gaps at the end of each street they could see the tremendous seas still breaking high on the beach. The town had rolled up its sleeves and gone to work repairing its glittering façade.

Farther down the island evidences of the gale's passage were more frequent and more striking. Beach-front cottages had been undermined and moved off their foundations. A graveled side street was half washed away and there were scattered pieces of driftwood as far inland as Ventnor Avenue.

Dread of what they might find made the Faulkners uneasy as they drove southward.

"There it is," said June with a sigh of relief. "Seems to be standing up all right."

"By George!" her father smiled. "Not even a shutter blown off! We're a lot luckier than some of the others."

They parked the roadster in the driveway and went toward the porch steps. Candy was trotting busily around the house, sniffing here and there at the battered hydrangeas. Suddenly he began to bark and dance up and down in excitement.

"What is it now, half pint?" June asked indulgently.

The spaniel was nosing at the bottom of the porch lattice. As soon as his mistress approached he plunged

Candy watched the road behind them.

through a hole that had been scraped there in the sand and raced around the cavern under the porch, still barking with obvious excitement.

"Look, Dad," June called. "What do you suppose dug this hole?"

Her father stooped down, peering at the sand. "The

rain has washed away all the tracks except Candy's," he
said. "But I'd guess a dog had been under there. Maybe
one of those stray curs we used to see hanging around.
Here, Candy—you rascal! Come back here!"

The little black dog had dashed out and away down
the street toward the beach. They got him back with
difficulty but he continued to bark eagerly as if he were
trying to tell his owners some thrilling secret.

They laughed at him, unlocked the front door and
went through the echoing rooms to make sure no damage had been done. At the end of a quarter of an hour
they came out to the car again. The little black dog was
nowhere in sight.

June called once or twice, then got in and drove toward the boardwalk. Candy was on the beach, sniffing
busily along the sand. A quarter of a mile away to the
northward the girl saw an old yellow mongrel loping off
at the edge of the surf. She collected the reluctant
cocker and carried him back to the roadster.

"You must have been right, Dad, about the dog
under the porch," she said. "I just saw one running off
as if he'd been caught trespassing."

They turned the car and set out once more for Philadelphia. Candy whined mournfully once or twice and
stood up with his forepaws on the back of the seat,
watching the road behind them as if he hoped to catch
a glimpse of something.

"I believe he'd like to stay, the way he acts," Ramsdell Faulkner chuckled. "Come, you funny little beggar. Get down here where you belong."

Candy obeyed, but he gave his master a reproachful look.

REUNION

Bat had not seen his friend the old mongrel for several days until that morning. Food had been increasingly difficult to find and both dogs were ranging farther than usual from their haunts. That was how they happened to meet, a little before noonday, on the beach at the northern end of Ventnor.

It was warm there in the sun. If Bat's belly had not been so empty he would have felt like romping a bit in the surf. Instead he hunted diligently back and forth across the beach at his companion's side. Noses to the sand, they quartered from the edge of the tide to the shadows under the boardwalk. Bat had found nothing more tempting than the sodden tip of a discarded ice cream cone when he heard an eager whimper from the yellow dog.

The cur was pawing away at the sand with both forefeet. In a moment Bat had caught the scent and was digging beside him. In some unaccountable way a grocer's carton of sliced bacon had found its way onto the beach and been covered by sand at high tide. They pulled the soggy treasure free and ripped away the cardboard and the clinging paper. Bat seized a limp rasher and bolted it with one snap of his jaws. It was salty and fat but his ravenous stomach welcomed it and cried for more.

It was at that moment, when they were both gobbling bacon as fast as they could, that Bat saw something move close beside him. Out of the corner of his eye he caught a glimpse of a pair of leather puttees and an outstretched arm. Even as he jumped aside, the arm came down and a heavy net settled over the yellow mongrel.

Bat's first impulse was to get away, but a yelp of entreaty from his struggling comrade made him change his mind. With a silent snarl he jumped at the burly figure in the puttees. The man swore and tried to beat him off with his free arm. Bat's teeth slid off the thick leggings but he found a hold in the loose cloth of the breeches above. Then the man's gauntleted hand caught him by the strap that was still around his neck and wrenched him loose, with a three-cornered piece of stout worsted clamped in his teeth.

The terrier found himself dangling in the air, half choked by the grip on his collar. The man was strong. He pulled the net tight around the mongrel and dragged his two captives grimly across the sand. There was another man waiting beyond the boardwalk, guarding a truck in which three or four other dogs were already imprisoned.

Bat made one more frantic struggle to get away, as
he saw the heavy wire door being opened. It was no use.
The man swore and threw him into the truck. The old
yellow cur followed an instant later and the door
slammed shut.

The rest of the captured dogs lay apathetically on the
jolting floor or yapped and howled in a futile chorus. As
soon as Bat recovered his wind he nosed up and down
the length of the truck body, hunting for a loose board
—a broken wire—anything that might offer a fighting
chance of escape. Finally he shouldered a path among
his doleful fellow-passengers and squatted as close to the
wire grille as he could get.

The truck rumbled on a few blocks and parked in
front of a hamburg-and-beer joint, where the dog-
catcher and his driver went in for refreshment. Time
went by. A hot sun burned down on the rear of the van
and its worried occupants panted thirstily. Boys passing
in the street stopped to stare and point. When one of
them tried an experimental whistle the dogs barked
and leaped eagerly against the wire. After that they
were tormented by whistles and calls of "Here, boy!
Here, Rover!" for the better part of an hour.

At last the big man and his companion came out
wiping their mouths. They laughed at the urchins,
chased them away from the truck, started up the engine
and proceeded on their rounds. It was late afternoon
when they came chugging back up Pacific Avenue. The

load had been augmented by half a dozen more forlorn waifs, and those that still had voices left were all yelping at once in a bedlam of sound.

It was when they turned west on Virginia Avenue that Bat caught sight of the shabby little roadster just pulling out from the curb. He rose on his hind legs, clawing at the wires, and forced a hoarse, desperate bark out of his dry gullet. They stopped at an intersection and the little car came nearer. He could see Tony standing up, pointing toward him, calling. Then the truck jarred into motion and his friends were gone.

Bat watched hopefully for half a dozen blocks before he had another glimpse of the roadster. It was flying up behind them, cutting in and out of traffic. As the next light turned red it skidded to a squealing stop beside the truck. Then a familiar voice reached him—a voice that dropped its h's in excitement.

" 'Ere, you!" Tim was shouting. "That's our dog you've got in your blarsted wagon!"

"Yeah?" the driver answered coldly. "That's too bad, Mister. If yer wanta git him now, yer'll hafta come to the pound."

As if to end the argument he shifted gears and rumbled forward with the changing light. The chase went on for another mile, but Bat was happy now. He couldn't understand why he hadn't been let out at once, but he had faith in Tim and Tony and Marie. As long as they followed he knew he would be safe.

At the gate of the dog-pound the two vehicles stopped side by side. Tim was out of the car at a bound, but the dog-catcher took his own time about clambering down.

"In a hurry, ain't you?" he asked sourly, with a glance at the roadster's license-plate. "You folks from the city go off an' leave your dogs runnin' loose down here, an' then expect me to stop in the middle o' town an' let 'em outa the truck. It'll cost you two dollars tax an' you'll have to sign for him in the office there. Which dog is it?"

Tony, with his face already pressed against the wire gate, pointed up at Bat. "That's Beppo—the white one!" he cried.

"Oh—that baby, eh?" the dog-catcher glowered. "Well, it'll be an extra two bucks to bail *him* out. Look what the beggar done to my pants." And he turned to exhibit the triangular rent in his clothing.

Marie gave the man her prettiest smile. "We're terribly sorry he did that," she said. "But I've got the four dollars right here. Can't you let him out now?"

"Soon as I git 'em all in the pound," replied the dog-catcher. His helper backed the truck up to a narrow door in the high wire fence and they opened the tail gate, letting an avalanche of dogs pour out into the enclosure.

"What happens to the others," Tony asked, "if nobody comes to take 'em home?"

"Oh, they stay here a week maybe, an' then the S.P. C.A. puts 'em out o' their misery."

The little cripple shivered. "Gee!" he murmured. "S'posin' we hadn't seen him!"

The receipt was duly signed, the four dollars handed over, and at last Tony was allowed to enter the pound. Bat was waiting just inside the gate. He looked up at the boy with sober gratitude, and his tongue, rough and dry, tried to return Tony's caress.

"Look at 'im," Tim growled. " 'E's thirsty. Give us a pan o' water, can't you, Bud?"

Bat lapped greedily at the proffered water, while the dogs inside the fence watched him with panting envy. The dog-catcher turned from Tim's accusing eyes. "They'll all git some in a minute," he said. "Don't worry—we treat 'em good enough. Better'n what most of 'em are used to."

Tim got into the car, opening the rumble seat for Tony and the terrier. As Marie took her place in front she looked once more at the dejected group beyond the wire. "That old yellow dog," she said. "I feel sorrier for him, somehow, than for any of the others. And yet he can't have had a very happy life."

"No," said Tim. " 'E's old an' sick an' mangy. 'E'll be better off if they put 'im away."

But the rescued bull terrier was still looking back when they turned the corner and left the pound behind.

Bat's emotions were mixed as he saw the familiar landmarks of the White Horse Pike appear one by one. His memories of this road were no longer happy ones, and yet he had an excited feeling that this time something pleasant might lie at the end of it. He was fond of Tony and his sister and deeply grateful for his release. But the homesick yearning that lay deepest in his heart was not for them.

"W'at time is it?" Tim asked, as they neared Berlin.

"A few minutes before six," the girl replied. "Why?" she teased. "Have you got a date tonight?"

"No—but I was thinkin' we might go right on out to the Main Line. If you know the address, that is."

"It's in Devon," she said. "I guess we can find it."

Dusk had fallen before they reached Philadelphia, and out beyond, on Lancaster Pike, the October leaves threw a halo of gold around each streetlight. Tony stared wide-eyed at the big, shadowy houses set back in their rolling lawns. "Gee," he murmured to the dog, "did you live in one o' those places, Beppo? I never knew there was anybody as rich as that!"

A policeman in Wayne told them how to reach the Faulkner estate. Bat knew where he was now. When they turned in between the great stone gateposts it was all Tony could do to keep him from leaping out of the car and racing ahead.

Tim followed the curving drive in silence, but as they chugged up to the door of the house Marie spoke in a whisper. "I'm scared," she said. "It's all so big—so grand."

He patted her arm. "Steady on, girl," he told her, with a hearty assurance he did not feel. "You've met 'em. They're just people, I 'ope—not royalties. 'Ere, I'll ring the bell myself. Come on. You an' Tony bring the pup."

He marched up the steps and pushed the button firmly. There was a pause during which they all listened so intently they could hear the blood pounding in their ears. Then the latch clicked and the heavy door swung open a few inches. Forbes, in his butler's livery, looked down his long nose at them.

Now that the moment had arrived, Tim stuttered, unable to phrase a sentence. It was Marie who spoke. "We were wondering," she said sweetly, "if Mr. Faulkner was at home."

The butler gave a disdainful glance at the little roadster. "You have some business to transact with Mr. Faulkner?" he asked coldly. "Perhaps the tradesmen's entrance would be—"

"No," Tim broke in, recovering the use of his tongue. "We'd like to see 'im in person. It's about findin' 'is dog, 'ere."

"Ah, his dog." Forbes stared at the battered and disreputable terrier and shook his head. "That," he said with finality, "is not Mr. Faulkner's dog. You've made a mistake, my man. And if I may say so, Mr. Faulkner

"That," he said, "is not Mr. Faulkner's dog."

is in no mood for any more mistakes of that sort. You'd best take yourselves off."

He was about to shut the door in their faces when Bat began to bark. There was a pleading, worried note in his voice that was like a call for help. And before the door could close they heard someone speak inside.

"What is it, Forbes?" asked a clear, girlish voice. "I thought I heard—"

Bat's charge was irresistible. He struck the heavy oak like a battering-ram and drove the startled butler back on his heels. The next instant he was crouched at June Faulkner's feet, his tail beating a muffled tattoo on the rug. He knew he was dirty and dilapidated. He knew it would be wrong to put his grimy paws on her dress, much as he wanted to. But with all the urgency of his adoring heart he was trying to tell her that at long last he had come home.

The girl gave a little gasp and dropped on her knees beside him. "Bat!" she sobbed as she caught him to her, "Bat—you poor darling—you've come back to me!"

For the big white dog the rest of that eventful evening passed like a rosy dream. Just being reunited with his mistress made him too happy to give his usual keen attention to all that was said and done. But there were some high spots that lived in his memory long afterward.

There was the moment when the master heard the commotion and came hurrying into the hall. He stared at Bat for long seconds and rubbed his hand across his eyes.

"Are you sure?" he said to his daughter dazedly. And laughing through her tears she told him of course she was sure. Then he sent Forbes to fetch McGill and turned to the embarrassed trio who stood just inside the door.

"Where did you find him?" he asked.

Haltingly and with some help from Marie and Tony, Tim told his story.

"Atlantic City!" Mr. Faulkner exclaimed. "Did you hear that, June?"

"Yes, Dad. He must have gone back to Ventnor to find us, poor lamb. Do you suppose—oh, Dad! Remember—that place under the porch! He was at the shore all the time—even during the northeaster! And we missed him. But Candy knew—oh, Dad, how could we be so stupid!"

They called Candy, then, and after seeing the cocker's transports of joy at greeting his old friend, nobody could doubt Bat's identity.

McGill arrived a moment later. He was breathless from hurrying and for once his dour Scotch features were radiant with delight. "Aye," he panted, holding the terrier's jaw in his hand and looking into his eyes. "It's the dog, right enough. But what a beatin' the poor lad must ha' taken! Look at his ribs—fair starved he is. An' the scars on him!"

Ramsdell Faulkner frowned and blew his nose with vigor. He seemed to have a little trouble controlling his voice. "I suppose," he said huskily, "we'll never be able to show him again?"

The kennel-man shook his head. "It's verra doubtful. We might do somethin' for the ears by croppin'. In a case like this we could get permission under the law. But his hide's been cut up bad."

"Who cares about showing?" June laughed. "We think you're still beautiful, don't we, Bat! And what a sire you'll make!"

She turned to Marie and put a friendly arm about her. "Won't you come into the library, Miss Donato?" she said. "You and Tony and your friend—while Dad writes that check? If you're willing I'd like to know you better. May I come to see you some time soon?"

"Yes, indeed, Miss Faulkner," Marie blushed. "I'd love to have you. You know—I didn't tell you before— but we'd planned to use the money for Tony. An operation to cure his lameness. It all seems too good to be true!"

Bat watched the proceedings with a preoccupied gladness. He nosed happily about the familiar rooms with Candy trotting by his side. In the sun-porch he found his own blanket bed still undisturbed. When he returned, Mr. Faulkner was tearing a piece of paper out of a book. He blew on it and handed it to Marie

Donato with a smile and some mumbled words about owing her an apology.

Then the three who had brought the terrier home rose to take their departure. At the door, Tony turned back suddenly. He knelt beside Bat and clutched him tight in a farewell embrace. "Oh, gosh, Beppo," he whispered. "I know you're goin' to have fun here, but maybe I'll never see you again!"

June wiped the tears from the boy's face with her own handkerchief.

"Yes, you will, Tony," she comforted him. "I'll bring him with me when I come to call. And I'm going to give you a puppy out of the very first litter that Bat gets."

"Gee!" the youngster grinned. "You mean a little white puppy that'll grow up just like him? Gosh, you're a swell lady!"

They got into the roadster and trundled away down the drive, the lights making a golden tunnel among the maples.

Bat rubbed his scarred head gently against June's knee and felt her fingers caressing his neck. His eyes closed in blissful contentment. The long weeks of suffering and despair seemed to drop away in that moment, and a new life began.

"Tomorrow," said June understandingly, "you're going to have the most tremendous bath in history. But tonight—" she kissed the crown of his head—"tonight you're just my dog!"

MAZO DE LA ROCHE

Short and Merry

Looking back at Hamish and you, I am interested in the difference between you as male and female.
I can see you now sitting side by side on the verandah,
your eyes fixed expectantly on the gap in the cedars
through which you could see the road. A dog trots by,
and, with two yells that sound as one, you hurl yourselves to the lawn, cross it as though shot from two cata-
pults, dart through the gap, and in a moment come
sounds of terror, rage, victory. The pair of you return
trippingly across the lawn. You hate to touch the sod,
you are so proud. You sit down, scarcely allowing your
sterns to touch the boards, you are so keen to be up and
at it again. There is an interval of the humming of bees
in the clover field, of the chirping of young birds in
the eave, of the gentle break of a slow wave. Then
two pairs of ears are pricked. A nurse, pushing a pram,
appears in the opening, another infant toddles beside.
This time there is no rush, but Hamish lifts his lip in a
sneer at the human young and you beat your tail and

beam in approval of it. A faint chatter comes from the
infants; Hamish's sneer becomes a growl. You rise, trot
down to the road, and prostrate yourself before the
babes. It is some time before you return, jogging contentedly along the path. There are crumbs on your lip.
The infant has been sharing its arrowroot biscuit with
you. Hamish meets you, licks off the crumbs, and you
settle down again side by side.

Another interval of peace, then across the field
comes the boy Edwin on his bicycle, bringing the daily
paper. This is the high spot of the day. You two preci-
pitate yourselves with one leap into the clover blooms.
You are on either side of him, raging at the pedals,
trying to tear them off, passionately desirous of rending
the solemn youth in twain. In Hamish's eye there is a
glitter that bodes danger when he is older. But, with
you, Edwin knows it is a game. One feels that if you did
tear him up, you would try most certainly to put him
together again.

You hated no one. Hamish hated all he did not love.
Of human beings he loved me best of all. Just why this
was I do not know, for I was the only one who was stern
with him. He would stand before me looking up at me
with wonder. When I had been away and returned, he
would greet me with a whine of joy so deep that it was
almost pain. He would regard me with a look as full of
awe as the gaze a human being might raise toward a
sunset or an approaching storm. He could never make

This is the high spot of the day.

out what I was going to do next and he made no effort
to do so. He just stood and stared. You knew all about
me. You were tolerant of, rather than thunderstruck at,
my humours. You understood him too, from stem to
stern, but you were not always tolerant of him. With
all the power that was in him he sought to understand
you, to share in your peculiar ecstasies. When you
caught up a green apple from the grass, tossed it, caught
it, tossed it again, rolled on it barking with delight, he
would sometimes find an apple for himself, walk dourly
around the apple tree with it in his teeth, and finally
take it away and lose it, returning with a sheepish air.
When you would lie sprawling, your belly to the sun,
wriggling in sensuous enjoyment of your nearness to
warm earth and warmer heaven, I have known him to
lie stiffly down beside you, roll over once, then get
quickly to his thin white legs, with a suspicious look
around, as though he feared what the sinister powers
about him might have done in the moment when he
had relaxed vigilance.

I am certain that his mind was beset by dangers of
which you recked nothing. I have seen the hair rise all
along his spine, as he sat by your side, while you gazed
tranquilly, savouring the amiability of the universe. But
in your rages your two spirits were as one. By the time
late summer came, "those black and white rascals" were
the terror of all the dogs about. I think it was the ferocity of your sudden rushes. You were like two wild High-

landers charging down the glen brandishing your battle-axes. I have seen you harry a great Dane the length of the beach, running in and out among his legs, leaping on him from either side, with snarls twice too fierce for your size. There were complaints. An angry lady came,

You caught up a green apple.

red-faced, declaring that you had driven her spaniel, which was larger than the two of you put together, out into the lake where he had had to swim for his life. While she complained, beating the air with a tennis racquet, you two sat on the verandah regarding her, Hamish with a concentrated sneer, you with obvious delight in her fluster. You wished she would go on and on, throw herself on the grass and roll. How gladly you would have rolled with her! But you were in disgrace and I was in disgrace, and it was only when the lady's dog took to biting people that I was comfortable again.

It was hard for you to settle down in the city. Hardest for Hamish, because all his freedom was gone. To be taken on the lead made him hysterical. Without it he was as impossible as a wolf cub in the streets. So in and out of the back garden he dived, up and down three flights of stairs he raced, in and out of all the rooms, as though hag-ridden. Only in the evenings he was quiet, sitting rigidly aloof in the black armchair in the corner. He had developed greatly in the summer. His breast now looked full and strong. He held his head as though the muscles in his neck were powerful. Yet he was so thin that there was always a suggestion of airy delicacy about him. Friends said of him that he looked like the female and you like the male. But to us who were familiar with the spirits of both, you looked as feminine as, in truth, you were and all his traits were pathetically masculine.

You still harried him when you were in the mood. There were times when you denied him the dignity of his own chair. You would rush at him without warning, uttering a sudden complaining scream that made him leap over the arm of the chair in panic. He would retire to a corner glowering while you would hop into his place and set about licking your paws till every ebony toenail shone. In the meantime he would establish himself, trembling, on the farthest chair. And, after a bit, something approaching serenity would appear in his eyes. Out of your deep dark ones you were watching him. You waited for that moment when his nerves relaxed, then, with another scream, you were after him. And so every chair he sought in turn.

But, when he chose, he had character. He was master and you knew it. This was where his share in me was in question. He and I had one pleasure we shared with no one else. The pleasure, I admit, was on his side; on mine it was mostly compassion and tenderness for him. This was to sit together on the end of the sofa and look out through the window of the drawing room into the street. The curtain must be well drawn back, regardless of crushing it, so that nothing should obstruct the view. I must sit near enough the end to leave barely room for him to stand, his sharp elbows resting on the slippery mahogany arm of the sofa, his chest pressed forward till he sometimes lost his balance and I only saved him from a fall by grasping his spiderish hind legs.

That room was one of the coldest I have ever known. When a spell of zero weather came, we used to shut it up and sit in the dining room, but rather than that he should miss this particular joy, I would retire there with him and stay until I could endure the cold no longer. I

must be near enough to him for our bodies to touch.
He needed the reassurance of that contact when he
looked out on a world so strange, exciting to the point
of hysteria. I would feel the stiffening of his spine, the
bristling hackle, as a dog passed down the street. A
group of dogs playing in the snow would enrage him
till his barking made them turn and stare at the window. He would be beside himself till they had sauntered
off, when he would settle down again on his breast-
bone to follow each pedestrian, each motorcar, with
his eager eyes. But always alert for the moment when
another dog should appear.

Sometimes you would follow us into the drawing
room and stand up with your paws against my knee,
making as though to join us. It was then that he would
turn on you with a snarl so ferocious, a sneer so terrible,
that you quickly retired and sat down on the floor, regarding him with submission in which there was the
hint of mockery. You knew that you might, perhaps
within the hour, trot along that (to him) so fabulous
a highway, be the admired centre of just such a group of
dogs as had now driven him into a fever.

He might have spent hours by the drawing-room window alone, but he would never go there except in my
company. And the moment I rose from the sofa, no
matter what might be passing in the street outside, he
jumped down without hesitation and escorted me from

the room, his bearing at these moments being one of dignified melancholy.

This was the winter when you ran away. What a fright you gave us! You had been turned into the garden as usual when the house was opened in the morning, but it was not noticed that the gale of the night before had blown open a back gate. When we came down to breakfast you were not there to meet us, and the open gate showed how you had gone. Every boy to be found was set searching. We walked till we were weary on false trails. The house was a hollow shell, echoing the restless movement that had raced through it. Consternation was in our hearts. We were bereft, not of two little devils, but of two small beings so perfect that sprouting wings had swept them away. We wrote advertisements for all the evening and morning papers. We advertised you separately and as a pair. "Scotch terrier, bitch, wearing silver collar." "White West Highland terrier, wearing plain leather collar." "Two terriers, White West Highland and Black Brindle Scottie, male and female." And, of course, warnings to those who might detain them; and, of course, rewards to those who returned.

The day passed somehow between doleful recallings of the enchantment of your presence and sudden rushings into the street after dogs that resembled one or the other of you. The evening and the night were like eternity. They were like nothing at all. We lay awake listening to the house crack under the frost. It was the coldest time of the winter.

Breakfast, with no waving paws or bright eyes begging for toast and bacon. The postman with letters which no one cared to read. A morning paper that held no interest because no one advertised a terrier found. Weary speculations as to whether or not you had survived the bitter night. Towards teatime a ring at the door, and the arrival of the man (he seemed more god than man) who came to tell us that you were safe and sound.

He was a carpenter living on the outskirts of the city quite three miles away. When he had gone home to his lunch, his wife, with an air of great mystery, had led him to the kitchen window and shown him two small dogs in the yard. They had run in there, she told him, just after he had left for work before seven. They had run gambolling, leaping about the yard. She had seen at once (God bless her for that!) that they were not common dogs, and had run and bolted her gate, shutting them in. She had tried to make friends with them, but the white one had frightened her by his fierce looks and she had not ventured into the yard. The man had carried food to them, and the black one had eaten as though famished and had let herself be stroked, but the white one had gone into a corner and stood there snarling. The man had gone out and bought a morning paper and found the advertisement. He told all this in a rambling, excited way.

It was a Saturday afternoon and it was not easy to find someone to fetch you. At last we were driven to hire a small lorry. Hamish's crate was put on this, and before dark we had you back again. It had taken the carpenter and the driver of the lorry together to catch Hamish and put him in the crate.

What a strange glamour there was about you two when once more you gambolled through the house! Mystery surrounded your doings for those twenty-four hours. How had you crossed all those innumerable streets and not lost each other? What miracle had saved you from death in those crossings? Had St. Francis, lover of animals, given a thought to you? In and out, up and down, you had stayed together. Somewhere in the bitter cold you had huddled together in the night. Were you afraid? Had you longed for home? Or did the great gust of freedom bear you along as two happy leaves? I pictured you running into the strange yard in the red winter sunrise, leaping, playing in the snow, with stomachs as empty as sea shells.

Hamish's ribs looked as though they would come through the skin. He was like a little famished white wolf. What a dinner we gave you! Vegetables, meat, and brown gravy, with a piece of toffee each to cap it off. You slept all the next day. There was no play in you.

After that there was something new in your relations to each other. You had shared strange dangers. You had passed a night of mystery in unknown streets. You would retire into a corner, sit close together, seeming to recall something.

Even when you romped together to the music of a gramophone record (a fox trot put on specially for you), moments of abstraction would still your gambols. You would lie in a tranced embrace, looking into each other's eyes, remembering, I feel sure, that day and night of vagabondage.

from JIM KJELGAARD'S

Big Red

*Ross Pickett, a trapper, and his son Danny live in
a little cabin on the estate of Mr. Haggin. The boy
is acting as caretaker for Big Red, one of Mr.
Haggin's champion dogs, and training him to flush
partridges. Danny has been a natural dog handler
since he was a baby, and now wants to be a profes-
sional dog trainer. He falls in love with the beautiful Irish Setter at first sight, and Big Red becomes
completely devoted to Danny. So much so that
when the setter is sent to New York to compete in
a show, the boy has to go along too, to keep the
dog from getting dispirited and missing a prize.
No wonder then that Danny is amazed when Big
Red suddenly begins to ignore him.*

SHEILAH MacGUIRE

Ross left the traps in the shed, entered the cabin,
and started a fire. He was in the midst of preparing supper when there was a knock at the door. Ross opened

it to confront Curley Jordan, one of the caretakers
from Mr. Haggin's estate. Curley thrust a yellow en-
velope at him.

"What is it?" Ross inquired.

"Telegram," Curley said.

Ross opened it, read it, thanked Curley, and shut
the door in his face. Then he retreated to the darkest
corner of the cabin to sit down on a chair with his chin
in his hands. His forehead creased, and he stared mood-
ily at the floor. He had always known that some day
such a thing was inevitable. But Danny was so young!
Not even eighteen!

Ross picked the telegram up, re-read it, and rose to
pace the floor. But when he heard Danny take his
snowshoes off and hang them beside the door he hastily
shoved the telegram under the bread box. Danny burst
in, his cheeks flushed and his eyes bright. Red padded
in behind him and wagged over to greet Ross, who was
puttering unconcernedly about the table.

"How's it out?" Ross said over his shoulder.

"Breakin'. The pussy-willow stalks are plumb green,
and there's an inch of water over the ice on the beaver
dam. Two more weeks of winter is the most we'll get."

"Yeh?"

Ross absently tossed a paring knife into the air and
caught it by the handle. His brow wrinkled in perplex-
ity. This wasn't something a man could bull or bluff his
way through. Young people were pretty sensitive about

their business, and apt to get huffy if somebody tried to run it for them. It was a time for subtlety. But Ross didn't know how to be subtle.

"Danny," he said bluntly, "do you trust me?"

"Why, why sure, Pappy."

"All right, I don't aim to mind your business for you. But if there's any way I can help you, I will."

"What you talkin' about?"

"I'm talkin' about this woman you met when you took Red to the dog show in New York! Danny, she's comin' here!"

"What!"

"Here it is," Ross insisted. He took the telegram from beneath the bread box and thrust it at Danny. "Read it yourself. I expect you to do whatever's right. But if this Haggin's aimin' to palm off one of his female relatives on a boy what don't know his own mind I'll . . ."

"Wait a minute." Danny opened the telegram and read, "MEET SHEILAH MACGUIRE ON 10 P.M. TRAIN AT WINTAPI. REGARDS. HAGGIN." He folded the telegram and stared over it. Then he began to laugh. "Pappy, that's no woman. It's a dog!"

"A huh?"

"A dog!" Danny repeated. "A mate for Red. Mr. Haggin said he'd send one up just as soon as he got one good enough! Just think, Pappy! We're goin' to raise pups here, good pups, show and field dogs! Man, oh man, Pappy! Just think!"

Ross scratched his head dubiously. "You sure?"

"Of course!" Danny danced around the table. "I was too busy at the dog show to meet any women in New York. Just think of the pups we're goin' to have, Pappy! Two years from now I bet one of 'em takes first in show at Madison Square! We'll have to keep her warm and everything, Pappy! And . . ."

"Sheilah MacGuire!" Ross snorted. "Who ever heard of a dog named that? Mebbe-so, if the cabin ain't comfortable enough for her, we can build a steam-heated house!"

"We don't need it," Danny said, blissfully unconscious of the sarcasm. "Let's see now, spring pups make awful good ones. By gosh, I can take a couple of 'em this fall and start 'em huntin' with Red. What time is it, Pappy?"

"Twenty to five."

"Whew! I better go!"

"You better," Ross said drily. "It's four whole miles to the Wintapi station, and you ain't got but five hours and twenty minutes to make it."

Nevertheless, Danny insisted on leaving at once, and when Red would have followed he ordered him back. The big dog went to his blanket beside Danny's bed, and looked resentfully out of his brown eyes. Ross snapped his fingers, and Red padded defiantly over to sit beside him. Ross addressed him with mock sympathy.

"I hope you got your wild oats all planted, Red. There's a woman comin' into your life."

From the doorway, Danny grinned. He left the cabin, strapped on his snowshoes, and started up the long valley that led over a mountain to the Wintapi station. A happy little song trailed from his lips as he travelled, and his feet seemed to bear wings. His brightest and most hopeful dreams were at last coming true; he was going to raise fine dogs. Maybe Sheilah MacGuire would bear a big litter, and all would be champions. Danny grinned ruefully. Maybe at least *one* would be. Danny snowshoed down to the Wintapi station, and for two hours shivered in the late-winter wind that swept it. He went inside the fireless station, and sat on a porcupine-chewed bench while an endless procession of wonderful red dogs gambolled and frolicked through his mind. Then, at long last, he heard the train whistle.

Danny rushed out to the platform, watched the train stab the darkness with its single headlight, and stamped his feet restlessly as it drew near. As it stopped, the door of the express car rolled open. The agent thrust his head out.

"Hey, are you waitin' for a dog?"

"Yup."

"Here it is."

He thrust a crate through the door, and Danny lowered it excitedly to the ground. His heart pumped crazily. From the brief glimpse he had had through the

slatted crate in the car's dim light, the dog within had
looked like none other than the setter that most nearly
approached Red's perfection, the one that had com-
peted with him for best of breed. But it couldn't be—
Mr. Haggin had said that no money could buy her.

The train rushed into the darkness and Danny knelt
beside the crate. The dog within whined, and pressed
her cold nose against Danny's questing hand. Her wagging tail bumped the side of the crate, and she whined
again. A short, sharp bark cut the night's silence, and
the dog scratched with her front paw at the gateway
of her prison. Danny murmured soothingly.

"Oh, sure, sure, Sheilah. Here's me lookin' at you,
and you wantin' to get out. I bet you're tired, cold, and
hungry."

He felt about in the darkness, found the wire that
held the crate's door shut, and untwisted it. He opened
the door, and the dog minced hesitatingly forward.
She sat down before Danny, and bent her long, finely
formed head upward as she looked at him. Danny
stroked her ears, and gently tickled her muzzle. His
hands went over her in the darkness, feeling her ribs,
her loins, her back, and her rear legs. A sigh escaped
him. You could tell almost as much by feeling a dog as
you could by looking at one, and if this wasn't Dr. Mac-
Gruder's bitch it was an exact replica. Danny took a
length of buckskin thong from his pocket, slipped it
under the dog's collar, and again spoke to her.

"This is only until we know each other, Sheilah. Right now we can't take a chance of losin' one another in the dark night."

He started up through the forest, retracing the snow-shoe trail he had made coming down, and for a space Sheilah floundered in the snow beside him. Gently but firmly Danny forced her behind, made her walk where his snowshoes had packed the snow. And he travelled slowly. Sheilah was not Red, who knew the tricks and ways of the forest. But she would learn.

Danny swung back down into the beech woods, to-ward the cabin, and Sheilah plunged and bucked as, for the first time in her life, the smell of wood smoke drifted to her sensitive nostrils. Danny knelt beside her, stroking her smooth sides with his hand and talking quietly. A balmy little breeze, fore-runner of the warmth that was to come, played up the valley and pushed the cold air before it. Danny heard Red's challenging bark. The hounds came out of their kennels and bayed sleepily. Ross stood framed in the open door.

"You got her, Danny?"

"Yeah. I'll fetch her in in a minute."

He knelt beside the trembling dog, stroking her sides and talking gently to her. Irish setters were a special breed in themselves, sensitive, intelligent, and proud. You had to handle them right or you couldn't handle them at all. Doubt or mistrust in their minds was very hard to overcome, and getting off to the right start with a new Irish setter was essential. The dog stopped trembling, laid her head on Danny's thigh, and sighed. For a few moments more he fussed over her.

When he rose, Sheilah walked confidently beside him and stayed very close to his knees while he took off his snowshoes. A little uncertain, but no longer trembling, she walked up the steps and into the cabin. Then her trepidation returned. She shrank against Danny, the being who had released her from the crate, the person who obviously had had most to do with terminating her long and onerous train ride.

"There she is," Danny said proudly.

"Whew!" Ross whistled. "Is that ever a dog! But she's scared, Danny."

"They're all high strung."

"Well, we got to calm her."

Ross dropped a piece of fat beef into the skillet and put it on the stove. It sputtered there, and when it was cooked he carried it over to hold it under the aristocratic nose of Sheilah MacGuire. She sniffed at it, licked it with her tongue, and finally accepted it. She smelled at Ross's trousers, his shirt, his hands, his shoes, etching in her keen mind an indelible picture of this man who, apparently, meant only to be kind and could be trusted. Danny knelt beside her, hand on her shining ruff.

"See how she acts with Red," Ross suggested.

Danny glanced around to see Red sitting before the

Getting off to the right start was essential.

stove, apparently engaged in a deep study of the cabin's opposite wall. He snapped his fingers.

"Come here, Red. Come over and meet Sheilah."

The big dog rose. Looking only at the open door, haughtily ignoring all other occupants of the cabin, he stalked regally into the night.

Danny stared, dumfounded. Sheilah wriggled a little closer to him, and opened her slender jaws to lick his hand. Danny looked out the open door, then up at Ross.

"What the dickens . . . ?"

"Haw, haw, haw!" Ross sat on a chair, bent double with laughter. He straightened to gasp, "You got him a mate, Danny. But you forgot to ask him if he wanted one!"

"What's the matter with him?"

"He's jealous, you loon! He's been king-pin 'round here long's he's been here. Now you got another dog to pet. That's what's eatin' him."

"Well, I'll be darned!"

Danny's gaze strayed from the slight Sheilah to the open door, and back again. He had known that Red would want to be boss of his own household, and that Sheilah would do as he thought best. But it never occurred to him that Red wouldn't even want a mate.

"What'll I do?" he appealed.

"I dunno." Ross shook his head lugubriously, but laughter still sparkled in his eyes. "Mebbe," he suggested helpfully, "you could write to one of these here newspaper people who give advice to all romantical things and . . ."

"I'm not foolin', Pappy."

"He'll come back if you kick her out."

"She'll run away."

"Likely she will," Ross agreed gravely, "but she sure ain't goin' to share Red's bed. Given she's in here at all, she can have all of it."

"Watch her," Danny said decisively. "I'm goin' out and see if I can argue with that old fool."

He took a flashlight and went outside. The yard about was tracked up, by both men and dogs, and there was no possibility of choosing Red's trail from among so many. Mike, leader of the hounds, sat sleepily in front of his cabin revelling in the warm breeze. Asa stood in his snowy pasture, letting the soft wind blow winter weariness away from his gaunt frame. Danny whistled, and Asa tossed his head up to look around. Danny cast the beam of his light in the direction Asa was looking, and saw Red framed in the black doorway of the mule's shed. Danny whistled again, and the dog ducked into the shed.

Danny plunged through the melting snow to the shed, and entered. Asa's stall, fresh and clean, confronted him. Asa's hay was packed on both sides of the stall, and filled all the rest of the shed. Stretched out, facing the wall and ignoring Danny, Red lay on a forkful of hay that had tumbled from the rack. Danny knelt beside the dog. His fingers tickled Red's ear in that place which the big dog found so difficult to reach with his own hind paw.

"You're actin' like a jug-head," Danny scolded softly. "Come on back to the house, Red."

Red swung his head to look steadily up at Danny, and turned away. Danny flinched. Ross had been right. Red was jealous, fiercely jealous that his beloved master's hands should even stroke another dog, to say nothing of taking her right into the house.

"You're wrong, Red," Danny protested. "I don't like her better'n you. But I got to keep her in the house. She don't know this place like you do, and she don't know yet that she's goin' to belong here. Come on back, Red. You're still king-pin. Come on, Red!"

He ran toward the door, and paused to throw his light back on the hay. Red had stretched full length in it, and did not even raise his head when Danny snapped his fingers and whistled. Danny went worriedly from the shed. Red was deeply insulted, and unless there was some way to atone that insult he would continue to sulk. But—just how might that be done? Danny went back into the cabin to be greeted daintily by Sheilah, who had been lolling against Ross's knees.

"Where is he?" Ross inquired.

"Sleepin' with Asa. He won't come out."

Ross wagged his head. "That dog's a proud 'un. I just dunno what you're goin' to do now."

"He'll come to his senses."

"Yeah?" Ross inquired skeptically. "I'll bet four dollars to an empty shotgun cartridge he never gives in to you."

"But, but he's got to!"

Danny sat down on a chair to stare hard at Sheilah MacGuire. He had wanted a fine dog, a mate for Red, but he had never wanted it to be like this. Red was Red, partridge dog extraordinary and the most satisfactory canine companion that a man could possibly have. If Red was going to stay mad at him why—why he might just as well not have any dog. If he let Sheilah out, and she ran away, she'd probably only go down to Mr. Haggin's. He voiced the thought to Ross.

Ross's mouth tightened sternly, and he shook his head. "Danny, did you find that dog chasin' 'round in the snow?"

"Why no. But . . ."

"Mr. Haggin ain't goin' to find it thataway, either," Ross pronounced firmly. "Given he'd wanted the dog down to his place, he'd of sent it there. But he sent it to us—to you. If you're not goin' to keep it, you see that he gets it back."

"I was just thinkin'," Danny said miserably. "Maybe we could toll him back with a bait of meat."

"Sure!" Ross scoffed. "You know him better'n that. That Red dog ain't goin' to do nothin' without he wants to."

"I guess you're right," Danny admitted.

Sheilah looked up at Ross, whom she seemed to have adopted as her special mentor, and sighed deeply. She laid her head on Ross's lap, and Ross scratched her ear. Danny sighed unhappily. Sheilah had taken to Ross as Red had taken to him, and now instead of having two dogs he hadn't any. He went to bed, and lay sleepless while the warm zephyrs played outside his window and the long night hours ticked by. A dozen times during the night he reached over the side of his bed for Red, who always slept on a blanket beside him. But the big dog was not there.

The next morning Red emerged from the mule shed and sat in the sun before it. Haggard and worn from lack of sleep, Danny saw him there when he went out to the wood lot for an arm-load of wood, and tried to whistle him into the house. But Red only turned his head toward the sound and looked away again. Danny took his load of wood and his breaking heart back into the house.

"What's he doin' this mornin'?" Ross inquired.

"Settin' by Asa's shed. He won't come to me."

Ross said gently, "Don't let it hit you too hard. I bet he'd like to come back in. But a proud dog's a lot like a proud man."

"If'n he wants to go on bein' a fool he can just be one. I don't care," Danny lied.

"That's the way to take it."

Danny cooked breakfast, and Sheilah went over to sit beside Ross with one paw on his knee as she received tidbits from his plate. Ross finished and pushed his plate back, and a little smile played around his lips as he looked fondly down at the dog. Danny watched, and even in the depths of his own misery found room for surprise. Ross was a man who had always hunted varmints, and preferred varmint hunting dogs. Obviously the delicate Sheilah would never hunt varmints, and maybe not anything, but just the same Ross was engrossed in her.

"Sure is a lot of dog under them red setters' hides," he observed. "We got to let her out to run a bit, Danny."

"Do you think she'll stay here?"

"Sure," Ross said confidently. "I think I can handle this dog. You had the right angle on 'em, Danny. You can't lick such dogs. But they'll do anything for you given they once want to."

He pushed his chair back and opened the door. The sun had climbed brightly over Stoney Lonesome, and great wet spots appeared on top of the snow. The depressions in the pasture were puddles, and the trunks of the trees gleamed wetly. Sheilah stood for a moment on the porch, and the hounds came out of their kennels

to bay at her. She glanced up at Ross, and gave the
hounds a wide berth as she padded down the steps.
Plainly she lacked Red's bravado—in the first five minutes of his stay at the Pickett household he had shown
Mike who was going to be boss of all the dogs there.
Ross, a slight smile still on his lips, climbed down the
steps with her and followed her about as she cast back
and forth in front of the cabin. They started toward the
beech woods, and Danny glanced at Red.

He was still sitting by the door of the mule shed, staring indifferently at Sheilah and Ross. Danny let his gaze
return to them, and saw Sheilah race toward a clump of
brush. Half a dozen partridges burst out of it. Two lit
in a hemlock, and the other four scattered in the beech
woods. Sheilah raced wildly about, dashing to and fro
as she sought to pin down exactly this new and entranc-
ing scent.

"Here, Sheilah," said Ross gently. "Come here, gal."

Sheilah went over and rubbed against Ross's legs.
Red left his seat by the mule shed, and at top speed
raced across the slush-filled pasture. Danny gasped, and
rose to shout. Red had gone mad; he was going to kill
this unwelcome trespasser. But he stifled the shout in
his throat as Red snapped to a perfect point in front of
the hemlocks. He held his point, tail stiff and foreleg
curved. Danny dashed in to get his shotgun, and ran
across the field.

He heard his father call to him, but paid no attention

to it. A hundred feet from Red he stopped running and edged up behind him.

"Get 'em out, Red," he said softly.

Red lunged forward and the two partridges thun-

Sheilah and Red.

dered up. Danny raised his gun, deliberately undershot the out-of-season birds, and lowered his shotgun.

"Missed!" he said dejectedly.

Red looked around, his eyes friendly once more and his tail wagging. He looked disdainfully toward the shrinking Sheilah. Red, prince of partridge dogs, had proven himself definitely superior to this puny female, and Danny had witnessed the entire performance. There could not now be the slightest doubt as to which dog was best. He shoved his muzzle deep into Danny's cupped hand and sniffed loudly. Then he went forward to meet Sheilah.

She advanced, uncertain but friendly, and they sniffed noses. Then together they set off toward the house.

JAMES THURBER

Snapshot of a Dog

I ran across a dim photograph of him the other day. He's been dead 25 years. His name was Rex (my two brothers and I named him) and he was a bull terrier. "An American bull terrier," we used to say, proudly; none of your English bulls. He had one brindle eye that sometimes made him look like a clown and sometimes reminded you of a politician with derby hat and cigar. The rest of him was white except for a brindle saddle and a brindle stocking on a hind leg. Nevertheless, there was a nobility about him. He was big and muscular and beautifully made. He never lost his dignity even when trying to accomplish the extravagant tasks my brother and I used to set for him.

One of these was the bringing of a ten-foot wooden rail into the yard through the back gate. We would throw it out into the alley and tell him to get it. Rex was as powerful as a wrestler, and he would catch the rail at the balance, lift it clear of the ground, and trot with great confidence toward the gate. Of course, the gate being only four feet wide, he couldn't bring the rail in broadside. He found that out when he got a few terrific jolts, but he wouldn't give up. He finally figured out how to do it, by dragging the rail, holding onto one end, growling. He got a great, wagging satisfaction out of his work.

He was a tremendous fighter, but he never started fights. He never went for a dog's throat but for one of its ears (that teaches a dog a lesson), and he would get his grip, close his eyes, and hold on. He could hold on for hours. His longest fight lasted from dusk to almost pitch-dark, one Sunday. It was fought with a large, snarly nondescript belonging to a large colored man. When Rex finally got his ear grip, the brief whirlwind of snarling turned to screeching. It was frightening to listen to and to watch. The Negro boldly picked the dogs up, swung them around his head, and finally let them fly like a hammer in a hammer throw, but although they landed ten feet away, with a great plump, Rex still held on. Working their way to the middle of the car tracks, two or three streetcars were held up by the fight. A motorman tried to pry Rex's jaws open with a switch rod; somebody lighted a stick and held it to Rex's tail but he paid no attention. Rex's joy of battle, when battle was joined, was almost tranquil. He had a kind of pleasant expression during fights, his eyes closed in what would have seemed to be sleep had it not been for the turmoil of the struggle. The Fire De-

He swung them around his head.

partment finally had to be sent for and a powerful stream of water turned on the dogs for several moments before Rex finally let go.

The story of that Homeric fight got all around town, and some of our relatives considered it a blot on the family name. They insisted that we get rid of Rex, but nobody could have made us give him up. We would have left town with him first. It would have been different, perhaps, if he had ever looked for trouble. But he had a gentle disposition. He never bit a person in the ten strenuous years that he lived, nor even growled at anyone except prowlers.

Swimming was his favorite recreation. The first time he ever saw a body of water, he trotted nervously along the steep bank for a while, fell to barking wildly, and finally plunged in from a height of eight feet or more. I shall always remember that shining, virgin dive. Then he swam upstream and back just for the pleasure of it, like a man. It was fun to see him battle upstream against a stiff current, growling every foot of the way. He had as much fun in the water as any person I have ever known. You didn't have to throw a stick into the water to get him to go in. Of course, he would bring back a stick if you did throw one in. He would have brought back a piano if you had thrown one in.

That reminds me of the night he went a-roving in the light of the moon and brought back a small chest of drawers he had found somewhere—how far from the house nobody ever knew. There were no drawers in the chest when he got it home, and it wasn't a good one—just an old cheap piece abandoned on a trash heap. Still it was something he wanted, probably because it presented a nice problem in transportation.

Swimming was his favorite recreation.

We first knew about his achievement when, deep in the night, we heard sounds as if two or three people were trying to tear the house down. We came downstairs and turned on the porch light. Rex was on the top step, trying to pull the thing up, but it had caught and he was just holding his own. I suppose he would have held his own until dawn if we hadn't helped him. Next day we carted the chest miles away and threw it out. If we had thrown it out nearby, he would have brought it home again, as a small token of his integrity in such matters.

There was in his world no such thing as the impossible. Even death couldn't beat him down. He died, it is true, but only, as one of his admirers said, after "straight-arming the death angel" for more than an hour. Late one afternoon he wandered home, too slowly and uncertainly to be the Rex that had trotted briskly homeward up our avenue for ten years. I think we all knew when he came through the gate that he was dying. He had apparently taken a terrible beating, probably from the owner of some dog he had got into a fight with. His head and body were scarred, and some of the brass studs of his heavy collar were sprung loose. He licked at our hands and, staggering, fell, but got up again. We could see that he was looking for someone. One of his three masters was not home. He did not get home for an hour. During that hour the bull terrier fought against death as he had fought against the cold, strong current of the creek. When the person he was waiting for did come through the gate, whistling, ceasing to whistle, Rex walked a few wabbly paces toward him, touched his hand with his muzzle, and fell down again. This time he didn't get up.

PHILIP CURTISS

The Eight-Dollar Pup

The Perriers had always given their dogs "real" names for, as Mrs. Perrier once pointed out, you would not call a child or even a faithful hired man "Spot" or "Dash." There had been, for example, Titus, the old Gordon setter whose almost centenarian existence had practically covered the span of the Perriers' own married life. Then, at various times, there had been Frank, the pointer, Emil, the dachshund, and Benjamin Cibber, a picturesque but not very responsive little Skye. There still was Charley, a big, mongrel police dog, and, although the Perriers had never really gone in for the family idea, they had once had a broody little Airedale named Mrs. Harris. Names seemed to suggest themselves as a rule as soon as an animal walked onto the premises, but when the black cow dog appeared, there was a pained and uncomfortable silence.

It was Andy Payson, a vociferous and determined gentleman on the other side of town, who was really responsible for the cow-dog craze in West Gosset; for just as a man who has been dining for weeks in the smartest hotels will suddenly have a craving for a dough-nut and a dill pickle, so did Andy break out one evening:

"You know, I'm getting awfully sick of these German schnautzhounds and Popperdene terriers that are judged merely by the length of their ears or the number of wrinkles on their noses. What has become of what we used to call ordinary 'shepherd dogs' twenty years ago? I don't mean collies, exactly, and I don't mean those long-haired English sheepdogs. I mean the kind of dog that you used to see in every farmyard, asleep under a lumber wagon. When I was a boy we had a dog like that, and I swear that he could do everything except read and write."

"I think I know where you could get one," replied August Perrier promptly. "There's a man in Vermont who has been advertising for years in the farm papers. He calls them just what you do—old-fashioned shepherds for driving sheep and cows. He'll sell you a male pup for eight dollars and a female for three."

The whole company burst into a laugh, headed by Molly Payson.

"But can't you just imagine," she hazarded, "what they would be like—at that price?"

"I'll bet," retorted her husband, "that they would be a lot better dogs than that little beast of an undersized Scotty for which you paid seventy-five last year. He didn't have a brain in his head and all he thought about was his own little self."

"Well, Scotties are like that sometimes," confessed Molly. "It's their temperament."

"But what I want," exclaimed Andy, "is a dog that will look up and thump the floor with his tail when I come into the room."

"Yes, I have noticed that trait in your make-up," replied Molly quietly.

"No, but I'm serious," retorted her husband. "You telephone me that address, Gus, and I'll risk eight dollars."

He was as good as his word, and so was August Perrier. Within a week there arrived at the West Gosset express office an ordinary wooden box which was labeled "Superior Baked Beans," but when the three crude slats were pried off the top, out stepped a dapper little gentleman whose composure and manners were so perfect that they brought tears even to Molly's eyes. "Ah yes," his demeanor announced, "you are the people I have come to see. Now if you will kindly show me where I can wash my hands . . ."

True to his boyhood memories, Andy named him "Shep," and within a week he was the sensation of the village. Everybody seemed, long ago, to have known a dog just like him. He was black, in the main, but with a white nose, white collar, and fluffy white shirt front. His legs and his jaws were faintly tinged with light brown, like autumn foliage, and over each eye was a single tan spot. As he grew in size, his tail became a great curving plume, and when he stood on a rock to gaze over the landscape he looked like a dog in a steel engraving of the year 1873. As Molly said, all he needed was three sheep, a sleeping child, and Melrose Abbey in the background and, underneath, the line "Man's Faithful Friend."

And brains? In the case of Shep it was libellous to say that he could do everything but talk. Given the key word and the right expression in your eye, you could make him wail up and down for minutes, like an old man complaining about his feet. Andy Payson, of course, was almost unbearable in his pride. He spent hours and hours teaching his protégé to walk at heel, carry newspapers, and open doors with complicated latches. About the only thing he didn't do was send him to Yale.

The next spring August Perrier himself caught the fever and sent his own check to the same address. What he got was—well, just about what he could expect for eight dollars. This time when Mrs. Perrier saw the box opened all she said was, "Oh." Inside was a crouching black creature that might have been a young Newfoundland and then again might have been a trained seal. If Shep, so to speak, had come off the train putting on his kid gloves, this little fellow gave the impression of having a lollipop in each hand. One could see in his coat and his attitude the whole history of his night's travel, and the general effect was that of a very dirty baby with his spirit ruffled, his milk bottle gone sour, and his bib twisted under one ear.

If it is true that intellect and untidiness go together, this little fellow was certainly an illustration of the role, for within a week it was obvious to the Perriers that he was like no other pup they had ever seen. He was a thinker, a hobbyist, an isolated and eccentric soul. If he had been a child he would shortly have begun to collect stamps or display an interest in mechanical drawing but, being what he was, he became that rather rare creature—a hermit dog.

He seldom played with other dogs, and the attempts which he did make were always followed by disaster. If there was a hole within two hundred yards, he would always manage to fall into it, and even when running by himself, his big back legs would suddenly cave in and go flop. When chasing another dog he would never seem to see the bush behind which the other dog had dodged, or else his ungainly frame could not stop in time, and he would go crashing into it. When, in his slow, tardy way, he would try to wrestle with neighboring pups, it would be like watching a fight in a dream. All his muscles seemed to be made of fluid or sand; his pushes, somehow, would never reach home, and his barks would never detonate. But, strangest of all, no matter what happened to him, he never changed ex-

pression. Pushed down the cellar hole or rolled in the
mud, his eyes would always remain thoughtful and ac-
ceptant.

As to his exterior aspects, alas, Helen Perrier had seen
the whole truth when she had opened the box. An exact
catalogue of his features might possibly make him seem
worse than he actually was, but in general his appearance was that of an ebony sheep. His body was large and
round, his head was small and pointed, and his coat was
a sort of curly chinchilla. He seldom trotted from place
to place, like other dogs, but almost any time one could
catch him on the skyline, going somewhere at a slow
walk. He may have been a little farsighted, or else some
of his ancestors had had hair over their eyes, for when
you spoke to him he would lift his head rather higher
than usual and gaze at you down the bridge of his nose,
like a man with his reading glasses still on.

To name such a dog was naturally a bit of a problem,
that is if one wanted a name that would really probe the
depths. For a week or two he was called simply "Pup"
or "Bub," but one day when Helen Perrier was watching him from the east terrace she suddenly called to her
husband:

"August! August! I know what I'm going to call him.
His name is Joel!"

Perrier appeared behind the screen door. "Why Joel?"

"I don't know," replied Helen, "but he *looks* like
Joel."

Strangely enough he did, and, as if he had only been waiting for this to be settled, he seemed to calm down from then on and live the part. He did not at once, of course, abandon all attempts to wrestle with dogs of the neighborhood, but more and more he apparently

To name such a dog was a bit of a problem.

realized his limitations and proceeded to carve out a life of his own. It was not a great life, but then, as he would have been the first to admit, he was not much of a dog.

Sitting on a little hilltop just behind the house seemed to be one of the major features of this new and permanent existence. Just what he found there to interest him one could not imagine. Possibly he was hop-

ing that someday there would appear over the horizon
some other dog who was interested in stamps. He had
no bones there, no rabbit thickets, yet there he would
remain for hours at a time. Frequently the Perriers
would leave him there when they went out in the car
after luncheon and find him still there when they
came back late in the afternoon. At their appearance,
to be sure, he would come galloping heavily to meet
them at the garage door; but that could not have been
the whole purpose of his lookout for, as soon as he
knew that they were safe in the house, back he would
go to his hilltop.

Then, little by little, he developed other occupations,
mostly agricultural. For one thing, he loved to watch
anyone plant anything, such as beans or onions, where
he could sit in contemplation at the head of the rows.
When the worker came up to his end of the field he
would give one short wag and then move over to the
next row. In his relations to the Perriers themselves he
could have been called neither affectionate nor unaffec-
tionate and he did not seem to care a great deal about
coming into the house. When patted on his coarse,
curly head he would look grateful and would wag his
tail, which meant in his case a slow, undulating movement of his whole hind quarters. On the other hand, he
did not demand to be a part of everything, as when visitors came to tea. After such visitors had exclaimed and
gushed over big Charley and put him through all his

He loved to watch anyone plant anything.

tricks, one of them might happen to glance out of the window and say, "Hullo! What's this?"

"Oh," one of the Perriers would answer, "that's our *other* dog."

Thus life drifted on for a couple of years, and so unobtrusively had Joel sunk into the background that the world failed to notice the day when the hilltop no longer remained his chief point of attraction. The Perriers' dining room was on the west side of the house, and one noon, at luncheon, Helen suddenly laid down her fork. Her eyes were fixed on the open window.

"I don't want to say anything," she remarked quietly, "but I do believe that a bit of scandal is developing in the neighborhood. That is the third time this week that Joel has been up to call on Miss Craggs."

With the liveliest interest August Perrier followed her look, since it was the most extraordinary thing for Joel even to leave the yard. Yet there he certainly was, coming slowly down the road, with his sheeplike body and his pensive walk. Unlike any other dog, he did not stop to sniff at any side attractions; he did not break into a frolic as he reached the gateway, or make any violent pretenses that he had not really left the place. Instead he continued straight ahead, with his calm, old-man's pace, and disappeared around the ell of the house.

"I thought there was something in the wind," continued Helen, "when I saw him walking up there the other day. At first I was going to call him back, but it was so unusual that I decided to watch him and see what would happen. And there's where he went, straight as an arrow. He turned in at the arbor and went up the front path, just as if he'd had a date."

"He probably had," laughed Perrier. "You don't suppose she has a Pekinese or something?"

"Not a thing," replied Helen promptly, "not even a cat. I believe it's Miss Craggs herself that is the attraction. She came out to meet him yesterday as he went in."

"Well, by George!" laughed Perrier. "If they wouldn't be an ideal couple! They're positively made for each other. She's got lots of money, and he'd give her a certain intellectual tone. Can't you see them, in the winter, driving around in her limousine in New York?"

"To the life!" agreed Helen. "Their habits would fit to a T. Every morning she could drop him at the dog department of the Metropolitan Museum or someplace where he could fuss around with a few old manuscripts on 'Dog Life Among the Assyrians.' Or he could lunch with that new Russian dog who had just arrived from Mongolia where he had dug up the most fascinating prehistoric bones, proving that the gazelle hound was really descended from the zebra."

"And at night," chuckled Perrier, "they could go back to that old house of hers in Fifty-seventh Street where they could sit in front of a fire with nobody but themselves and the servants. She could do lacework and talk about her rheumatism, and Joel could correspond with a few famous savants or write up the notes that he had made during the day."

"Of course," added Helen, "there would be a few old friends with whom they would dine occasionally. And two or three times a winter they would go out to some staid old opera like *Tristan* or *Die Meistersinger*."

"But never," suggested Perrier, "to anything like *The Follies* or Eugene O'Neill."

"Oh, never!" agreed Helen.

"As nearly as I can see," said Perrier, "Joe's future is settled. What do you suppose we ought to do to bring them together? Perhaps Charley ought to give them a tea."

"We'd better do nothing," said Helen emphatically, "if I know Miss Craggs!"

Having been a neighbor for at least twelve summers, it could fairly be accepted that Helen Perrier was an authority on Miss Craggs, but as a matter of fact, it was shortly evident that no pushing on anyone's part was needed to forward the budding romance. Every morning, without looking either to right or to left, Joel would go solemnly up the road, and Miss Craggs, meeting Helen one afternoon, confessed, almost blushing, "You know, I've never cared much for animals but I do rather like to have him around." In a week the affair was flaunting and open, and in another week, due to Perrier's efforts, it was the talk of the town. Andy Payson, in particular, seized on the idea and spent whole hours laying out great plans for what he called "the love life of the Joel Perriers."

"I think I'd like to have them married under the apple trees," he commented one evening, "but considering the age and dignity of both parties, we don't want anything of a splurge—just, perhaps, a few of his colleagues from Harvard and the University of Michigan and a few of her oldest friends from Washington Square. We must have a bishop, of course, and I have no doubt that they'll get a cablegram from the Duchess of Kent."

"And as they come out to their carriage," suggested Perrier, "six handsome greyhounds should be lined up, forming an arch of crossed mutton bones."

None of these remarks, naturally, was allowed to come to the ears of Miss Craggs herself, for hitherto Miss Annie Craggs had not been an individual with whom West Gosset had taken many liberties. She was, as Perrier's comments might have implied, a person now well in the autumn of life, and her career in the village had been marked by that peculiar combination of a soft heart and a cantankerous manner that seems to be the unfortunate handicap of many wealthy old ladies. In her appearance, certainly, there was nothing very redoubtable, but, possibly because she had lived all her life in the fear of being imposed upon, there had grown up around her a tradition of causticity that had resulted in her being left severely alone.

That this isolation might possibly be undeserved it had apparently remained for Joel to discover. How he had nosed out Miss Craggs's front porch in the first place could never be learned, but, having once formed a habit of going there, it was easy to see why it was a place exactly after his own heart. There was so much neatness at Miss Craggs's house and such complete silence. There were no other dogs there to irritate him with their continual fighting and not even a cat to make an occasional pass at his nose. It was so peaceful after breakfast to go up to that perfect piazza and sink down with a heavy thump. Or, in the long afternoons, there was no better place in West Gosset for a dog to sit, panting slightly and thinking of this and that. Even if Miss Craggs or one of the maids patted him occasionally or urged him to move, it was done with such timidity and hesitation that a dog had time to prepare his nerves.

For a time August Perrier half expected that Miss Craggs would offer to buy Joe, in which case he was prepared to toy with the idea of offering him as a gift. It was not that he didn't like the black pup, but he could recognize destiny when he saw it and would never have been willing to stand in the way of a larger and finer career. Lacking, however, any such overtures from Miss Craggs, Perrier wisely refrained from taking the first step. Having sprung, himself, from much the same New Englandish atmosphere, perhaps he understood the old lady better than his wife did. Any definite or final suggestion might very easily have frightened her into an attitude of resistance that would have ended Joel's summer then and there.

So matters rested, with great tact on both sides, until one lazy afternoon when Helen Perrier lay reading in a steamer chair on the terrace. Suddenly she felt a shadow cross the bricks at her feet and, looking up, saw an elderly parlormaid with a light cape thrown over her uniform.

"Please, Mrs. Perrier," said the maid, "Miss Craggs sends her compliments and she wants to know whether anything has happened to Joel."

Helen hitched up in her chair with apprehension. "Joel? Why, not that I know of. He was here for his dinner. I saw him not long ago."

"He wasn't up at the house yesterday," explained the maid, "and he wasn't today. Miss Craggs didn't know . . ."

If Joel was not at Miss Craggs's there was only one other place where he could possibly be, and Helen rose hastily. Sure enough, there was Joel on his hilltop, his head on his paws and his back to the sun. Helen gave a shrill whistle, and Joel vaguely lifted his head. The signal was repeated and, realizing at last that it was really for him, Joel, slowly rose, shook himself, and came down the hill. At sight of the maid he gave a guarded wiggle but that was as far as he went.

"Take him up now if you wish to," suggested Helen, and quite eagerly the maid urged:

"Come on, Joel."

Again Joel gave his little wiggle but he did not move from his tracks.

"Go on, Joel," added Helen. "Go see Miss Craggs."

For answer Joel turned his head and looked up at her eyes. "Is this an order?" he seemed to be asking, and when Helen assured him that it was, he waddled off in the wake of the maid. Yet, half an hour later, when Helen looked up from her book, there was Joel again at the top of the hill.

When Perrier came home his wife related the incident, and, as a first guess, Perrier pulled up Joel's forehead to look at the whites of his eyes.

"Oh, he's not sick," broke in Helen quickly. "I thought of that, but he's eaten all his meals."

"Perhaps the chauffeur kicked him or squirted the hose on him," suggested her husband.

"Never in the world," answered Helen, "not that nice old Garrity. No," she insisted, "for some reason or other he's simply 'off' Miss Craggs. In some way she must have hurt his feelings."

"Poor Miss Craggs!" grinned Perrier. "Can't she even get on with the dogs?"

For about two days longer the mystery continued, then one morning Perrier burst into his wife's dressing room.

"I believe I've got it," he exclaimed, "—what's wrong with Joel! He's got a rival. He's simply jealous!"

Helen looked up with the fixed expression of one who at last hears the truth. "Not another dog?"

"Dog nothing!" said Perrier. "Another man. I just saw Miss Craggs going by in her car, and on the seat beside her was the foppiest little old gentleman with a very red face and a snow-white mustache."

"George Dallingham Smith!" murmured Helen. "I might have known it. I've heard that he's been trying to marry her for thirty years. He *is* the kind of man who would kick a dog—not nastily, I mean, but if the dog tried to jump up on him or lick his spats."

"They ought to go out in a field," suggested Perrier, "and shoot it out."

"But what a fool!" laughed Helen. "I mean Joel—to go off and sulk. As nearly as I can see, he has made more progress in two months than George Dallingham Smith has made in thirty years."

"Why don't you go and tell him that?" suggested Perrier, but his wife gave him a wicked little look.

"Is it ever any use," she asked, "to try to tell anything to anyone who's jealous?"

Nevertheless, between them they seemed to have arrived at a correct diagnosis as, from then on, the pres-

ence or non-presence of George Dallingham Smith in
West Gosset could be fairly judged by the actions of
Joel. It might very well have been that Joel never
actually *had* tried to jump on George Dallingham's
trousers or lick his spats, but there were plenty of other
minds in West Gosset that could state emphatically
that no household was ever the same after George Dallingham Smith was once in it. If Miss Annie Craggs
represented the chill and cautious side of old Victorian
life, George Dallingham Smith represented the
sprightly. He was the kind of man who would spring
about like a grasshopper all his days and then, at the end
of them, would write his memoirs. He was probably the
most endless talker that Heaven ever created and he
loved to joke at his friends with roars and chuckles. He
was the kind of man who was always popping up to re-
arrange and suggest things and, if the truth were known,
he had probably tried to show his appreciation of Joel
by poking him with his walking stick or rolling him over
by his ears. At any rate, whatever the facts, Joel made
it perfectly evident that between Miss Craggs's piazza
plus George Dallingham Smith and his hilltop minus
that gentleman, he for his part preferred the hilltop.

If Joel had only been a little more intimate with
George Dallingham Smith's private affairs he might
perhaps have been more tolerant; for it was distinctly
to the old gentleman's credit that while, for many
years, he had been very eager to marry Miss Annie

Craggs, it was only recently that it had become at all necessary that he should marry her. It was not George Dallingham's fault that he had been born with a sociable nature, a love for travel, and very little else, nor was it to his discredit that an income which thirty years before had been regarded as ample, not to say magnificent, had slowly shrunk into very ominous proportions. With his familiar world evaporating all about him, it was only natural that he should cling with greater and greater tenacity to the few friendly firesides which remained, and if he suddenly appeared three times in West Gosset in a single summer, it was only what he would have been glad to do thirty-five years before when, in his way, he had been quite a dashing beau and Miss Annie Craggs had been principally known as a gaunt, reserved, and not very popular girl.

But all this Joe, naturally, had not quite the vision to see. All that he could grasp was the fact that George Dallingham Smith was a very noisy and trivial person, and that when he was present Miss Craggs's piazza was gone all to pot. When G. D. was out of town, with the regularity of clockwork, Joel would go up again and live with Miss Craggs; when G. D. returned Joel would go back to his hilltop and, with that uncanny instinct which is one of the most mysterious facts of dog nature, he never mixed his dates.

The Perriers, for their part, scarcely knew with which one to side, for while Joel's point of view was obvious,

yet, as the summer wore on, they found themselves falling into an amazing fondness for George Dallingham
Smith. Unlike Miss Annie Craggs, George Dallingham
could not spend a week in a given neighborhood without becoming on intimate terms with its principal fam-
ilies. He formed the habit of dropping in at all hours
of the day and, seen thus at a closer view, his friendly,
guileless little ways became most disarming. Underneath his pomposities and his affectations he really
had a very kindly, simple nature, and, as the tragedy of
his situation became more apparent, the Perriers began
to root openly for his suit.

It was, in fact, this sociability of George Dallingham's that in the end threw Joel completely off his
stride and precipitated the climax. One afternoon,
while Joel was napping lazily on his hilltop, Miss Annie's open car came out of her driveway and down the
road with two figures plainly visible, the chauffeur at
the wheel and beside him George Dallingham Smith.
Now, if there is one thing that a modern dog learns
sooner than anything else, it is to distinguish the sound
of a familiar car from any other, and at the well-known
hum Joel sat up with interest. Then, seeing who occupied the front seat, the light in his eyes grew suddenly
dull. Slowly turning his head, he watched the car until
it had passed a turn in the road and then he sank down
again to his meditations. It is not acutally on record

that he said, "You little squirt!" but it might just as well have been.

Half an hour later the same familiar hum came back up the highway, and again Joel roused himself at the sound. This time, however, he did not merely remain in a sitting position but, with a glad, incredulous bound, he rose to his feet. "Can this really be true?" he seemed to ask himself, for now the car contained but a single figure, that of old Garrity, the chauffeur. Previously this had meant only one thing, and, still not believing his good luck, Joel watched the car in every inch of its progress, his ears drinking in each change in its tune as it shifted gears, turned up Miss Annie's steep drive, and passed around the other side of her house. When finally he heard a rumbling crunch as the garage doors rolled shut, it seemed completely conclusive. With a leap that was almost kittenish, Joel galloped up the road.

But George Dallingham Smith had not left town. He had merely gone to the railroad station to send a telegram, a telegram so exultant and so personal that he had sent it in French. Then, overcome by the splendor of the day and his own private happiness, he had been seized with the idea of walking home and, almost bursting with a boyish eagerness to confide in someone, he stopped in to chat with his new friends, the Perriers.

One look at his face told Helen the whole story. The

merest hint on her part caused the honest old gentleman to babble forth the great news, and Perrier rushed to the house for champagne. The Paysons dropped in before it was properly iced and, as the presence of a bottle of champagne on the lawn in the middle of the afternoon was a thing that called for explanations, they also were shortly in possession of the truth. One good bottle called for another; George Dallingham Smith was presently elected a member in full standing of the ancient and honorable community of West Gosset; and even when, standing up with his glass in his hand, he made a speech beginning, "My dear, good friends . . ." and recited forty lines from *Lucille*, everybody cheered. Only when the party began to break up did Helen glance a little anxiously at the guest of honor and suggest tactfully to her husband:

"August, you haven't had a bit of exercise all day. Why don't you stroll up the road with Mr. Smith?"

The lift of her eyebrow was not lost on Perrier, and most genially he agreed; but Helen's precautions had been entirely unnecessary, for the two men had not walked a dozen steps when Perrier saw that George Dallingham's flush and a certain dampness of the eye were entirely due to honest sentiment and not to Sillery 1914. At Miss Annie's gate the younger man was quite ready to turn back, but the blissful Romeo would not hear of this for an instant.

"Oh, come on, come on, my dear boy, come up to the house," he insisted, the note of the proprietor already in his voice. "My blessed Annie will be delighted to see you. I told her I was going to tell the whole universe and you *must* say a word."

Linking his arm boisterously into Perrier's, he led the way up the path, then, suddenly overcome with natural confusion, he began to hesitate. On the piazza sat Miss Annie Craggs in her favorite straight-backed wicker chair, and at her feet was Joel.

"My dear——" began George Dallingham Smith, but at that moment Joel looked up. Before him he saw the human being he most despised on earth—and not only that, but arm-in-arm with a man whom, up to that moment, he had believed he could respect and trust.

"If it had only been any other dog," as Perrier said afterwards, "you might have known what to expect. Old Titus, for instance, would have leaped at his throat, and Charley . . . well, Charley would have ordered another bottle of champagne."

But this was not Titus, the crusty setter, nor was it Charley, the prince of mongrels and friend of the world. It was only Joel, the hermit shepherd, and, without a look, without a turn of his head, Joel rose to his feet and walked slowly away. Not many times in his life had Joel been called upon to express emotion, but he was certainly a master of sheer, cold contempt.

Half an hour later Perrier himself followed, and at his own gate he found his wife waiting. She asked but a single word:

"Well . . . ?"

Perrier laughed in a confused, unsettled sort of fashion. "From somewhere out of a pious youth," he answered, "I seem to remember a sermon I once heard on The Prodigal Son. 'And amidst all the feasting and rejoicing there was one who had no gladness in his heart, who did not.approve of the festivities and had no intention of taking part.' And you know," concluded Perrier, "it has always been the elder brother for whom I myself have had a sneaking sympathy."

"You have the gift of tongues," replied Helen, "but you still leave me hazy."

"It was Joel," explained Perrier. "He was there on the piazza when we arrived, and you ought to have seen his expression. He looked, he sniffed, and he folded his tents. Honestly, I thought he was going to hand me back his collar and license."

"Oh, the poor darling!" exclaimed Helen. "Where is he? We must find him at once."

Rapidly she led the way around the house and, of course, there was Joel, again on his hilltop, his head on his paws, his nose toward Miss Craggs's house and the setting sun. As Helen came up the slope he turned one lusterless eye and gave his tail one thump in the dust, but, with a manner she had never yet used to this queer gallumux, Helen lifted his head and held it in her lap.

"Poor Joel!" she said, "I know how you feel. But don't mind, old man. At any rate, *we* love you and you still have us."

"By Jove!" exclaimed Perrier, looking down at them. "You know, I don't believe that we really *could* have given him up."

Gently parting the big woolly ears, Helen leaned over and kissed the flat chinchilla spot on the top of Joel's head.

"There now," she said, as she rose to her feet, "perhaps you'd like to be left alone."

"At a time like this," agreed Perrier, only faintly smiling, "I imagine that one does not exactly want to chatter."

He slipped his arm through his wife's and they started down the hill, but, when they were a dozen steps away, again Joel lifted his head and looked thoughtfully after them. Then, probably, he did the strangest thing that he had yet done in his life. Slowly he rose to his feet and followed them—straight into the house.

Such as Walk in Darkness

In all the trade of the city you might not find such another quaint business firm as Solomon John and Billy Wigg. The senior partner was a gentle old giant; the junior a brisk and shaggy little dog. It was Solomon John's business to stand on a roaring corner and sell papers; it was Billy Wigg's business to take care of him while he did it, for he was blind. It was our business— Dr. Harvey's and mine—to pay for our papers and pass on, but we seldom strictly minded it. Instead, we would stop to talk to Solomon John, to the detriment of trade, and to be patronized by Billy Wigg, who was much puffed up with self-importance, conceiving himself to be principal owner of the earth and sole proprietor of Solomon John. In the half of which he was correct.

I was very fond of Billy Wigg, despite his airs of superiority. Harvey preferred old Solomon; but this was a semi-professional interest, for my medical friend had contracted the pamphlet habit, which he indulged before scientific bodies made up of gentlemen with weak eyes who knew more about ophthalmology than can be found in many fat tomes. Solomon John was a remarkable case of something quite unpronounceable, and Harvey used to gaze into his eyes with rapt intensity, while Billy Wigg fidgeted and struggled against the temptation to gnaw such portions of him as were within reach; for Billy Wigg didn't understand, and what he didn't understand he disapproved of on principle. In the light of subsequent events I believe Billy's uneasiness to have been an instance of animal prevision.

To see Billy Wigg conduct his master across that millrace of traffic that swirled between curb and curb, as he did every morning in time for business, was an artistic pleasure. Something more than a mere pilot was the dog; rather the rudder to whose accurate direction old Solomon responded with precise and prompt fidelity. A tug of the trouser leg from behind would bring the ancient newsboy to a halt. A gentle jerk forward would start him again, and in obedience to a steady pull to one side or the other he would trustingly suffer himself to be conducted around a checked wagon or a halted car. All the time Billy Wigg would keep up a running conversation made up of admonition, warning, and encouragement.

"Come on, now"—in a series of sharp yaps as they started from the curb. "Push right ahead. Hold hard. That's all right; it's by. Hurry now. Hurry, I said. *Will* you do as I tell you?" Then, to a too-pressing cabby, in an angry bark, "What's the matter with you, anyway? Trying to run folks down? Hey? Well"—apologetically, in response to a jerk on his string—"these fool drivers do stir me up. Wait a bit. Now for it. And here we are."

How many thousand times dog and man had made the trip in safety before the dire day of the accident not even Solomon John can reckon. Harvey and I had started downtown early, while our pair of paper-vending friends chanced to be a little late. As we reached the corner they were already halfway across the street, and Billy Wigg, with all the strength of terror, was striving to haul Solomon John backward.

"What's the matter with Billy?" said Harvey, for from the sidewalk we could not then see the cause of his excitement.

A second later the question was answered, as there plunged into view from behind a car the galloping horse of a derelict delivery wagon.

"Good heavens! Look at the old man," I cried, and in the same breath, "Look at the dog," gasped Harvey.

With one mighty jerk Billy Wigg had torn the leash from his master's hand. Bereft of his sole guidance in the thunder and rush of traffic, the blind man stretched

The blind man stretched out piteous hands.

out piteous hands, warding the death he could not see.

"Billy," he quavered, "where are you, Billy? Come back to me, Billy-dog."

For once Billy Wigg was deaf to his master's voice. He was obeying a more imperious call, that unfathomed nobility of dog-nature that responds so swiftly to the summons. He was casting his own life in the balance to save another's. Straight at the horse's throat he launched himself, a forlorn hope. It was a very big horse, and Billy was a very little dog. The upstroke of the knee caught him full; he was flung, whirling, fell almost under the wheels of a cab, rolled into the gutter, and lay there quiet. The horse had swerved a little, not quite enough. There was a scream, and the blind man went down from the glancing impact of the shoulder. Harvey and I were beside him almost as soon as the crosswalk policeman. The three of us carried him to the sidewalk.

"No need to call an ambulance, officer," said Harvey. "I'm a physician and the man is a friend of mine."

"Bedad, then, the dog is a friend of mine," said the big fellow. "Couldn't you take him along too, sir?"

"Well—rather," said Harvey heartily. "Where is he?" He turned to look for the dog.

Billy Wigg came crawling toward us. Never tell me that dogs have no souls. The eyes in Billy's shaggy little face yearned with a more than human passion of anxiety and love, as, gasping with pain—for he had been cruelly shaken—he dragged himself to his partner's face. At the touch of the warm, eager tongue, Solomon John's eyes opened. He stretched out his hand and buried it in the heavy fur.

"Hello, Billy," he said weakly. "I was afraid you were hurt. Are you all right, old boy?" And Billy, burrowing a wet nose in Solomon John's neck, wept for joy with loud whines.

Some rapid and expert wire-pulling on the part of Harvey landed our pair of friends in a private hospital, where Solomon John proved a most grateful and gentle patient, and Billy Wigg a most tumultuous one until arrangement was made for the firm to occupy one and the same cot. Then he became tractable, even enduring the indignity of a flannel jacket and splints with a sort of humorous tolerance. Every day Harvey came and gazed soulfully into Solomon John's glazed eyes—which is a curious form of treatment for a broken collar bone, not sanctioned by any of the authorities who have written on the subject. It soon became evident that Harvey didn't care anything about the rib; he had other designs. On a day he came to the point.

"Solomon John, would you like to have your sight back?"

The blind man sat up in his cot and pressed his hands to his head.

"Do you mean it, sir?" he gasped. "You—you

wouldn't go to fool an old man about such a thing?"

"Will you let me operate on you tomorrow?"

"Anything you think best, sir. I don't quite seem to take it all in yet, sir—not the whole sense of it. But if it does come out right," added Solomon John in the simplicity of his soul, "won't Billy Wigg be surprised and tickled!"

Billy Wigg raged mightily and rent the garments of his best friends, because he was shut out during the operation. When he was admitted after it was over he howled tumultuously, because Solomon John was racked with ether sickness, which he mistook for the throes of approaching dissolution. Followed then weeks during which Solomon John wore a white bandage, in place of the old green eye-shade, and at frequent intervals sang a solemn but joyous chant which Billy Wigg accompanied with impatient yelps, because he couldn't make out what it meant.

> *We're going to have our sight again,*
> *Billy Wigg, Billy Wigg:*
> *We're going to see the world again,*
> *Billy, my dog.*

It was a long, nerve-trying wait, but the day finally came when the white bandages were removed. After the first gasp of rapture, Solomon John looked about him eagerly.

"Let me see my dog," he said. "Billy, is this you?" as the junior partner looked with anxious and puzzled eyes into his face. "Well, you're certainly a mighty handsome doggy, old boy." (Billy Wigg was homelier than a stack of hay in January, but the eyes that looked on him were as those of a mother when she first sees her babe.)

Unhappiness was the portion of Billy in the days that followed. A partner who wandered about unchaperoned and eluded obstacles without relying on his sense of touch was quite beyond his comprehension. So he sulked consistently until the time came for leaving the hospital. Then he chirked up a bit, thinking, presumably, that Solomon John would resume his old habit of blind reliance upon him when once the doors had closed behind him. Poor Billy!

It was three weeks after the operation that he left, Solomon John being discharged as cured. Harvey exulted. He said it was a great operation and proved things. I thought, myself, it was a mean trick on Billy Wigg. My unprofessional diagnosis was that he was on the road to becoming a chronic melancholiac.

The partners called on Harvey soon after the departure from the hospital. They were a study in psychological antithesis; Solomon John bubbling over with boyish happiness, Billy Wigg aged with the weight of woe he was carrying. The old man was touchingly grateful, but his ally surreptitiously essayed to bite a piece out of Harvey's leg when his back was turned. He nursed an unavenged wrong.

Months passed before we saw the pair again. We returned from our European vacation confident of finding them on the same old corner, and sure enough, there they were. But as we approached Harvey seized me by the arm.

"Good heavens! Bob! Look at the old man!"

"What's wrong with him?" said I. "He looks just the same as he used to."

"Just the same as he used to," echoed Harvey bitterly. "Eyeshade and all. All my work gone for nothing. Poor old boy!"

"Billy Wigg's all right, anyway," said I, as that superior animal greeted us with every indication of excitement.

"Think so?" said Harvey. "It strikes me that it isn't exactly welcome that he's trying to express." Then in a louder voice to Solomon John, "How did it happen, old Sol?"

At the sound of his voice Solomon John whirled about and started to thrust up his shade, as if involuntarily. Then he held out tremulous hands, crying:

"What! Is that you, Dr. Harvey?" God bless you, sir! And is Mr. Roberts with you? Well, well, but this does me good. You're a sight for sore eyes!"

"Not for yours, Solomon John."

"And why not, then? Whist! I forgot," he broke off scaredly, jerking his head toward Billy Wigg, who held us all under jealous scrutiny. "Wait a breath."

Thrusting his hand into his pocket, he whipped it out suddenly. A flight of coins scattered and twinkled and rolled diversely on the sidewalk. "Dear, dear!" cried the old man cunningly. "The old fool that I am! I'll never be rich this way. Pick them up, Billy-boy."

Sure enough, there they were.

Billy hated it, for picking small coins from a smooth pavement with lip and tooth is no easy job; hated worse leaving his partner to two such unscrupulous characters as he well knew us to be. But he knew his business, and set about it with all his energies.

"Whisper now," said the senior partner as Billy swore under his breath at a slithery and elusive dime. "I've as fine a pair of eyes as you'd want for star-gazing at noon-day."

"Then what on earth—"

"Sh-h-h! Soft and easy! The beast's cocking his little ear this way. Sure 'twas all on his account, sirs."

"On Billy's account?" we both exclaimed in a breath.

"You didn't think I'd be faking it?" he asked re-proachfully.

We didn't; and we said so. But we required further enlightenment.

"All on account of Billy Wigg there, sirs. The eye-sight was a million blessings to me, but 'twas death to poor Billy. Not a pleasure in life would he take after we left the hospital. When I'd walk free and easy along the streets that looked so pretty to my old eyes, the dog'd be crazy with fear that some harm would come to me through him not leading me. At the last he just laid down and set out to die. He'd not sleep, he'd not eat; and the eyes of him when he'd look at me were fit to make a man weep. I sent for a dog doctor—you being away, sir," put in Solomon John in polite parenthesis to my friend. "He says, 'The dog's dying of a broken heart. I've seen it before,' he says. 'What'll I do?' says I. 'He'll not be content till you are as you were before,' says the dog doctor. It was a minute before I sensed what he meant. Then my heart got thick and sick inside me. 'Blind?' I says. 'Is that what you mean?' 'You old fool,' says the dog doctor, 'can't you do a bit of play-acting? You've had enough practice in the part,' he says.

"Over I went and got my stick and put on the old shade that I hadn't ever thought to use again, thanks to you, sir, and tap-tapped across the floor to Billy Wigg. 'Come on, Billy,' says I, 'I want you to take me out for a walk.' Billy jumped up with a kind of choky bark, and I hugged Billy and Billy hugged me, and—we've been doing business on the corner ever since."

There was a long pause. Harvey's expression was queer. I felt a little queer myself. It was a queer story, you know. Finally I asked the old man if business was good. Not that I particularly yearned to know, but it seemed to be time to say something.

"Nicely, sir, thank you," said Solomon John, "but I want to ask you, Is it a dishonesty, think you, for me to be wearing my shade like a blind man, and me able to see a flea on the end of Billy Wigg's tail the length of a block away? The Lord's been mighty good to me, sir—you and the Lord—giving me back my sight," said Solomon John simply, turning to Harvey, "and I wouldn't want to do anything that wasn't square."

"I wouldn't let it weigh on my mind," said Harvey.

"I'd been thinking of a bit of a sign," proceeded Solomon John. "A friend of mine printed it out for me, but the idea's my own."

After some fumbling under his coat he produced a placard artfully designed in large and flourishy letters. This was the order of it:

> I am NOT Blind
> but
> The Dog
> Thinks I Am.

Billy Wigg seemed pleased because Harvey kicked me. No doubt he would have been equally pleased if I had kicked Harvey. But it happened to be I who laughed. Harvey covered it up by soberly telling Solomon John that the sign was sure to be a grand success.

It was a grand success; quite stupendous, in fact. Old Solomon did a business on the strength of it that would have made his eyes pop out if he hadn't kept them tight shut out of respect to Billy's prejudices. Reporters found his simplicity and naïve honesty a mine of "good stuff," and the picture of the firm was in all the papers. Billy Wigg began to suffer from swelled head; became haughty, not to say snobbish. But the fierce light of publicity wore upon the simple soul of Solomon John. He discarded the extraordinary placard, and was glad when he faded away from fame. Billy wasn't. He liked notoriety as well as authority. Billy continued to exercise his authority. Perhaps tyranny would be nearer the mark. But even so meek a soul as Solomon John has limits of endurance beyond which it is not well to press. Only the other day it was that the old man said to Harvey, while Billy Wigg was otherwise engaged:

"It's as bad as being a henpecked husband, sir. Last night, as I was quietly stepping out the window to take a mug of ale with some friends, Billy wakes up, and the fuss he makes rouses the neighborhood. Sure, he wouldn't bark to my going at all. You can see his teeth marks on my shin this minute, sir. Could you give me something harmless to put in his food that'd make him sleep the sounder?"

Harvey said he'd think about it. He wasn't obliged to. Less than a week later he got a note in the mail:

"Dear Sir—I could not stand it any longer. I have Absconded to Buffalo to Take a Rest. Please be Good to Billy Wigg. I enclose his Board and Lodging any place you Put him. He is a good Dog, but too Bossy. I am Going to See Things till my Eyes get Tired. I will come Back in Future.

    "Yrs. respectfully,

        "SOLOMON J. BOLES.

"P.S.—I know you will Treat Billy Good."

The enclosure was a twenty-dollar bill. It was the price of freedom, and cheap at the price.

RUDYARD KIPLING

Garm—A Hostage

One night, a very long time ago, I drove to an Indian military encampment called Mian Mir to see amateur theatricals. At the back of the Infantry barracks a soldier, his cap over one eye, rushed in front of the horses and shouted that he was a dangerous highway robber. As a matter of fact, he was a friend of mine, so I told him to go home before any one caught him; but he fell under the pole, and I heard voices of a military guard in search of some one.

The driver and I coaxed him into the carriage, drove home swiftly, undressed him and put him to bed, where he waked next morning with a sore headache, very much ashamed. When his uniform was cleaned and dried, and he had been shaved and washed and made neat, I drove him back to barracks with his arm in a fine white sling, and reported that I had accidentally run over him. I did not tell this story to my friend's sergeant, who was a hostile and unbelieving person, but to his lieutenant, who did not know us quite so well.

Three days later my friend came to call, and at his heels slobbered and fawned one of the finest bull-terriers—of the old-fashioned breed, two parts bull and one terrier—that I had ever set eyes on. He was pure white, with a fawn-colored saddle just behind his neck,

Two parts bull and one terrier.

and a fawn diamond at the root of his thin whippy tail. I had admired him distantly for more than a year; and Vixen, my own fox-terrier, knew him too, but did not approve.

" 'E's for you," said my friend; but he did not look as though he liked parting with him.

"Nonsense! That dog's worth more than most men, Stanley," I said.

" 'E's that and more. 'Tention!"

The dog rose on his hind legs, and stood upright for a full minute.

"Eyes right!"

He sat on his haunches and turned his head sharp to the right. At a sign he rose and barked twice. Then he shook hands with his right paw and bounded lightly to my shoulder. Here he made himself into a necktie, limp and lifeless, hanging down on either side of my neck. I was told to pick him up and throw him in the air. He fell with a howl and held up one leg.

"Part o' the trick," said his owner. "You're going to die now. Dig yourself your little grave an' shut your little eye."

Still limping, the dog hobbled to the garden edge, dug a hole and lay down in it. When told that he was cured, he jumped out, wagging his tail, and whining for applause. He was put through half a dozen other tricks, such as showing how he would hold a man safe (I was that man, and he sat down before me, his teeth bared, ready to spring), and how he would stop eating at the word of command. I had no more than finished praising him when my friend made a gesture that stopped the dog as though he had been shot, took a piece of blue-ruled canteen-paper from his helmet, handed it to me and ran away, while the dog looked after him and howled. I read:

Sir—I give you the dog because of what you got me out of. He is the best I know, for I made him myself, and he is as good as a man. Please do not give him too much to eat, and please do not give him back to me, for I'm not going to take him, if you will keep him. So please do not try to give him back any more. I have kept his name back, so you can call him anything and he will answer, but please do not give him back. He can kill a man as easy as anything, but please do not give him too much meat. He knows more than a man.

Vixen sympathetically joined her shrill little yap to the bull-terrier's despairing cry, and I was annoyed, for I knew that a man who cares for dogs is one thing, but a man who loves one dog is quite another. Dogs are at the best no more than verminous vagrants, self-scratchers, foul feeders, and unclean by the law of Moses and Mohammed; but a dog with whom one lives alone for at least six months in the year; a free thing, tied to you so strictly by love that without you he will not stir or exercise; a patient, temperate, humorous, wise soul, who knows your moods before you know them yourself, is not a dog under any ruling.

I had Vixen, who was all my dog to me; and I felt what my friend must have felt, at tearing out his heart in this style and leaving it in my garden.

However, the dog understood clearly enough that I was his master, and did not follow the soldier. As soon as he drew breath I made much of him, and Vixen, yelling with jealousy, flew at him. Had she been of his own sex, he might have cheered himself with a fight, but he only looked worriedly when she nipped his deep iron sides, laid his heavy head on my knee, and howled anew. I meant to dine at the Club that night, but as darkness drew in, and the dog snuffed through the empty house like a child trying to recover from a fit of sobbing, I felt that I could not leave him to suffer his first evening alone. So we fed at home, Vixen on one side, and the stranger-dog on the other; she watching his every mouthful, and saying explicitly what she thought of his table manners, which were much better than hers.

It was Vixen's custom, till the weather grew hot, to sleep in my bed, her head on the pillow like a Christian; and when morning came I would always find that the little thing had braced her feet against the wall and pushed me to the very edge of the cot. This night she hurried to bed purposefully, every hair up, one eye on the stranger, who had dropped on a mat in a helpless, hopeless sort of way, all four feet spread out, sighing heavily. She settled her head on the pillow several times, to show her little airs and graces, and struck up her usual whiney sing-song before slumber. The stranger-dog softly edged towards me. I put out my hand and he licked it. Instantly my wrist was between Vixen's teeth, and her warning *aarh!* said as plainly as speech, that if I took any further notice of the stranger she would bite.

I caught her behind her fat neck with my left hand, shook her severely, and said:

"Vixen, if you do that again you'll be put into the veranda. Now, remember!"

She understood perfectly, but the minute I released her she mouthed my right wrist once more, and waited with her ears back and all her body flattened, ready to bite. The big dog's tail thumped the floor in a humble and peace-making way.

I grabbed Vixen a second time, lifted her out of bed like a rabbit (she hated that and yelled), and, as I had promised, set her out in the veranda with the bats and the moonlight. At this she howled. Then she used coarse language—not to me, but to the bull-terrier—till she coughed with exhaustion. Then she ran around the house trying every door. Then she went off to the stables and barked as though some one were stealing the horses, which was an old trick of hers. Last she returned, and her snuffing yelp said, "I'll be good! Let me in and I'll be good!"

She was admitted and flew to her pillow. When she was quieted I whispered to the other dog, "You can lie on the foot of the bed." The bull jumped up at once, and though I felt Vixen quiver with rage, she knew better than to protest. So we slept till the morning, and they had early breakfast with me, bite for bite, till the horse came round and we went for a ride. I don't think the bull had ever followed a horse before. He was wild with excitement, and Vixen, as usual, squealed and scuttered and sooted, and took charge of the procession.

There was one corner of a village near by, which we generally pass with caution, because all the yellow pariah-dogs of the place gathered about it. They were half-wild, starving beasts, and though utter cowards, yet where nine or ten of them get together they will mob and kill and eat an English dog. I kept a whip with a long lash for them. That morning they attacked Vixen, who, perhaps of design, had moved from beyond my horse's shadow.

The bull was ploughing along in the dust, fifty yards behind, rolling in his run, and smiling as bull terriers will. I heard Vixen squeal; half a dozen of the curs closed in on her; a white streak came up behind me; a cloud of dust rose near Vixen, and, when it cleared, I saw one tall pariah with his back broken, and the bull wrenching another to earth. Vixen retreated to the protection of my whip, and the bull padded back smiling more than ever, covered with the blood of his enemies. That decided me to call him "Garm of the Bloody Breast," who was a great person in his time, or "Garm" for short; so, leaning forward, I told him what his temporary name would be. He looked up while I re-

peated it, and then raced away. I shouted "Garm!" He
stopped, raced back, and came up to ask my will.

Then I saw that my soldier friend was right, and that
that dog knew and was worth more than a man. At the
end of the ridge I gave an order which Vixen knew and
hated: "Go away and get washed!" I said. Garm understood some part of it, and Vixen interpreted the
rest, and the two trotted off together soberly. When I
went to the back veranda Vixen had been washed
snowy-white, and was very proud of herself, but the
dog-boy would not touch Garm on any account unless
I stood by. So I waited while he was being scrubbed,
and Garm, with the soap creaming on the top of his
broad head, looked at me to make sure that this was
what I expected him to endure. He knew perfectly that
the dog-boy was only obeying orders.

"Another time," I said to the dog-boy, "you will
wash the great dog with Vixen when I send them
home."

"Does *he* know?" said the dog-boy, who understood
the ways of dogs.

"Garm," I said, "another time you will be washed
with Vixen."

I knew that Garm understood. Indeed, next wash-
ing-day, when Vixen as usual fled under my bed, Garm
stared at the doubtful dog-boy in the veranda, stalked
to the place where he had been washed last time, and
stood rigid in the tub.

But the long days in my office tried him sorely. We three would drive off in the morning at half-past eight and come home at six or later. Vixen, knowing the routine of it, went to sleep under my table; but the confinement ate into Garm's soul. He generally sat on the veranda looking out on the Mall; and well I knew what he expected.

Sometimes a company of soldiers would move along on their way to the Fort, and Garm rolled forth to inspect them; or an officer in uniform entered into the office, and it was pitiful to see poor Garm's welcome to the cloth—not the man. He would leap at him, and sniff and bark joyously, then run to the door and back again. One afternoon I heard him bay with a full throat —a thing I had never heard before—and he disappeared. When I drove into my garden at the end of the day a soldier in white uniform scrambled over the wall at the far end, and the Garm that met me was a joyous dog. This happened twice or thrice a week for a month.

I pretended not to notice, but Garm knew and Vixen knew. He would glide homewards from the office about four o'clock, as though he were only going to look at the scenery, and this he did so quietly that but for Vixen I should not have noticed him. The jealous little dog under the table would give a sniff and a snort, just loud enough to call my attention to the flight. Garm might go out forty times in the day and Vixen would never stir, but when he slunk off to see his true

A soldier scrambled over the wall.

master in my garden she told me in her own tongue. That was the one sign she made to prove that Garm did not altogether belong to the family. They were the best of friends at all times, *but*, Vixen explained that I was never to forget Garm did not love me as she loved me.

I never expected it. The dog was not my dog—could never be my dog—and I knew he was as miserable as his master who tramped eight miles a day to see him. So it seemed to me that the sooner the two were re-united the better for all. One afternoon I sent Vixen home alone in the dog-cart (Garm had gone before), and rode over to cantonments to find another friend of mine, who was an Irish soldier and a great friend of the dog's master.

I explained the whole case, and wound up with:

"And now Stanley's in my garden crying over his dog. Why doesn't he take him back? They're both unhappy."

"Unhappy! There's no sense in the little man any more. But 'tis his fit."

"What *is* his fit? He travels fifty miles a week to see the brute, and he pretends not to notice me when he sees me on the road; and I'm as unhappy as he is. Make him take the dog back."

"It's his penance he's set himself. I told him by way of a joke, afther you'd run over him so convenient that night, whin he was drunk—I said if he was a Catholic he'd do penance. Off he went wid that fit in his little head *an'* a dose of fever, an' nothin' would suit but givin' you the dog as a hostage."

"Hostage for what? I don't want hostages from Stanley."

"For his good behaviour. He's keepin' straight now, the way it's no pleasure to associate wid him."

"Has he taken the pledge?"

"If 'twas only that I need not care. Ye can take the pledge for three months on an' off. He sez he'll never see the dog again, an' *so* mark you, he'll keep straight for evermore. Ye know his fits? Well, this is wan of them. How's the dog takin' it?"

"Like a man. He's the best dog in India. Can't you make Stanley take him back?"

"I can do no more than I have done. But ye know his fits. He's just doin' his penance. What will he do when he goes to the Hills? The docthor's put him on the list."

It is the custom in India to send a certain number of invalids from each regiment up to stations in the Himalayas for the hot weather; and though the men ought to enjoy the cool and the comfort, they miss the society of the barracks down below, and do their best to come back or to avoid going. I felt that this move would bring matters to a head, so I left Terrence hopefully, though he called after me:

"He won't take the dog, sorr. You can lay your month's pay on that. Ye know his fits."

I never pretended to understand Private Ortheris;
and so I did the next best thing—I left him alone.

That summer the invalids of the regiment to which
my friend belonged were ordered off the Hills early,
because the doctors thought marching in the cool of
the day would do them good. Their route lay south to
a place called Umballa, a hundred and twenty miles or
more. Then they would turn east and march up into
the Hills to Kasauli or Dugshai or Subathoo. I dined
with the officers the night before they left—they were
marching at five in the morning. It was midnight when
I drove into my garden, and surprised a white figure
flying over the wall.

"That man," said my butler, "has been here since
nine, making talk to that dog. He is quite mad. I did
not tell him to go away because he has been here many
times before, and because the dog-boy told me that if
I told him to go away, that great dog would immediately slay me. He did not wish to speak to the Pro-
tector of the Poor, and he did not ask for anything to
eat or drink."

"Kadir Buksh," said I, "that was well done, for the
dog would surely have killed thee. But I do not think
the white soldier will come any more."

Garm slept ill that night and whimpered in his
dreams. Once he sprang up with a clear, ringing bark,
and I heard him wag his tail till it waked him and the
bark died out in a howl. He had dreamed he was with

his master again, and I nearly cried. It was all Stanley's silly fault.

The first halt which the detachment of invalids made was some miles from their barracks, on the Amritsar road, and ten miles distant from my house. By a mere chance one of the officers drove back for another good dinner at the Club (cooking on the line of march is always bad), and there we met. He was a particular friend of mine, and I knew that he knew how to love a dog properly. His pet was a big retriever who was going up to the Hills for his health, and, though it was still April, the round, brown brute puffed and panted in the Club veranda as though he would burst.

"It's amazing," said the officer, "what excuses these invalids of mine make to get back to barracks. There's a man in my company now asked me for leave to go back to cantonments to pay a debt he'd forgotten. I was so taken by the idea I let him go, and he jingled off in an *ekka* as pleased as Punch. Ten miles to pay a debt! Wonder what it was really?"

"If you'll drive me home I think I can show you," I said.

So he went over to my house in his dog-cart with the retriever; and on the way I told him the story of Garm.

"I was wondering where that brute had gone to. He's the best dog in the regiment," said my friend. "I offered the little fellow twenty rupees for him a month ago. But he's a hostage, you say, for Stanley's good conduct. Stanley's one of the best men I have—when he chooses."

"That's the reason why," I said. "A second-rate man wouldn't have taken things to heart as he has done."

We drove in quietly at the far end of the garden, and crept round the house. There was a place close to the wall all grown about with tamarisk trees, where I knew Garm kept his bones. Even Vixen was not allowed to sit near it. In the full Indian moonlight I could see a white uniform bending over the dog.

"Good-bye, old man," we could not help hearing Stanley's voice. "For 'Eving's sake don't get bit and go mad by any measley pi-dog. But you can look after yourself, old man. *You* don't get drunk an' run about 'ittin' your friends. You takes your bones an' eats your biscuit, an' kills your enemy like a gentleman. I'm goin' away—don't 'owl—I'm goin' off to Kasauli, where I won't see you no more."

I could hear him holding Garm's nose as the dog drew it up to the stars.

"You'll stay here an' be'ave, an'—an' I'll go away an' try to be'ave, an' I don't know 'ow to leave you. I don't think—"

"I think this is damn silly," said the officer, patting his foolish fubsy old retriever. He called to the private who leaped to his feet, marched forward, and saluted.

"You here?" said the officer, turning away his head.

"Yes, sir, but I'm just goin' back."

"I shall be leaving here at eleven in my cart. You come with me. I can't have sick men running about all over the place. Report yourself at eleven, *here*."

We did not say much when we went indoors, but the officer muttered and pulled his retriever's ears.

He was a disgraceful, overfed doormat of a dog; and when he waddled off to my cookhouse to be fed, I had a brilliant idea.

At eleven o'clock that officer's dog was nowhere to be found, and you never heard such a fuss as his owner made. He called and shouted and grew angry, and hunted through my garden for half an hour.

Then I said:

"He's sure to turn up in the morning. Send a man in by rail, and I'll find the beast and return him."

"Beast?" said the officer. "I value that dog considerably more than I value any man I know. It's all very fine for you to talk—your dog's here."

So she was—under my feet—and, had she been missing, food and wages would have stopped in my house till her return. But some people grow fond of dogs not worth a cut of the whip. My friend had to drive away at last with Stanley in the back seat; and then the dog-boy said to me:

"What kind of animal is Bullen Sahib's dog? Look at him!"

I went to the boy's hut, and the fat old reprobate was lying on a mat carefully chained up. He must have heard his master calling for twenty minutes, but had not even attempted to join him.

"He has no face," said the dog-boy scornfully. "He is a *punniar-kooter* [a spaniel]. He never tried to get that cloth off his jaws when his master called. Now Vixen-baba would have jumped through the window, and that Great Dog would have slain me with his muzzled mouth. It is true that there are many kinds of dogs."

Next evening who should turn up but Stanley. The officer had sent him back fourteen miles by rail with a note begging me to return the retriever if I had found him, and, if I had not, to offer huge rewards. The last train to camp left at half-past ten, and Stanely stayed till ten talking to Garm. I argued and entreated, and even threatened to shoot the bull-terrier, but the little man was firm as a rock, though I gave him a good dinner and talked to him most severely. Garm knew as well as I that this was the last time he could hope to see his man, and followed Stanley like a shadow. The retriever said nothing, but licked his lips after his meal and waddled off without so much as saying "Thank you" to the disgusted dog-boy.

So that last meeting was over, and I felt as wretched as Garm, who moaned in his sleep all night. When we went to the office he found a place under the table close to Vixen, and dropped flat till it was time to go home. There was no more running out into the verandas, no slinking away for stolen talks with Stanley. As the weather grew warmer the dogs were forbidden to run beside the cart, but sat at my side on the seat. Vixen with her head under the crook of my left elbow, and Garm hugging the left handrail.

Here Vixen was ever in great form. She had to attend to all the moving traffic, such as bullock-carts that blocked the way, and camels, and led ponies; as well as to keep up her dignity when she passed low friends running in the dust. She never yapped for yapping's sake, but her shrill, high bark was known all along the Mall, and other men's terriers ki-yied in reply, and bullock-drivers looked over their shoulders and gave us the road with a grin.

But Garm cared for none of these things. His big eyes were on the horizon and his terrible mouth was shut. There was another dog in the office who belonged to my chief. We called him "Bob the Librarian," because he always imagined vain rats behind the bookshelves, and in hunting for them would drag out half the old newspaper-files. Bob was a well-meaning idiot, but Garm did not encourage him. He would slide his head round the door panting, "Rats! Come along, Garm!" and Garm would shift one forepaw over the other, and curl himself round, leaving Bob to whine at a most uninterested back. The office was nearly as cheerful as a tomb in those days.

Once, and only once, did I see Garm at all contented

with his surroundings. He had gone for an unauthorized walk with Vixen early one Sunday morning, and a very young and foolish artilleryman (his battery had just moved to that part of the world) tried to steal both. Vixen, of course, knew better than to take food from soldiers, and, besides, she had just finished her breakfast. So she trotted back with a large piece of the mutton that they issue to our troops, laid it down on my veranda, and looked up to see what I thought. I asked her where Garm was, and she ran in front of the house to show me the way.

About a mile up the road we came across our artilleryman sitting very stiffly on the edge of a culvert with a greasy handkerchief on his knees. Garm was in front of him, looking rather pleased. When the man moved leg or hand, Garm bared his teeth in silence. A broken string hung from his collar, and the other half of it lay, all warm, in the artilleryman's still hand. He explained to me, keeping his eye straight in front of him, that he had met this dog (he called him awful names) walking alone, and was going to take him to the Fort to be killed for a masterless pariah.

I said that Garm did not seem to me much of a pariah, but that he had better take him to the Fort if he thought best. He said he did not care to do so. I told him to go to the Fort alone. He said he did not want to go at that hour, but would follow my advice as soon as I had called off the dog. I instructed Garm to take

him to the Fort, and Garm marched him solemnly up
to the gate, one mile and a half under a hot sun, and I
told the quarter-guard what had happened; but the
young artilleryman was more angry than was at all necessary when they began to laugh. Several regiments,
he was told, had tried to steal Garm in their time.

That month the hot weather shut down in earnest,
and the dogs slept in the bathroom on the cool wet
bricks where the bath is placed. Every morning, as
soon as the man filled my bath, the two jumped in, and
every morning the man filled the bath a second time. I
said to him that he might as well fill a small tub especially for the dogs. "Nay," said he smiling, "it is not
their custom. They would not understand. Besides, the
big bath gives them more space."

The punkah-coolies who pull the punkahs day and
night came to know Garm intimately. He noticed that
when the swaying fan stopped I would call out to the
coolie and bid him pull with a long stroke. If the man
still slept I would wake him up. He discovered, too,
that it was a good thing to lie in the wave of air under
the punkah. Maybe Stanley had taught him all about
this in barracks. At any rate, when the punkah stopped,
Garm would first growl and cock his eye at the rope,
and if that did not wake the man—it nearly always did
—he would tiptoe forth and talk in the sleeper's ear.
Vixen was a clever little dog, but she could never con-
nect the punkah and the coolie; so Garm gave me

grateful hours of cool sleep. But he was utterly wretched—as miserable as a human being; and in his misery he clung so close to me that other men noticed it, and were envious. If I moved from one room to another Garm followed; if my pen stopped scratching, Garm's head was thrust into my hand; if I turned, half awake, on the pillow, Garm was up at my side, for he knew that I was his only link with his master, and day and night, and night and day, his eyes asked one question—"When is this going to end?"

Living with the dog as I did, I never noticed that he was more than ordinarily upset by the hot weather, till one day at the Club a man said: "That dog of yours will die in a week or two. He's a shadow." Then I dosed Garm with iron and quinine, which he hated; and I felt very anxious. He lost his appetite, and Vixen was allowed to eat his dinner under his eyes. Even that did not make him swallow, and we held a consultation on him, of the best man-doctor in the place, a lady-doctor, who had cured the sick wives of kings; and the Deputy Inspector-General of the veterinary service of all India. They pronounced upon his symptoms, and I told them his story, and Garm lay on a sofa licking my hand.

"He's dying of a broken heart," said the lady-doctor suddenly.

" 'Pon my word," said the Deputy Inspector-General, "I believe Mrs. Macrae is perfectly right—as usual."

The best man-doctor in the place wrote a prescription, and the veterinary Deputy Inspector-General went over it afterwards to be sure that the drugs were in the proper dog-proportions; and that was the first time in his life that our doctor ever allowed his prescriptions to be edited. It was a strong tonic, and it put the dear boy on his feet for a week or two; then he lost flesh again. I asked a man I knew to take him up to the Hills with him when he went, and the man came to the door with his kit packed on the top of the carriage. Garm took in the situation at one red glance. The hair rose along his back; he sat down in front of me, and delivered the most awful growl I have ever heard in the jaws of a dog. I shouted to my friend to get away at once, and as soon as the carriage was out of the garden Garm laid his head on my knee and whined. So I know his answer, and devoted myself to getting Stanley's address in the Hills.

My turn to go to the cool came late in August. We were allowed thirty days' holiday in a year, if no one fell sick, and we took it as we could be spared. My chief and Bob the Librarian had their holiday first, and when they were gone I made a calendar, as I always did, and hung it up at the head of my cot, tearing off one day at a time till they returned. Vixen had gone up to the Hills with me five times before; and she appreciated the cold and the damp and the beautiful wood fires there as much as I did.

"Garm," I said, "we are going back to Stanley at Kasauli. Kasauli—Stanley; Stanley—Kasauli." And I repeated it twenty times. It was not Kasauli really, but another place. Still I remembered what Stanley had said in my garden on the last night, and I dared not change the name. Then Garm began to tremble; then he barked; and then he leaped up at me, frisking and wagging his tail.

"Not now," I said, holding up my hand. "When I say 'Go,' we'll go, Garm." I pulled out the little blanket coat and spiked collar that Vixen always wore up in the Hills to protect her against sudden chills and thieving leopards, and I let the two smell them and talk it over. What they said of course I do not know, but it made a new dog of Garm. His eyes were bright; and he barked joyfully when I spoke to him. He ate his food, and he killed his rats for the next three weeks, and when he began to whine I had only to say "Stanley—Kasauli; Kasauli—Stanley," to wake him up. I wish I had thought of it before.

My chief came back, all brown with living in the open air, and very angry at finding it so hot in the Plains. That same afternoon we three and Kadir Buksh began to pack for our month's holiday, Vixen rolling in and out of the bullock-trunk twenty times a minute, and Garm grinning all over and thumping on the floor with his tail. Vixen knew the routine of travelling as well as she knew my office-work. She went to the station, singing songs, on the front seat of the carriage, while Garm sat with me. She hurried into the railway carriage, saw Kadir Buksh make up my bed for the night, got her drink of water, and curled up with her black-patch eye on the tumult of the platform. Garm followed her (the crowd gave him a lane all to himself) and sat down on the pillows with his eyes blazing, and his tail a haze behind him.

We came to Umballa in the hot misty dawn, four or five men, who had been working hard for eleven months, shouting for our dâks—the two-horse travelling carriages that were to take us up to Kalka at the foot of the Hills. It was all new to Garm. He did not understand carriages where you lay at full length on your bedding, but Vixen knew and hopped into her place at once; Garm following. The Kalka road, before the railway was built, was about forty-seven miles long, and the horses were changed every eight miles. Most of them jibbed, and kicked, and plunged, but they had to go, and they went rather better than usual for Garm's deep bay in their rear.

There was a river to be forded, and four bullocks pulled the carriage, and Vixen stuck her head out of the sliding-door and nearly fell into the water while she gave directions. Garm was silent and curious, and rather needed reassuring about Stanley and Kasauli. So we rolled, barking and yelping, into Kalka for lunch, and Garm ate enough for two.

The road wound among the Hills.

After Kalka the road wound among the Hills, and we took a curricle with half-broken ponies, which were changed every six miles. No one dreamed of a railroad to Simla in those days, for it was seven thousand feet up in the air. The road was more than fifty miles long, and the regulation pace was just as fast as the ponies could go. Here, again, Vixen led Garm from one carriage to the other; jumped into the back seat and shouted. A cool breath from the snows met us about five miles out of Kalka, and she whined for her coat, wisely fearing a chill on the liver. I had had one made for Garm too, and, as we climbed to the fresh breezes, I put it on, and Garm chewed it uncomprehendingly, but I think he was grateful.

"Hi-ye-ye-ye!" sang Vixen as we shot around the curves; "Toot-toot-toot!" went the driver's bugle at the dangerous places, and "Yow! Yow! Yow! Yow!" bayed Garm. Kadir Buksh sat on the front seat and smiled. Even he was glad to get away from the heat of the Plains that stewed in the haze behind us. Now and then we would meet a man we knew going down to his work again, and he would say: "What's it like below?" and I would shout: "Hotter than cinders. What's it like above?" and he would shout back: "Just perfect!" and away we would go.

Suddenly Kadir Buksh said, over his shoulder: "Here is Solon"; and Garm snored where he lay with his head on my knee. Solon is an unpleasant little cantonment, but it has the advantage of being cool and healthy. It is all bare and windy, and one generally stops at a rest-house near by for something to eat. I got out and took both dogs with me, while Kadir Buksh made tea. A soldier told us we should find Stanley "out there," nodding his head towards a bare, bleak hill.

When we climbed to the top we spied that very Stanley, who had given me all this trouble, sitting on a rock with his face in his hands, and his overcoat hanging loose about him. I never saw anything so lonely and dejected in my life as this one little man, crumpled up and thinking, on the great gray hillside.

Here Garm left me.

He departed without a word, and, so far as I could see, without moving his legs. He flew through the air bodily, and I heard the whack of him as he flung himself at Stanley, knocking the little man clean over. They rolled on the ground together, shouting, and yelping, and hugging. I could not see which was dog and which was man, till Stanley got up and whimpered.

He told me that he had been suffering from fever at intervals, and was very weak. He looked all he said, but even while I watched, both man and dog plumped out to their natural sizes, precisely as dried apples swell in water. Garm was on his shoulder, and his breast and feet all at the same time, so that Stanley spoke all through a cloud of Garm—gulping, sobbing, slavering Garm. He did not say anything that I could understand, except that he had fancied he was going to die, but that now he was quite well, and that he was not going to give up Garm any more to anybody under the rank of Beelzebub.

Then he said he felt hungry, and thirsty, and happy.

We went down to tea at the rest-house, where Stanley stuffed himself with sardines and raspberry jam, and beer, and cold mutton and pickles, when Garm wasn't climbing over him; and then Vixen and I went on.

Garm saw how it was at once. He said good-bye to me three times, giving me both paws one after another, and leaping on to my shoulder. He further escorted us, singing Hosannas at the top of his voice, a mile down the road. Then he raced back to his own master.

Vixen never opened her mouth, but when the cold twilight came, and we could see the lights of Sumla across the hills, she snuffled with her nose at the breast of my ulster. I unbuttoned it, and tucked her inside. Then she gave a contented little sniff, and fell fast asleep, her head on my breast, till we bundled out of Simla, two of the four happiest people in all the world that night.

ERNEST THOMPSON SETON

Snap:
The Story of a Bull Terrier

I

It was dusk on Halloween when first I saw him. Early in the morning I had received a telegram from my college chum Jack: "LEST WE FORGET. AM SENDING YOU A REMARKABLE PUP. BE POLITE TO HIM; IT'S SAFER." It would have been just like Jack to have sent an infernal machine or a skunk rampant and called it a pup, so I awaited the hamper with curiosity. When it arrived I saw it was marked "Dangerous," and there came from within a high-pitched snarl at every slight provocation. On peering through the wire netting I saw it was not a baby tiger but a small white bull terrier.

He snapped at me and at anyone or anything that seemed too abrupt or too near for proper respect, and his snarling growl was unpleasantly frequent. Dogs have two growls: one deep-rumbled and chesty; that is polite warning—the retort courteous; the other mouthy and

much higher in pitch: this is the last word before actual
onslaught. The terrier's growls were all of the latter kind.
I was a dog man and thought I knew all about dogs, so,
dismissing the porter, I got out my all-round jackknife-
toothpick-nail-hammer-hatchet-toolbox-fire-shovel, a spe-
cialty of our firm, and lifted the netting.

Oh, yes, I knew all about dogs. The little fury had
been growling out a whole-souled growl for every tap of
the tool, and when I turned the box on its side, he made
a dash straight for my legs. Had not his foot gone
through the wire netting and held him, I might have
been hurt, for his heart was evidently in his work; but I
stepped on the table out of reach and tried to reason with
him. I have always believed in talking to animals. I
maintain that they gather something of our intention
at least, even if they do not understand our words; but
the dog evidently put me down for a hypocrite and
scorned my approaches. At first he took his post under
the table and kept up a circular watch for a leg trying to get down. I felt sure I could have controlled him
with my eye, but I could not bring it to bear where I
was, or rather where he was; thus I was left a prisoner.

I am a very cool person, I flatter myself; in fact, I rep-
resent a hardware firm, and, in coolness, we are not ex-
celled by any but perhaps the nosy gentlemen that sell
wearing apparel. I got out a cigar and smoked tailor
style on the table, while my little tyrant below kept
watch for legs. I got out the telegram and read it:

"Remarkable pup. Be polite to him; it's safer." I think
it was my coolness rather than my politeness that did
it, for in half an hour the growling ceased. In an hour
he no longer jumped at a newspaper cautiously pushed
over the edge to test his humor; possibly the irritation
of the cage was wearing off, and by the time I had lit
my third cigar, he waddled out to the fire and lay down;
not ignoring me, however, I had no reason to complain
of that kind of contempt. He kept one eye on me, and
I kept both eyes, not on him, but on his stumpy tail. If
that tail should swing sidewise once, I should feel I
was winning; but it did not swing. I got a book and put
in time on that table till my legs were cramped and
the fire burned low.

About 10 P.M. it was chilly, and at half-past ten the
fire was out. My Halloween present got up, yawned and
stretched, then walked under my bed, where he found a
fur rug. By stepping lightly from the table to the dresser,
and then on to the mantel shelf, I also reached bed, and,
very quietly undressing, got in without provoking any
criticism from my master. I had not yet fallen asleep
when I heard a slight scrambling and felt "thump-
thump" on the bed, then over my feet and legs; Snap
evidently had found it too cool down below, and pro-
posed to have the best my house afforded.

He curled up on my feet in such a way that I was
very uncomfortable and tried to readjust matters, but
the slightest wriggle of my toe was enough to make him

snap at it so fiercely that nothing but thick woolen bedclothes saved me from being maimed for life.

I was an hour moving my feet—a hair's-breadth at a time—till they were so that I could sleep in comfort; and I was awakened several times during the night by angry snarls from the dog—I suppose because I dared to move a toe without his approval, though once I believe he did it simply because I was snoring.

In the morning I was ready to get up before Snap was. You see, I call him Snap—Gingersnap in full. Some dogs are hard to name, and some do not seem to need it—they name themselves.

I was ready to rise at seven. Snap was not ready till eight, so we rose at eight. He had little to say to the man who made the fire. He allowed me to dress without doing it on the table. As I left the room to get breakfast, I remarked:

"Snap, my friend, some men would whip you into a different way, but I think I know a better plan. The doctors nowadays favor the 'no-breakfast cure.' I shall try that."

It seemed cruel, but I left him without food all day. It cost me something to repaint the door where he scratched it, but at night he was quite ready to accept a little food at my hands.

In a week we were very good friends. He would sleep on my bed now and allow me to move my feet without snapping at them. The no-breakfast cure had worked

wonders; in three months we were—well, simply man
and dog, and he amply justified the telegram he came
with.

He seemed to be without fear. If a small dog came
near, he would take not the slightest notice; if a me-
dium-sized dog, he would stick his stub of a tail rigidly
up in the air, then walk around him, scratching contemptuously with his hind feet, and looking at the sky,
the distance, the ground, anything but the dog, and
noting his presence only by frequent high-pitched
growls. If the stranger did not move on at once, the
battle began, and then the stranger usually moved on
very rapidly. Snap sometimes got worsted, but no
amount of sad experience could ever inspire him with a
grain of caution. Once, while riding in a cab during the
dog show, Snap caught sight of an elephantine St. Bernard taking an airing. Its size aroused such enthusiasm
in the pup's little breast that he leaped from the cab
window to do battle, and broke his leg.

Evidently fear had been left out of his make-up and
its place supplied with an extra amount of ginger, which
was the reason of his full name. He differed from all
other dogs I have ever known. For example, if a boy
threw a stone at him, he ran, not away, but toward the
boy, and if the crime was repeated, Snap took the law
into his own hands; thus he was at least respected by
all. Only myself and the porter at the office seemed to
realize his good points, and we only were admitted to

the high honor of personal friendship, an honor which I appreciated more as months went on, and by midsummer not Carnegie, Vanderbilt, and Astor together could have raised money enough to buy a quarter of a share in my little dog Snap.

II

Though not a regular traveler, I was ordered out on the road in the autumn, and then Snap and the landlady were left together, with unfortunate developments. Contempt on his part—fear on hers; and hate on both.

I was placing a lot of barb-wire in the northern tier of States. My letters were forwarded once a week, and I got several complaints from the landlady about Snap.

Arrived at Mendoza, in North Dakota, I found a fine market for wire. Of course my dealings were with the big storekeepers, but I went about among the ranchmen to get their practical views on the different styles, and thus I met the Penroof brothers' cow outfit.

One cannot belong in cow country now without hearing a great deal about the depredations of the ever wily and destructive gray wolf. The day has gone by when they can be poisoned wholesale, and they are a serious drain on the rancher's profits. The Penroof brothers, like most live cattlemen, had given up all attempts at poisoning and trapping, and were trying various breeds of dogs as wolf hunters, hoping to get a little sport out of the necessary work of destroying the pests.

Foxhounds had failed—they were too soft for fighting; great Danes were too clumsy, and greyhounds could not follow the game unless they could see it. Each breed had some fatal defect, but the cowmen hoped to succeed with a mixed pack, and the day when I was invited to join in a Mendoza wolf hunt, I was amused by the variety of dogs that followed. There were several mongrels, but there were also a few highly bred dogs —in particular, some Russian wolfhounds that must have cost a lot of money.

Hilton Penroof, the oldest boy, "the Master of Hounds," was unusually proud of them, and expected them to do great things.

"Greyhounds are too thin-skinned to fight a wolf, Danes are too slow, but you'll see the fur fly when the Russians take a hand."

Thus the greyhounds were there as runners, the Danes as heavy backers, and the Russians to do the important fighting. There were also two or three foxhounds, whose fine noses were relied on to follow the trail if the game got out of view.

It was a fine sight as we rode away among the Badland Buttes that October day. The air was bright and crisp, and though so late, there was neither snow nor frost. The horses were fresh, and once or twice showed me how a cow pony tries to get rid of his rider.

The dogs were keen for sport, and we did start one or two gray spots in the plain that Hilton said were wolves or coyotes. The dogs trailed away at full cry, but at night, beyond the fact that one of the greyhounds had a wound on his shoulder, there was nothing to show that any of them had been on a wolf hunt.

"It's my opinion yer fancy Russians is no good, Hilt," said Garvin, the younger brother. "I'll back that little black Dane against the lot, mongrel an' all as he is."

"I don't unnerstan' it," growled Hilton. "There ain't a coyote, let alone a gray wolf, kin run away from them greyhounds; them foxhounds kin folly a trail three days old, an' the Danes could lick a grizzly."

"I reckon," said the father, "they kin run, an' they kin track, an' they kin lick a grizzly, *maybe*, but the fac' is they don't want to tackle a gray wolf. The hull darn pack is scairt—an' I wish we had our money out o' them."

Thus the men grumbled and discussed as I drove away and left them.

There seemed only one solution of the failure. The hounds were swift and strong, but a gray wolf seems to terrorize all dogs. They have not the nerve to face him, and so each time he gets away, and my thoughts flew back to the fearless little dog that had shared my bed for the last year. How I wished he was out here, then these lubberly giants of hounds would find a leader whose nerve would not fail at the moment of trial.

At Baroka, my next stop, I got a batch of mail including two letters from the landlady; the first to say that "that beast of a dog was acting up scandalous in my room," and the other still more forcible, demanding his immediate removal.

"Why not have him expressed to Mendoza?" I thought. "It's only twenty hours; they'll be glad to have him. I can take him home with me when I go through."

III

My next meeting with Gingersnap was not as different from the first as one might have expected. He jumped on me, made much vigorous pretense to bite, and growled frequently, but it was a deep-chested growl and his stump waggled hard.

The Penroofs had had a number of wolf hunts since I was with them, and were much disgusted at having no better success than before. The dogs could find a wolf nearly every time they went out, but they could not kill him, and the men were not near enough at the finish to learn why.

Old Penroof was satisfied that "thar wasn't one of the hull miserable gang that had the grit of a jack rabbit."

We were off at dawn the next day—the same procession of fine horses and superb riders; the big blue dogs, the yellow dogs, the spotted dogs, as before; but there was a new feature, a little white dog that stayed close by me, and not only any dogs, but horses that came too near were apt to get a surprise from his teeth. I think he quarreled with every man, horse, and dog in the country, with the exception of a bull terrier belonging to the Mendoza hotel man. She was the only one

A little white dog stayed close by me.

smaller than himself, and they seemed very good friends.

I shall never forget the view of the hunt I had that day. We were on one of those large, flat-headed buttes that give a kingdom to the eye, when Hilton, who had been scanning the vast country with glasses, exclaimed:

"I see him. There he goes, toward Skull Creek. Guess it's a coyote."

Now the first thing is to get the greyhounds to see the prey—not an easy matter, as they cannot use the glasses, and the ground was covered with sagebrush higher than the dogs' heads.

But Hilton called, "Hu, hu, Dander," and leaned aside from his saddle, holding out his foot at the same time. With one agile bound Dander leaped to the saddle and there stood balancing on the horse while Hilton kept pointing. "There he is, Dander; sic him—see him down there." The dog gazed earnestly where his master pointed, then seeming to see, he sprang to the ground with a slight yelp and sped away. The other dogs followed after, in an ever-lengthening procession, and we rode as hard as we could behind them, but losing time, for the ground was cut with gullies, spotted with badger holes, and covered with rocks and sage that made full speed too hazardous.

We all fell behind, and I was last, of course, being least accustomed to the saddle. We got several glimpses of the dogs flying over the level plain or dropping from sight in gullies to reappear at the other side. Dander, the greyhound, was the recognized leader, and as we mounted another ridge we got sight of the whole chase —a coyote at full speed, the dogs a quarter of a mile behind, but gaining. When next we saw them the coy-

We rode as hard as we could behind them.

ote was dead, and the dogs sitting around panting, all but two of the foxhounds and Gingersnap.

"Too late for the fracas," remarked Hilton, glancing at these last foxhounds. Then he proudly petted Dander. "Didn't need yer purp after all, ye see."

"Takes a heap of nerve for ten big dogs to face one little coyote," remarked the father sarcastically. "Wait till we run onto a Gray."

Next day we were out again, for I made up my mind to see it to a finish.

From a high point we caught sight of a moving speck of gray. A moving white speck stands for antelope, a red speck for fox, a gray speck for either gray wolf or coyote, and which of these is determined by its tail. If the glass shows the tail down, it is a coyote; if up, it is the hated gray wolf.

Dander was shown the game as before and led the motley mixed procession—as he had before—greyhounds, wolfhounds, foxhounds, Danes, bull terrier, horsemen. We got a momentary view of the pursuit; a gray wolf it surely was, loping away ahead of the dogs. Somehow I thought the first dogs were not running so fast now as they had after the coyote. But no one knew the finish of the hunt. The dogs came back to us one by one, and we saw no more of that wolf.

Sarcastic remarks and recrimination were now freely indulged in by the hunters.

"Pah! scairt, plumb scairt," was the father's disgusted

comment on the pack. "They could catch up easy enough, but when he turned on them, they lighted out for home—pah!"

"Where's that thar onsurpassable, fearless, scaired-o'-nort tarrier?" asked Hilton scornfully.

"I don't know," said I. "I am inclined to think he never saw the wolf; but if he ever does, I'll bet he sails in for death or glory."

That night several cows were killed close to the ranch, and we were spurred on to another hunt.

It opened much like the last. Late in the afternoon we sighted a gray fellow with tail up, not half a mile off. Hilton called Dander up on the saddle. I acted on the idea and called Snap to mine. His legs were so short that he had to leap several times before he made it, scrambling up at last with my foot as a halfway station. I pointed and "sic-ed" for a minute before he saw the game, and then he started out after the greyhounds, already gone, with energy that was full of promise.

The chase this time led us, not to the rough brakes along the river, but toward the high open country, for reasons that appeared later. We were close together as we rose to the upland and sighted the chase half a mile off, just as Dander came up with the wolf and snapped at his haunch. The gray wolf turned round to fight, and we had a fine view. The dogs came up by twos and threes, barking at him in a ring, till last the little white one rushed up. He wasted no time barking, but rushed straight at the wolf's throat and missed it, yet seemed to get him by the nose; then the ten big dogs closed in, and in two minutes the wolf was dead. We had ridden hard to be in at the finish, and though our view was distant, we saw at least that Snap had lived up to the telegram, as well as to my promises for him.

Now it was my turn to crow, and I did not lose the chance. Snap had shown them how, and at last the Mendoza pack had killed a gray wolf without help from the men.

There were two things to mar the victory somewhat: first, it was a young wolf, a mere cub, hence his foolish choice of country; second, Snap was wounded—the wolf had given him a bad cut in the shoulder.

As we rode in proud procession home, I saw he limped a little. "Here," I cried, "come up, Snap." He tried once or twice to jump to the saddle, but could not. "Here, Hilton, lift him up to me."

"Thanks; I'll let you handle your own rattlesnakes," was the reply, for all knew now that it was not safe to meddle with his person. "Here, Snap, take hold," I said, and held my quirt to him. He seized it, and by that I lifted him to the front of my saddle and so carried him home. I cared for him as though he had been a baby. He had shown those cattlemen how to fill the weak place in their pack; the foxhounds may be good and the greyhounds swift and the Russians and Danes fighters, but they are no use at all without the crown-

He rushed straight at the wolf's throat.

ing moral force of grit, that none can supply so well as
a bull terrier. On that day the cattlemen learned how
to manage the wolf question, as you will find if ever
you are at Mendoza; for every successful wolf pack there
has with it a bull terrier, preferably of the Snap-Men-
doza breed.

IV

Next day was Halloween, the anniversary of
Snap's advent. The weather was clear, bright, not too
cold, and there was no snow on the ground. The men
usually celebrated the day with a hunt of some sort,
and now, of course, wolves were the one object. To the
disappointment of all, Snap was in bad shape with his
wound. He slept, as usual, at my feet, and bloody stains
now marked the place. He was not in condition to fight,
but we were bound to have a wolf hunt, so he was be-
guiled to an outhouse and locked up, while we went
off, I, at least, with a sense of impending disaster. I
knew we should fail without my dog, but I did not realize how bad a failure it was to be.

Afar among the buttes of Skull Creek we had roamed
when a white ball appeared bounding through the sagebrush, and in a minute more Snap came, growing and
stump-waggling, up to my horse's side. I could not send
him back; he would take no such orders, not even from

me. His wound was looking bad, so I called him, held down the quirt, and jumped him to my saddle.

"There," I thought, "I'll keep you safe till we get home." Yes, I thought; but I reckoned not with Snap. The voice of Hilton, "Hu, hu," announced that he had sighted a wolf. Dander and Riley, his rival, both sprang to the point of observation, with the result that they collided and fell together, sprawling, in the sage. But Snap, gazing hard, had sighted the wolf, not so very far off, and before I knew it, he leaped from the saddle and bounded zigzag, high, low, in and under the sage, straight for the enemy, leading the whole pack for a few minutes. Not far, of course. The great greyhounds sighted the moving speck, and the usual procession strung out on the plain. It promised to be a fine hunt, for the wolf had less than half a mile start and all the dogs were fully interested.

"They've turned up Grizzly Gully," cried Garvin. "This way, and we can head them off."

So we turned and rode hard around the north side of Hulmer's Butte, while the chase seemed to go round the south.

We galloped to the top of Cedar Ridge and were about to ride down, when Hilton shouted, "By George, here he is! We're right onto him." He leaped from his horse, dropped the bridle, and ran forward. I did the same. A great gray wolf came lumbering across an open

plain toward us. His head was low, his tail out level, and
fifty yards behind him was Dander, sailing like a hawk
over the ground, going twice as fast as the wolf. In a
minute the hound was alongside and snapped, but
bounded back, as the wolf turned on him. They were
just below us now and not fifty feet away. Garvin
drew his revolver, but in a fateful moment Hilton in-
terfered: "No; no; let's see it out." In a few seconds
the next greyhound arrived, then the rest in order of
swiftness. Each came up full of fight and fury, determined to go right in and tear the gray wolf to pieces;
but each in turn swerved aside, and leaped and barked
around at a safe distance. After a minute or so the Russians appeared—fine big dogs they were. Their distant
intention no doubt was to dash right at the old wolf;
but his fearless front, his sinewy frame and death-deal-
ing jaws, awed them long before they were near him,
and they also joined the ring, while the desperado in
the middle faced this way and that, ready for any or
all.

Now the Danes came up, huge-limbed creatures, any
one of them as heavy as the wolf. I heard their heavy
breathing tighten into a threatening sound as they
plunged ahead, eager to tear the foe to pieces; but when
they saw him there, grim, fearless, mighty of jaw,
tireless of limb, ready to die if need be, but sure of this,
he would not die alone—well, those great Danes—all

three of them—were stricken, as the rest had been, with a sudden bashfulness: yes, they would go right in presently—not now, but as soon as they had got their breath; they were not afraid of a wolf, oh, no. I could read their courage in their voices. They knew perfectly well that the first dog to go in was going to get hurt, but never mind that—presently; they would bark a little more to get up enthusiasm.

And as the ten big dogs were leaping round the silent wolf at bay, there was a rustling in the sage at the far side of the place; then a snow-white rubber ball, it seemed, came bounding, but grew into a little bull terrier, and Snap, slowest of the pack, and last, came panting hard, so hard he seemed gasping. Over the level open he made, straight to the changing ring around the cattle killer whom none dared face. Did he hesitate? Not for an instant; through the ring of the yelping pack, straight for the old despot of the range, right for his throat, he sprang; and the gray wolf struck with his twenty scimitars. But the little one, if foiled at all, sprang again, and then what came I hardly knew. There was a whirling mass of dogs. I thought I saw the little White One clinched on the gray wolf's nose. The pack was all around; we could not help them now. But they did not need us; they had a leader of dauntless mettle, and when in a little while the final scene was done, there on the ground lay the gray wolf, a giant of his kind, and clinched on his nose was the little white dog.

We were standing around within fifteen feet, ready to help, but had no chance till we were not needed.

The wolf was dead, and I hallooed to Snap, but he did not move. I bent over him. "Snap—Snap, it's all over; you've killed him." But the dog was very still, and now I saw two deep wounds in his body. I tried to lift him. "Let go, old fellow; it's all over." He growled feebly, and at last let go of the wolf. The rough cattle-men were kneeling around him now; old Penroof's voice was trembling as he muttered, " I wouldn't had him hurt for twenty steers." I lifted him in my arms, called to him and stroked his head. He snarled a little, a farewell as it proved, for he licked my hand as he did so, then never snarled again.

That was a sad ride home for me. There was the skin of a monstrous wolf, but no other hint of triumph. We buried the fearless one on a butte back of the ranch-house. Penroof, as he stood by, was heard to grumble: "By jingo, that was grit—cl'ar grit! Ye can't raise cattle without grit."